MW00655448

BREAKING

BOOK TWO AFTER THE THAW

TAMAR SLOAN
HEIDI CATHERINE

SEQUEL HOUSE

For Jesse and Nathan

NOVA

*N*ova blinks in the bright white of the lab room, flashes of all the moments that brought her here shadowing her like an eclipse.

Not insisting enough that Kian take her blocks.

Choosing to stitch both arms because she couldn't leave Sam to bleed.

Wanting to push the barrel of pods off the raft because she didn't want to risk the others' lives.

Never realizing they were all working toward the same goal with the raven eggs in the final test.

Failing to understand she couldn't make herself more than what she is.

All culminating in one moment. One decision. One irreversible severing of far more than a finger.

Unbound.

Nova is Unbound.

She tries to tuck her numb left hand under her arm but she winces, the movement feeling too much. Is this what ice felt like? An aching cold that slices straight to the marrow? So jagged and sharp you're too scared to move?

The door on the other end of the room slides open even though she's nowhere near it, a signal she needs to get going.

The others are waiting.

From where she's standing, Nova can see an open-roofed tunnel, one which was never there before. It looks so much like the life that's now been molded for her—unexpected, solid.

Inescapable.

Although light streams down from above, the tunnel stretching before Nova feels like a nightmare. At the end is her future.

A future she was too scared to imagine.

Knowing it's inevitable, she starts walking. Her body is so frozen with shock that her movements are jerky and uneven, but she doesn't allow herself to stop. She needs to maintain what little momentum she's gained. The thought of curling up in this empty space without any plans to get up is calling to her. If she stops she may never start again.

The door at the other end appears too soon, a smooth white rectangle waiting to swallow her.

Nova raises her left hand, eyes stinging when the sight of her missing ring finger is unmistakable. The gap is so garish, the stump cauterized and raw.

It's living proof she's been forever altered. Deficit. One less than everyone she loves.

How did she think this wasn't going to happen? Did she really believe she'd be anything more than...Unbound?

She wishes the word would go away. That it never existed.

But its serrated edges slice through her, like some sick whirlpool in her head. Shredding her from the inside out.

It's probably a good thing everything is frozen. This is painful enough as it is.

Eyes averted from her disfigurement, Nova passes her hand over the sensor. The door slides open with little more than a whisper. It's like all her senses are slowly shutting down.

The nightmare continues and Nova walks onto the stage, wishing she could close her eyes. She knows the first face she's going to see. He'll be expecting her. Probably wondering what's taken so long.

Just as she predicted, Kian rushes forward, face so alive with anticipation that the shards that now make up her body shift and scrape restlessly.

She should lift her hand to show him, but she can't bring herself to. Moving hurts too much.

She tries to smile, to soften the blow that's about to come, but holding in her ocean of tears is taking every ounce of her energy.

Kian's eyes travel down her arm, apprehension bringing the lines of the face she loves into sharp relief.

She knows when he sees it.

He freezes, too.

Then the inevitability Nova was dreading happens—his gaze flies to hers. He mouths one word.

"No."

The world fractures and falls away. It's just the two of them, faces anguished, hearts disbelieving, souls aching.

Nova is Unbound.

They will never be together. Never live the future the two of them dreamed as one.

The crowd moves, Nova assumes they're clapping, maybe cheering. That's what happens whether you're Bound or Unbound. Both are a gift in Askala.

There are others there. Sweet Terra, her mother. She's smiling just like a High Bound should. Except her eyes are wide, confused almost. Her lip trembles and Nova quickly looks away before she has to watch the devastation shatter her, too.

Then there's Shiloh, who has her hand clapped to her mouth. Dex is holding Wren as they look as stricken as each other. Nova's glad they have someone to cling to as they absorb the ramifications. Whatever ties she'd woven, whether over a lifetime with Dex, or over a sweet, short week with Wren, have now been severed.

Just like her ability to have Kian's children.

Nova looks back to Kian to see he hasn't moved. The crowd around him is like an overflowing ocean and yet he's a statue.

It only adds to the agony that she knows how he feels.

Callix brushes her elbow, breaking the connection. He smiles as he indicates for Nova to leave the stage on the left. Nova gives herself a moment to study his face. He's one of the few who wouldn't have been surprised. He knew this was coming. Does he even realize how this will change her world? Does he even care?

Callix's gaze flickers for the briefest of seconds but he doesn't look away, remaining stoic under her scrutiny. His smile looks like it could be carved from stone.

Nova blinks, unable to hold his gaze. Just another reason she couldn't have been Bound—she could never hurt someone so deeply and continue to look at them like that.

She winces as she turns. Callix would know that. He already knew she didn't make the cut.

It's a relief to leave the stage. Every pair of eyes on her did nothing but amplify her shame. Their gazes simply fed the humiliation.

Except she's walking away from Kian and every dream she's ever hoped for.

As she steps down, Nova finds Felicia waiting for her, her face tear-streaked and soft with compassion. She folds around Nova, her arms cradling her.

Felicia is the one person who understands how much effort is necessary to hold herself together right now.

Except Nova can't bring herself to hug her back, even though she wishes she could. Felicia needs comfort now, too.

4

But that would involve raising her arms, bringing her shame closer to her face.

Seeing that they're both like this now.

Felicia releases her and Nova finds herself slipping to the back of the room. She wants to disappear. She wants to lose the weight of the eyes on her.

Curling around herself, Nova tucks behind the lines of people. Kian is probably pushing up on his toes, craning his neck trying to find her.

Nova startles. Surely he wouldn't come looking for her, wanting to talk. Not when there's nothing to say. No matter how much her soul cries out for it to be different, her spirit's now like her body—never to be whole again.

The crowd seems to stop, and Nova's eyes widen. She can't see Kian again. Not so soon.

Except it isn't Kian's voice that has the crowd hushing.

"As many of you know"—it's Magnus, his voice rich with celebration—"today is auspicious for two reasons. Not only have this year's Bound and Unbound been announced, but today is the Selection." He raises his arms in the air." The new leaders of Askala are about to be declared. Those bright, kind minds who are our future will have the responsibility of caring for something so much bigger than us—Earth. I now call upon all the Bounds eligible for High Bound status to please move to the front."

The crowd surges with excitement, pulling even further away from Nova.

The High Bounds. The ten who scored highest on the Proving over this generation. The best of the best. It is they who will lead Askala until the next generation takes over.

Kian's never said it, but Nova knows it's his deepest wish to follow in the footsteps of his parents. To be one of the ultimate leaders of Askala.

She hopes he's chosen.

But Nova won't be there to see it. She can't.

No matter the decision, watching the Bounds celebrate the next generation of High Bounds would break her. They're beginning a future she won't be part of.

The door at the back of the room beckons her and without glancing back, Nova slips out, never once looking at her hand as it passes over the sensor.

On the other side, she pauses. She was thinking she'd go home, to the cabin she shared with her mother in the lower decks of the Oasis.

But she no longer belongs there. She'll never go back.

The first tear breaks through, finding the cracks in her tightly held control. She ducks her head as she spins in the opposite direction, taking some measure of pride that she's held them back till now. Crying on the stage would've brought her mother so much shame. Being Unbound isn't supposed to be a curse.

Her body trembling with the effort, Nova walks away.

Away from her mother and the Bounds.

Away from Kian.

Toward her new home.

Dragging her shattered body up the stairs, Nova repeats to herself what she's been told so many times. The Unbound are lucky. They're cared for. Their time is their own. They're free of the shackles of responsibility.

But the words don't have the healing properties she was hoping for. Instead, they feed the tears that come with more force. The muted world becomes blurry and Nova stumbles.

Strong hands capture her. "Nova?"

She looks up, recognizing the voice. "Sam."

His bushy brows sit high on his weathered face. "What are you—" He glances down and his brows slam back down. "Bloody fools. How the hell could they think you're Unbound?"

Nova doesn't know what to say to that. Sam knows better

than anyone that she would never have become Bound. After all, it was him she broke the rules for and stitched the cut on his head.

Sam wraps his arm around her shoulders. "Come 'ere, angel. I'll show you where you need to go."

Nova nods silently, wishing she could do this with some dignity, but now that the tears have started, they won't stop. There's an ocean of pain overflowing down her cheeks.

Loud laughter filters through Nova's fog, only to suddenly stop. "Hey, Sam!" It's a voice Nova doesn't know, slightly slurred. One of the other Unbound. "Who you got there?"

Sam folds protectively around her. "You'll see soon enough. Get back to your drinking."

Nova doesn't look up because she doesn't want to know.

Sam leads her down the hall. "Every Proving we clean up a few cabins, knowing others are about to join our lucky ranks." The last two words are snarled through his beard. "They're just down here."

Nova lets Sam lead her, noticing the air is less stale than the rooms below deck that house the Bound. The Bounds take the responsibility of caring for the Unbound seriously—it's logical that they receive the more comfortable living quarters.

Like Sam said, they're lucky.

Nova swallows. She's lucky.

Sam stops at one of the doors down the hall and lifts his hand to the scanner. The tears surge. The hand with only four fingers.

The hand like hers.

It slides open to reveal a room much like the one she had below deck—a bed against the wall, a bowl for washing, a small desk. Except everything is larger, the room is bigger. More comfortable.

Lonelier.

Nova hesitates in the doorway. Coming out of the tunnel

7

was her birth into this new life. Entering this room will be the step that completes the metamorphosis.

One that every cell in her body is refusing to accept.

That's because every cell in her body is screaming for Kian.

Sam brushes her left arm. "You'll need to keep an eye on your hand. The machines are sterile and infections are rare, but they can still happen."

Nova can't bring herself to look at the stump that used to be her ring finger. The anesthetic's wearing off and it's beginning to throb. She wonders absentmindedly if the sap could've helped all those who have gone through this before her.

"Thank you, Sam." If she could feel anything apart from heart-shattering grief right now, she'd be touched by the care he's shown her.

Sam shuffles beside her. "You going in? It's as clean as it gets, to be honest."

Nova knows she needs to enter the room. There's nowhere else for her to go. This is her home now.

Another reason she would never have been Bound—she doesn't have the ability to face what needs to be done with stoicism and strength.

"I just need to be alone." Nova's voice, choked with tears, is full of apology.

Sam nods with understanding. "We all felt like that, angel."

With a gentle brush of her back, Sam leaves.

Nova is alone. Hurting.

Unbound.

She pulls in a shuddering breath.

One step is all it takes.

The door slides closed behind her.

Nova's knees collapse as the first sob cracks through her chest.

How is she ever going to be happy again?

KIAN

*N*ova is gone.

The moment she blended into the back of the crowd and he lost sight of her, he knew she'd leave. A sweet, soft person like her can only take so much.

Every shred of his being wants to go to her. His heart demands it. His soul rages for it.

But his mind knows he has to stay.

A hand clamps on Kian's shoulder, making him wince. Dex is shaking his head, looking shell-shocked. "I'm so sorry, Kian. It wasn't meant to be this way."

He's right. Never once did he imagine this scenario without Nova in it. It was a given. Right now, they should be holding hands so tightly their fingers would be aching, but they wouldn't care. They'd just hold tighter. Nova's smile would be so bright the ancient chandeliers above would be redundant. Anticipation of what the remainder of the day, the upcoming night, what the rest of their life will look like would be dancing around them.

Now everything feels incomplete. A vital part of this moment has been torn away.

Wren is frowning ferociously. "How could they do this?"

Kian doesn't have the ability to defend Askala right now. Callix and the High Bound didn't make this choice. Their results did.

The inevitability of what's coming next saves Kian from needing to answer. The retiring High Bounds have already stepped onto the stage, and each are holding a carved box.

Ten people, two of which are his parents, line up before the crowd. Including Nova's mother. Kian notes Thea's shoulders are so far back she looks like she's about to snap. Her self-control seems as tightly wound as his.

It's then that he notices she's not holding a box. Kian doesn't know if he's more surprised or troubled. Is this some statement because her daughter has been made Unbound?

Dex leans forward, whispering over Kian's shoulder. "Three of them don't have boxes."

He's right. Only seven are clasping the timber cases that hold High Bound rings.

A murmur ripples through the crowd as others must notice, too.

His father lifts a hand and the room silences. "Today is an unusual Selection, my friends. As you know, only the top ten who reach the highest pinnacle of intelligence and kindness are selected to be High Bound. This year, seven reached that mark. Because Earth deserves only the most exceptional of the exceptional, we were unwilling to lower the cutoff to maintain the tradition of ten High Bound. This generation, seven will lead us."

A few people glance at each other and Kian wonders what people are thinking. Are they noting the high standard his father is maintaining? Or are they wondering what happens if the numbers are low again next Selection? Or even lower...

His gut clenches. The importance of Bound and High Bound needing to breed is inescapable.

Children were always in his future. Children with Nova.

Except Nova's chip would be leaching its chemicals through her system as he stands here. She's probably sterile already.

His father raises his hand, his gold High Bound ring catching the light. "As we face these changes, I thought it would be valuable for us to remember." Kian stills, although he's not surprised his father is going to do this now. Losing three High Bound places is going to unsettle a lot of people. "We must remember."

A few voices repeat the words quietly as if it's a prayer.

His father surveys the crowd, his hand held high. "Remember that continents baked and burned. And all that remained was charred soil and blackened bodies."

Kian's chest tightens as the next words echo through his mind.

"We remember that cities were battered by storms so violent and frequent there was never enough time to rebuild before the next one hit." His father's voice gains momentum. "We must remember that the lucky had their homes swallowed by a rising, toxic sea because they had time to escape."

Kian mouths the next lines along with his father.

"Governments collapsed, borders were erased.

Sentient life was decimated. Extinction was the new order."

His father's arm is like a beacon held high as his voice soars with conviction.

"In the end, what humans thought was important—technology, money, possessions—were the fuel of their own demise. We must never forget it was nothing but greed and self-indulgence that did this."

His father's gaze combs the crowd, coming to settle on Kian, alight with emotion.

Kian's chest expands as the last lines reverberate through him. They've been said so many times as he was raised, they were like their nightly prayer before they went to sleep in their small, stuffy cabin.

"We are fortunate.

We have food. Safety. A future.

We also have a responsibility. To endure. To repair. To sacrifice."

There's a pause even though every person in the room knows the final words.

"For Earth."

Every voice in the room echoes his father's promise. "For Earth."

Kian's eyes sting and he's not sure why. It's like those words were for him, and not because they've reduced the number of High Bound.

It's because of Nova.

His father looks away as he steps back in line with the other High Bound lined up on the stage. His mother reaches out to brush his hand.

Knowing it's time, the Bound of this generation form an orderly line to the right of the stage. Kian heads to the back, an instinctive movement as it's what Bounds do, but also because he needs time to process this.

He'd always dreamed of being High Bound.

But not like this.

Wren looks to Dex. "I'm getting this over and done with." She heads to the front of the line, striding with purpose as she slips behind the first couple of Bound.

Dex takes a step to follow, only to stop.

Kian indicates with his chin for him to keep going. "You go with her. She acts like this is easy, but it's not."

Dex shakes his head. "I'm staying with you."

"Nothing can make this better, Dex." Kian tries to smile so he can soften the truth. "You can help her more than you can help me right now."

Dex hesitates, clearly torn.

Kian gives him a gentle shove. "To be honest, I need a bit of time."

Alone isn't possible right now, so the back of the line is the closest he can get.

Dex's eyes are heavy with understanding. He's grown up knowing that Kian and Nova were forged from one heart. "I'll see you after."

Dex joins Wren at the front of the line and Kian wonders if Wren realizes how her shoulders relaxed when Dex arrived beside her. Kian swallows against the flash of agony that rips through him. Kian used to love watching the way Nova did that whenever he was near her.

A brush of his elbow has Kian turning.

"Kian." Shiloh shifts closer to him. "I'm so sorry. I'm here if you need me."

Kian straightens, the movement pulling him away. He doesn't respond, not knowing what to do with the intensity in Shiloh's blue gaze. She's close enough to have heard what he just said to Dex.

She offers a small smile, not seeming to need an answer as she goes to line up behind him. Kian quickly steps back, indicating she slip in front of him. Shiloh's smile grows as she ducks her head.

The first Bound steps up to the stage, one of the older males within their group. He stops at the first High Bound like he's in a rush, but then pauses. He's probably weighing up his odds. Only seven people scored high enough to be selected, and women have always outnumbered men.

The Bound scans his hand over the box held out in front of him and the crowd seems to hold its breath, but the lid remains tightly shut. Keeping his shoulders back, he steps off the stage.

The line moves forward and another person approaches the High Bound. Kian watches as if from a distance. Maybe this is all some twisted dream. Maybe he took the two of them passing for granted, and his conscience is trying to show him what that harrowing world could be like.

For a split second, Kian allows himself the relief of that fantasy.

Except Nova isn't beside him. She's not even in the room. Shiloh's in front, glancing back occasionally with an encouraging smile, and there's nothing but empty space behind him.

He almost doubles over as it hits him all over again. Nova's hand. Her beautiful, precious body has been forever altered.

They can never be together.

The only thing that keeps him upright are his father's words.

For Earth...

The next Bound steps onto the stage, her shoulders slumping as she fails to open a box. She steps off the stage and the first male who went through wraps his arms around her shoulders. Kian looks away, not able to watch him comfort her.

Wren is next and she strides right up onto the stage, facing this like she has everything else, whether it was a leatherskin or a polar grizzly.

Or Callix.

As if she doesn't have time for fear.

As Wren walks straight past the other High Bound, Kian glances at Dex, finding him looking just as surprised. *Surely not...*

But Wren seems to have her sights set on Dex's father as she heads to the end of the line.

She only pauses when she passes Thea. Wren glances at her, opens her mouth only to shake her head and keep moving. Thea stares straight ahead, looking as if she's been carved from grief.

Wren stops in front of Callix, looking up at him in that unflinching way of hers.

Is she aware that Dex may have wanted to choose his father? Does she know that if she's High Bound, it's the ring in Callix's box that she'll take and wear?

14

Kian's eyes widen. Or is she doing this to protect Dex so he doesn't have to face his father?

Wren lifts her hand as she angles her chin, defiance and determination evident in the one movement.

For the first time, Kian wonders whether Wren will be High Bound. A week ago, he wouldn't have thought it possible that she, a Remnant, would be Bound. But she scored consistently well on the tests of the Proving, even on the ones she didn't try to score well on. She was smarter than them all.

And when she stopped being so obnoxious, she revealed a heart that's fiercely protective of those she cares about.

But is that enough to be High Bound?

He holds his breath as she lifts her hand to scan over the box, her silver ring tightly wrapped around her finger.

When the box doesn't move, the lid remaining still and shut, Kian rocks back, realizing he'd been leaning forward. Of course, Wren wouldn't be High Bound. Being Bound was a privilege in itself considering she wasn't born of Bound genes.

Wren turns to leave, only to suddenly spin back. Pushing up on tiptoes, she grinds out whispered words meant only for Callix. The only sign he heard are his hands tightening around the box.

Kian's muscles lock as he realizes why Wren chose to scan his box. She didn't expect to be High Bound, she may have been protecting Dex, but that wasn't all. Although Kian couldn't hear what Wren said, he could make out the last word. The final world that was practically spat at Callix.

Nova.

Wren was telling Callix what she thinks of the decision that Nova be made Unbound.

Kian's face feels like the skin has been pulled taught across his skull. He tries to swallow but his whole body is wound too tightly.

He wishes he lived in a world where he could do that, too...

The line shuffles forward again, meaning it's Dex's turn. This time Kian is on high alert as he studies Callix. Not only is he Dex's father, but he already knows the outcome. Except Callix stands stoic like the other High Bound, staring straight ahead as he holds one of the seven timber boxes.

Dex walks up the steps to the stage, his shoulders back, his arms by his side. Kian realizes it's the strongest and surest he's ever seen him. There's not a hint of Dex wanting to hide his stump. It seems being Bound has given him the confidence he needed.

Kian watches as Dex approaches Callix. After him is Kian's mother then father, the last remaining High Bound holding boxes. At least Wren not receiving a golden ring means Dex can potentially receive his from Callix.

Except Dex doesn't stop when he reaches his father. He doesn't even look at him.

Instead, he stops at the next person. Amity.

Kian's mother.

She hides her surprise as Dex turns to face her.

Why would Dex do this? Is he using the opportunity to show Callix that his father never chose him first? Is it because he's worried he's not High Bound and he knows it'll be easier facing Kian's mother?

Or is it because of Nova... Is Dex telling his father he's not okay with what happened, just like Wren did?

Kian's mother extends her box and Dex waves his stump over the lid. The click is audible in the cavernous room, a pinpoint of noise that has everyone cheering.

The first High Bound has been announced.

And it's Dex!

Kian's mother's smile is radiant as she helps Dex remove his silver ring and replace it with a gold.

"You are High Bound," she says. "Bound to Askala. Bound to the future. Our planet depends on you."

Dex nods as he hands back the box. "I accept my duty."

Dex turns to the crowd, looking shocked. He raises his hand and the cheering climbs as the Bounds do the same. Kian feels the flicker of something positive as he claps for his cousin. At least this has worked out for someone.

Dropping his hand, Dex leaves the stage, but not before Kian sees a frown flicker over his face.

The next Bound steps up, then another, and another. For the most part, the boxes remain silent and closed. For the few who pass their hands over the lid and they click open, they glow at the privilege they've been deemed good enough for. They are the next leaders of Askala.

As they come to the last remaining Bound, Kian notes that he barely feels a thing. Whenever he imagined this moment, he'd pictured his heart hammering at his ribs. He'd be excited, nervous, then excited again. Now, there's moments he's not even sure his heart is beating. His chest feels...hollow.

Up ahead, someone steps to the side, glancing apologetically at the person behind them. With four hurried steps he slips behind Kian.

It's Finn, and even if Kian didn't know it already, it's apparent he's Jay's older brother—just as tall and lanky and awkward. Kian wishes he could say something about the loss of his younger brother, but now isn't the time.

Finn swallows, his Adam's apple bobbing. "Sorry. I could use a few more minutes."

Kian nods, understanding the feeling. It seems they've both lost someone precious to the Proving.

Two more Bounds go up. Two more Bounds step off the other side of the stage, their rings remaining silver.

When it's almost Shiloh's turn, she turns back to Kian as she pulls in a steadying breath. "Wish me luck," she whispers.

Kian doesn't have the energy to hold the frown out of his

voice. "It's not about luck, Shiloh. You've either scored high enough or you haven't."

Shiloh flushes. "Of course. I just meant..." She looks away. "With two boxes left and all..."

Kian realizes she's right. There's three of them in line, and two boxes still unopened, up on the stage. What is it about Shiloh that seems to wind him up tight? He's about to apologize but she moves away, holding herself proud and tall as she steps on to the stage.

The two final boxes are held by Kian's father and Dorian, an older High Bound. Kian isn't surprised that Shiloh walks toward Dorian. In fact, he suspects everyone in the line left their leader, Magnus, alone.

Because Kian is in the line.

There's the slightest of tremors as Shiloh brushes her hand over the top of the carved box. A second later it clicks open. Shiloh looks up to Dorian's face, her own alive with disbelief. Dorian nods, smiling gently as he lifts the box. With trembling hands, Shiloh swaps her rings.

Silver for gold.

She turns around and raises her hand, looking like she could float away on the cheers of the crowd. Shiloh turns, her gaze like a laser as she finds Kian's.

A single tear trickles down her cheek. Relief? Celebration? Elation?

Kian wishes he could smile, he really does. It's what Shiloh's moment deserves. But his face is like cement. Why does it feel like his pain just compounded?

Instead, he nods, which seems enough for Shiloh. Her smile dials up even brighter before she turns away and walks off the stage.

It leaves his father with the remaining unopened box. One High Bound ring, two of them in line.

"Jay would've hated this," mutters Finn from behind.

Kian grasps Finn's arm. "He was braver than any of us realized."

Finn nods as his eyes well with tears. "He sacrificed for Askala. It's our duty."

Kian turns away, conscious that the room has gone quiet once more. Far quieter than it has been since the Selection began.

They're all waiting for the final High Bound to be announced.

Kian holds his shoulders straight as he climbs the steps, feeling like all of the weight of Askala is sitting on them. Everyone is watching.

Everyone but Nova.

He reaches his father, the silence starting to suffocate him.

His father's chest moves with calm, even breaths. He studies Kian in that wise way of his, his dark eyes glittering.

Kian looks away, not wanting to decipher what's in there. Not wanting his father to see how much he's hating this.

He stares at the box, knowing a gold ring of the High Bound is in there. Knowing the odds are in his favor.

How can he do this? How can he act like everything is okay?

Silver or gold, it no longer feels like this matters. Nova will never wear a ring.

Kian's center of gravity starts to shift. He shouldn't be here, acting like his heart isn't torn and bleeding. He should be with the girl he loves, the girl who would be falling apart right now.

Alone.

His father's hands slide down to balance the box on his palms as if it's an offering. Kian looks up to see him mouth two words.

"For Earth."

His father's gaze holds his, his dark eyes alive with layers.

He knows Kian's hurting.

He understands his anger.

But his father is telling him this is the greatest test of his Proving. And he's waiting for Kian to pass it.

For Earth.

For the briefest of moments, Kian allows his eyes to flutter closed. He welcomes the whiplash of pain as it slices through his chest. He wonders how no one hears his soul screaming in the too-silent room.

When he opens his eyes again, Kian knows what he has to do. Without breaking his father's gaze, he swipes his hand over the intricately carved lid. There's a pause.

A click.

And his future is decided.

Kian doesn't need to look down to know the truth. He's not even sure he wants to touch the gold ring.

He's High Bound.

It's all he's ever wanted.

Except he's High Bound without Nova.

Which means somehow he has to lead Askala when half his heart is missing.

DEX

*W*alking into the boardroom straight from the Selection is the last thing Dex wants to do. He needs time.

Time to process everything that just happened.

Time to check the people he loves are going to be okay.

Time to accept the decisions his father made.

He follows the straight line of Kian's back off the stage. His cousin's shoulders are pulled tight, his head held high. To anybody who doesn't know him, he looks proud.

But Dex knows him. And that's how he knows Kian's confident posture is being used to disguise his shattered heart and dreams.

Nova had no need to pull off such a charade. Her eyes had betrayed her devastation when she'd emerged onto the stage. He hadn't needed to look at her mutilated hand to know the outcome of her Proving.

Sweet Nova. Had his father been drinking some of the Unbound's wine when he'd interpreted the test results?

Dex shakes his head. Of course, he hadn't been drinking. But did he have another motivation? Because that result will never make sense, no matter how much he thinks about it.

This was the reason Dex hadn't been able to look his father in the eye, choosing instead to accept his High Bound ring from Amity. The aunt who's been more of a parent to him than his own father.

Which brings him back to the words that have been echoing around his head since his father spoke them. It was only the night before, even if it feels like he said them a lifetime ago.

We're on the cusp of something big.

Askala is about to change.

His father had said they needed to get today out of the way. Then they could talk.

Which is another reason Dex needs time. Sitting through this meeting will be excruciating. How will he be able to make any kind of decision knowing that one of his best friends is a broken mess somewhere on the upper levels of this claustrophobic ship?

But this meeting is necessary. It's time for the new High Bound to assign responsibilities and take control. It doesn't matter whether or not Dex is ready for it, it's happening anyway.

They file into the boardroom and Dex stands behind the seat closest to the door, trying to fool himself that he has the option of leaving. At least he'll be able to get out of here first when the formalities are over to see if he can find Nova.

And Wren. Although, he half suspects he'll find them together. There's no way Wren will be celebrating with the other new Bounds. This thought brings him some comfort. Nova won't be alone.

The table before him is long and rectangular, made from timber. The scratches and dents in it are the most obvious evidence of its age, but if Dex looks closely he can see the top of it is sagging. Perhaps that's more a result of the decisions that have been made sitting in this room, like the weight of them has started to take its toll.

It was right here at this table that Magnus had announced his decision to burn the bridge and isolate them from the Outlands. It was also here that the decision had been made to ensure an Unbound could never again be mistaken as a Bound.

Although, almost two decades on, Dex has come to doubt those choices. It's clear his father has, too. If he'd even agreed with them in the first place.

If there are people like Wren in the Outlands, was cutting themselves off the smartest idea?

And is removing a finger really an effective way to make sure nobody can pose as a Bound? Surely, there are other far less brutal options.

Rubbing at his stump, Dex questions the outcome of his Proving once more. His father has the power to manipulate the results. It's very possible Dex is the first Unbound to pose as a Bound since that decision was made and he doesn't even know it.

Magnus is standing at the head of the table. He clears his throat as he waits for the seven new High Bound to find their places.

Kian is ready. Standing behind a chair at the opposite end of the table to Dex, his hands folded neatly in front of him, his eyes glazed over, waiting for this to start.

Waiting for this to end.

Shiloh's beside Kian, standing just a little closer to him than necessary, her blue eyes blinking innocently. She's recovered quite well after the trauma of the Proving and is back to her pretty self. Wren did them all a huge favor introducing them to the wonders of mangrove pine sap.

Dex glances at the three empty chairs, wondering how it's possible that only seven of them made the cut. Surely, Wren should be here! There's no way Dex could have scored higher than Wren. Just another thing that makes him suspect the results were manipulated.

The four other High Bound are a little older than them. Dex is pleased about that. Perhaps they'll have clearer heads, having had time to accept the results of their own Provings.

Time. There it is again. That intangible concept that he wants to reach out and grab hold of so he can make it stop.

"Let's begin, shall we?" says Magnus, making it clear that Dex can't hit pause on time, no matter how much he might want it to.

There are nods all around the table.

"Congratulations, High Bounds." Magnus's deep voice bounces off the walls and Dex wonders how he must be feeling to be stepping down as leader. It mustn't be easy. "As you know, you've been selected from all your peers as having the highest levels of both intelligence and empathy, as determined by your Provings."

The word empathy sticks in Dex's chest. Nobody in Askala is more empathetic than Nova. And she's most definitely not stupid. Even if she hadn't scored as highly in intelligence, surely her empathy was enough to boost her score, if not to High Bound level, then at least enough to be Bound. There's nothing about it that makes any sense.

"You're a very special group of people," Magnus continues. "But one of you must take over from me as leader of Askala."

He pulls out the seat he's been standing behind and sweeps his eyes around the table.

Dex sucks in a breath when Magnus's eyes catch his, wondering just how far his father might have taken things. Surely not that far? It's believable that Dex might be Bound. Acceptable he might be High Bound. But the leader. No, that's just plain ridiculous.

"I call on Kian to take my place as leader," says Magnus, his eyes alight with pride as they rest on his son. "Kian is not just my son, but he received the highest overall score of any participant in the last generation of Provings. Congratulations, Kian."

Dex feels the tension slip from his chest and he smiles. His faith in Askala has been restored just a little. Kian was born for this role. He has so many of Magnus's qualities, but just as many of his mother's. The future of Askala will surely be safe with Kian at the helm, no matter how much change his own father seems to think lies ahead.

Kian steps forward, his movements almost robotic as he goes to his father and shakes his hand.

Magnus pulls out the chair a little more and Kian takes his place at the head of the table. Dex catches sight of the silver ring on Magnus's finger. It's a contrast to the gold rings they all now wear and a symbol of the change in power. Magnus is no more than a regular Bound now. His duty to Askala as their leader is now done.

"I leave you now to lead us well," says Magnus, stepping away.

He strides from the room, the confidence in his steps his final act as Askala's leader. And as much as Dex loves his uncle, he finds himself glad his reign is over. It's time for the new generation to take control. The ones who'll be here to see the consequences of any decisions they make.

"Please, take your seats," says Kian in a voice that has a hollow quality to it.

There's the sound of six chairs scraping on the floor as everyone sits down.

"Our first task as the new High Bound is to assign roles." Kian glances around the table. "This is going to be a little more challenging given there are only seven of us. Does anyone have a role in mind they'd like to take on?"

Shiloh's hand shoots into the air.

"No need to raise your hand," says Kian. "This is just a conversation. I'm guessing you want to run the…"

Dex sees Kian's throat working, unable to get out the word he needs to say. He's about to assign the role Nova had dreamed of for herself.

"The infirmary," says Shiloh, saving him the trouble. "I've already been working there, which makes me the logical choice."

Kian nods, as he scans to see if anyone has any objections. "Very well. Shiloh is now in charge of the infirmary."

She beams at him, seeming to grow a few inches in her chair. Dex is glad that Nova isn't here to witness this. Although, if she were, then that wouldn't have just happened.

"Who'll look after the pteropods?" asks Zali, one of the older High Bounds. "Because I wouldn't mind learning about that."

Kian's mouth falls open just slightly as his eyes widen. Dex knows this is the other job Kian was torn between. They don't need someone to learn about the pods. They need someone who's grown up with them. They need Kian.

Dex leans forward, enjoying the freedom of no longer feeling the need to disguise his stump. "Given that there are only seven of us, wouldn't it make sense for Kian to do that job as well? If you don't feel it's too much, of course."

Kian nods. "Yes. I'm sorry, Zali but Dex is right. I'll be in charge of the pteropods as an additional responsibility. I've worked there my whole life. I know how to keep the population thriving."

Zali smiles, the empathy that made her a High Bound shining through. "I understand. The kitchens, then? May I please be assigned the kitchens? I could take on the gardens, too. Those jobs are linked anyway."

"That would be wonderful." Kian makes a note on an open ledger in front of him. "I'm sure you'll do a terrific job."

Dex shuffles in his chair, knowing he needs to speak up for himself in the same way he did for Kian. But does he want the role that everyone expects him to take? A role that holds responsibility for the entire next generation of Askala by determining if they'll be Bound or Unbound? It feels…too much.

"Dex, how do you feel about taking over from your father in the Provings?" asks Kian, forcing his decision to the table.

"Oh, yes," says Shiloh, leaning forward. "Dex would be wonderful in that role."

"He would." Kian gives him a gentle smile. "You're smart, you're logical, you're good with numbers."

Dex narrows his eyes, wondering since when he's been good with numbers.

Kian looks directly at him, seeming to be trying to tell him something. "You'll be able to use the results of our generation of Provings and help us move forward."

"It's an interesting idea," says Dex, trying to buy a few moments, given that time is so stubbornly insisting on marching forward.

Kian blinks as he waits for him to decide and the subcontext of what he just said washes over Dex. He'll be able to use the results of the last Provings to help them move forward.

He'll be able to see what went wrong with Nova.

Kian would never ask that of him directly. He's too committed to Askala. But there's one thing he loves more than the colony he lives for. And it's a girl who Dex has no doubt needs some answers.

Just like he does. But would taking on the Provings give him the answers to all the questions his father's so far refused to answer? There's only one way to find out. Besides, he'd hate to be stuck with responsibility for the water systems. Or even worse, the waste.

"Well?" asks Kian.

"It would be my honor." Dex smiles. "Thank you for your confidence in me."

"I'm pleased. Thank you, Dex."

Kian moves onto the next role, assigning the water and

waste systems to Aarov, who strangely seems happy about this, proving to Dex just how different they all are.

But it's hard to concentrate without getting distracted by thoughts of what Wren will think of Dex's new role. She had such suspicion for his father during the Proving. Will she choose to direct that animosity at Dex now instead? It was hard enough leaving the stage without her. There has to be a way to keep her not only on-side, but by his side.

"Milli, would you like to take responsibility for the Unbound?" Kian asks one of the two remaining High Bound yet to be assigned a role.

"I'd like that," says Milli, her dark eyes creasing in the corners as she smiles. "We have a responsibility to ensure they're well cared for."

"May I interrupt for a moment?" asks Dex, an idea lighting his mind.

"You just did," says Kian, shaking his head.

"Normally a High Bound is selected to assist with the Provings," he says. "We need someone to take over from Lana."

"We don't have enough High Bounds for that this time." Kian scratches his chin as he looks down the ledger. "With two of us already taking on extra responsibilities, we're going to need to put Trista in charge of resources. If that's all right with you, Trista?"

Trista nods and Dex notices her hands are shaking. It's a huge task to take on responsibility for the Oasis being supplied with all the resources it needs for them to function as a society. But given Trista was Selected as a High Bound for her intelligence, it's a task Dex is certain she's up to. Kian clearly agrees or he wouldn't have asked her.

"I'll try my hardest." Trista's smile looks more like a grimace.

"Thanks," says Kian. "You'll be terrific and you'll have the support of everyone around this table."

28

Everyone nods in response and a weight seems to lift from Trista's shoulders.

"So, getting back to Lana..." Dex hesitates, wanting to choose his words carefully.

"I'm sorry, Dex," says Kian. "But Lana's job won't exist anymore. I think you'll need to step up and run the Provings on your own moving forward."

"Of course, but I'd like to choose a Bound to assist me," says Dex, nodding. "One who can help me to gain a new perspective on things to help strengthen our tests."

"I see." Kian draws in a breath, having figured out exactly where Dex is heading with this. "Someone who wasn't born here?"

"You don't mean the Remnant, do you?" asks Milli.

"We don't use that term anymore," says Kian firmly. "I never want to hear that term again. Wren showed us that people from the Outlands are capable of a lot more than we realized. In terms of both intelligence and heart. There's a lot we can learn from them as well as the other way around."

Milli seems surprised, but keeps her lips sealed as she accepts Kian's words.

If Dex had the ability to clap, he would. Seeing Kian come full circle with Wren over the course of the Proving had been a miraculous thing to watch. They'd gone from archenemies, to almost having a revered respect for each other.

"It's a wonderful idea, Dex," says Kian. "Wren should absolutely help you with the Provings. Frankly, I'm a little surprised she's not here to suggest the idea herself."

Dex leans back in his chair, feeling very pleased with himself for finding a way to keep Wren in his life. Perhaps he's better at solving problems than he realized. Maybe he does deserve his place at this table.

"I'm sorry, Kian," says Zali. "But are you certain that's the right decision to have a...an Outlands person in the Provings?"

"Shiloh, would you like to answer that?" Kian turns as Shiloh jumps at the sound of her name. "I feel I've already said my piece."

"I understand how you feel," Shiloh says to Zali. "Why you might not trust someone from the Outlands. To be honest, at the start of the Proving, we didn't trust her either. But I can vouch for her. As can Kian and Dex. If you talk to Nova when you get to the upper decks to check on the Unbound, then I'm sure she'll vouch for Wren, too."

Dex notices she doesn't mention Felicia. There won't be any full circles for Wren and Felicia, that's for sure. Shiloh is smart enough to know that.

Kian is rubbing at his temples now, the mention of the words *Nova* and *Unbound* in the same sentence clearly taking their toll.

"With that decided, perhaps we should wrap things up for now?" asks Dex, knowing this is what Kian would want, but also knowing that he'd never put his personal needs above the needs of Askala.

"I agree," says Shiloh, shooting Kian a coy smile. "It's been such a long day. I'm keen to get back to my cabin. Alone, of course."

Kian rubs his temples a little harder before letting his head spring up. Shiloh is going to be a problem he'll need to resolve carefully. Although, Dex doubts that she's ranking on his list of immediate concerns.

"Thank you, everyone." Kian flashes a tired smile around the room. "It *has* been a long day. Please, have a think about your roles to make sure you're happy with them and if you have any ideas for improvements you'd like to make. Spend some time with the retiring High Bound to learn as much from them as possible. A good handover is always important."

"Thank you, Kian," says Aarov.

"It's an honor to be your leader," says Kian. "I promise you that I'll do my best to lead you well."

Dex smiles at his cousin, his heart bursting with pride for this boy he grew up beside, who now sits at the head of the table. No longer a boy, but a man. Kian's heart may be broken and his soul forever damaged, but perhaps these things will make him stronger in the same way that losing his own mother forced Dex to be brave.

He lets out a long sigh. Who's he kidding? There's no silver lining in Nova being Unbound.

Staying in his seat as the other High Bound rise and leave the room, he realizes there'd been no point in taking the seat closest to the door. Because there's no way he's leaving this room without Kian. He cannot be left alone at a time like this, no matter how much he might insist on it. And better that Dex take care of him than Shiloh, who also remains in her seat.

"Thanks, Shiloh," says Kian. "Please, return to your cabin now. Get some rest."

"You'll be a great leader," she gushes, as she rises. "Oh, and I'm very sorry about Nova."

Dex highly doubts that. Shiloh does have a kind heart. She wouldn't be here if she didn't. But she has to be happy that Kian will be in need of someone to have children with. Someone who's still able to do that for him. Someone who wears a ring on their finger just like Shiloh's, instead of a gruesome gap where her finger once was.

Poor Nova.

Dex's heart breaks all over again at the thought of what must have run through her mind when she'd pulled her hand from that machine. He wishes he'd been there to comfort her.

How is he going to sit behind the screens in the lab and watch the pain of the next generation as they go through the same thing? There may be a lot of advantages to the role he just agreed to, but the disadvantages are going to weigh heavily on him.

31

Shiloh leaves and at last Dex and Kian are alone.

Dex gets out of his chair, closes the door, then goes to his cousin.

"Bring it in," he says, holding out his arms.

Kian looks up at him, his eyes shining with tears.

"Come on," says Dex. "I don't just give these hugs away for nothing. They're quite popular with the girls. Apart from Shiloh, of course."

A hint of a grin crosses Kian's face as he stands. "You calling me a girl?"

"Never. This is strictly a bro hug. We'll call it a brug."

Kian steps forward and Dex pulls him in tight, wrapping his arms around him.

"You did good." Dex pats Kian firmly on the back. "You held it together as long as you had to. I'm proud of you."

"Is that enough brugging yet?" asks Kian, not making any moves to let go.

"Almost," says Dex, trying to pour as much love as he can into his broken cousin's soul.

Kian pulls away, wiping at his eyes with the back of his hand. "It feels like a bad dream."

"I'll find out what happened," says Dex. "I promise."

"You can't break any of the rules." Kian straightens his spine, as if remembering the position he was just handed. "Askala has rules for a reason."

Dex nods, realizing that now's not the right moment to have the conversation they're going to need to have.

It's true that Askala has rules for a reason. But maybe the reasons no longer make sense. Maybe Dex's father is right. They could very well be on the cusp of something big.

Because there's no doubt in Dex's mind that Askala is about to change.

Perhaps it already has.

WREN

*W*ren paces her small cabin with one thing on her mind.

Find Nova.

That poor girl is broken. And even though Wren doesn't have the glue to put her back together, she knows she has to try.

It's not right. None of this is. How can a society that prides itself on being kind separate people into two groups? Never in the history of humankind has that ended well. It promotes hate, not peace. Is the future of the planet really more important than the people who live on it?

It was harder to get away from the ballroom than she'd expected. The doors had been closed at the beginning of the High Bound Selection and apparently aren't meant to be opened until the crowd is able to see who emerges as their new leader.

Wren had no interest in waiting. It's obvious Kian will lead. If not, then this system is even more screwed up than she originally thought. He's the obvious choice.

She'd watched the new High Bound file through a door off to the side of the ballroom. It'd been odd seeing Dex turn his back and walk away, when normally his eyes seek out hers whenever they're in the same room. Maybe that's how it's going to be from now on?

Eventually, she'd convinced the Bound at the door to let her out by telling him she was having women's issues and needed to get back to her cabin. After some flushing and stammering on his part, he'd insisted on walking her to the cabin she'd stayed in before the Proving. A small lonely space with cracked walls and a blinking light that she'd swap in a heartbeat for a blanket underneath Dex's bed.

But she's stuck with this depressing space for now. Located on the lower deck with the other Bound, her cabin feels anything but home. The Bound aren't her people. If they were then why was she the only one to be escorted from the ballroom?

Earning the trust of her fellow Bounds is going to take time. Although, in truth, they're probably wise not to trust her.

There are new clothes laid out on her bed with an apple perched on top. A cup containing two pteropods is sitting on the desk. There's a small bathroom connected to the cabin where a wash basin and comb have been left for her. Deciding to make the most of having to return to her room, she strips off her clothes and uses the hemp cloth beside the bowl, doing her best to wipe away the nervous energy that's been clinging to her skin all morning.

Wishing she had her leather vest and pants to slip back into, she picks up the clean clothes and puts them on. At least they make up in comfort what they lack in style. Ensuring her pendant is tucked into her shirt, she drags the comb through her tangle of hair, giving up after it gets caught in a knot.

Catching sight of herself in a mirror she decides that will have to do. She's not here to win a beauty pageant.

Her empty stomach groans, so she takes a few bites of the apple. It's floury and tasteless but will ease her hunger pains for now. Although, if she wants any nutrition, she's going to have to face those two squishy creatures in the cup.

Holding her nose and tipping back her head, she lifts the cup and swallows the pods in one gulp. There's no way she's biting down on them like she did on the raft. She imagines the look on her face must've been deserving of Dex's howls of laughter. They were disgusting!

She peers through the peephole, seeing that the hallway is clear, so presses her chip to the sensor. The door slides open and she steps out.

The Bound who'd escorted her here hadn't said she had to stay put, even if it was obvious he preferred she did. And she hadn't promised she would, either.

She strides down the hallway to the stairwell, heading for the upper decks. A place she's heard wild stories of during the Proving but hasn't yet seen for herself.

With each step she takes, it becomes more and more apparent that finding Nova isn't going to be easy. According to the signs on the walls, there are multiple levels. She knew that the Unbound outnumber the Bound, but by this much?

Unsure which level to try first, she stops at one of the landings.

"Hey, little Bound."

Wren spins around to see a man sitting on the next flight of stairs, watching her. He's at least twice her age, wire thin with gray skin and a receding hairline. There's clearly no wash basin in his cabin. The smell of him brings Wren right back to the Outlands. A place where getting clean is as impossible as having roast turkey for Thanksgiving.

"Is the little Bound lost?" He lets out a peel of laughter as he breaks into song. "*Mary had a little Bound, little Bound, little Bound. Mary had a little bound, its...hair was dark as...dirt.*"

Great. He's not just filthy. He's drunk.

"Do you know where the new Unbound were taken today?" she asks, not really expecting him to be able to help her.

"Oh!" His face lights up and her eyebrows raise in response. Maybe she'd been too quick to judge.

"I sang the wrong song!" He slaps himself on the forehead. *"Little Bound Peep has lost her sheep and—"*

"Forget about it." Wren turns her back on him and scans her wrist on the sensor, deciding that this level is as good a place to start looking as any.

The noise that greets her as the door slides open is only slightly less startling than the smell. She feels like if she breathes in deeply enough it's possible she might start singing nursery rhymes about lost sheep. That's some wine they must make up here.

Tucking her left hand in her pocket, she steps into the hallway.

"New girl!" a woman screeches, rushing up to her. The woman's hemp shirt is unbuttoned to her waist and she has flowers tucked into a messy bun piled on top of her head. She looks like she just got out of bed, despite the late hour. Perhaps she has. Although, Wren doubts she's been sleeping.

"Oh, it's a pretty one." A man in his twenties, who hasn't bothered with a shirt at all, sidles up beside the woman and slings an arm around her shoulders.

They study Wren like the fresh prey she is.

"Wanna join the party?" the woman asks, not seeming to mind that the man's hand has found its way inside her gaping shirt.

"I'm looking for someone." Wren takes a small step back and gives them a polite smile.

"Aren't we all, love, aren't we all." The woman laughs, turning to the man and running her tongue up his cheek. That's all the encouragement he needs and he pushes her against the wall and slips the rest of her shirt from her shoulders.

Wren scurries down the hallway. She's seen plenty of people like these in the Outlands. It's just a shock to find them in Askala. She'd thought everyone was like the Bounds who roam the lower decks.

How is sweet Nova going to survive up here?

The sound of beating drums draws her further down the hall to a large open space that looks like it might have once been a dining hall. The windows have been blacked out and Wren blinks as her eyes adjust, looking for anyone with blonde hair to see if it might be Nova.

The room is heaving with people in various states of undress with their hands in the air gyrating to the sound of the drums like they're in a trance. Three men are standing on a bar with drums strapped to their chest, beating out the hypnotic rhythm. The smell of smoke fills the air, and Wren notices people are taking turns to press a pipe to their mouths, sending clouds of white smoke billowing from their o-shaped lips.

A man grabs Wren by the arm and pulls her into the center of the room. Resisting the urge to send a knee into his crotch, Wren nods at the circle of people forming around her. She'll get out of here a lot faster if she doesn't make a scene. She knows when she's outnumbered.

A woman is saying something Wren can't make out, although her friends seem to hear just fine as they break into laughter, clutching their skinny bellies as they point and stare. She passes Wren a bottle and Wren pretends to drink, a small sip of the liquid somehow making it past her teeth.

She swallows it down and winces at the strength of the alcohol. It's far more potent than anything they make in the Outlands. It's got enough kick to power a flamethrower.

Smiling as she passes the bottle back, the woman nods her approval before taking a large slug of the liquid herself, letting out a loud whoop as she raises the bottle in the air and spins around in a circle. That guy in the stairwell had been positively sober by comparison.

The drums pick up a faster beat and the people cheer as they march around Wren like she's some kind of prize, brushing past her with their sweat-stained skin and yellow teeth. These aren't people who care about the future of the planet. They don't even care about the future of their own lives. They're living for the moment. A result of having been clearly told that they're not worthy of saving.

A result of the system Askala seems to think is fair.

There's no way Wren's going to find Nova here. This is a useless quest.

With her hand still in her pocket, Wren slips off her Bound ring. Clenching her left hand into a fist, she raises both arms in the air and joins the Unbound in their dance, tossing her head back and laughing as she stomps her feet and hopes there's enough smoke in the air that they won't notice her fully formed hand.

Slowly and subtly, Wren manages to maneuver herself out of the throng of revelers and back toward the exit. But each time she gets close to disentangling herself, someone notices and sweeps her back in.

A scream ripples through the crowd and Wren snaps around ready to fight, only to see one of the drummers tumble from the bar and land awkwardly on the floor.

Taking this as her chance, Wren moves quickly to the exit and down the hallway, slipping into a room she hopes is unoccupied.

Her shoulders slump to see two men playing cards at a table. She's heard of cards. She even saw a packet once in the Outlands. But never has she seen anybody actually play with them. In her world, games are a luxury that don't exist.

Deciding that these two men look more harmless than anyone else she's encountered on these upper levels, she sinks into a chair in the back of the room, needing a moment to center herself.

"You okay, love?" One of the men sets down his cards and turns in his chair. He's the oldest person Wren's seen in Askala. But he has a kind smile.

Wren nods. "I'm okay. Just looking for someone."

"Maybe I can help." The man leans forward. "I know most people around here."

"Come on, Sam," the other man complains. "Any excuse to get out of the game. You're not going to be able to help her."

"Don't listen to him." Sam pushes back his chair and flashes Wren a smile. "I was going to beat him anyway."

The other man folds his arms and huffs, clearly unimpressed, but Sam is undeterred.

"Now, tell Old Sam who you're looking for." He gives her another one of his grins and Wren tries not to notice how many teeth he has missing, focusing instead on the scar on his forehead.

"The new Unbound," she says. "Do you know where they were taken?"

Sam's four-fingered fist pumps in the air as he turns back to his card opponent. "See! I can help her. I know exactly where they are. Took one of them to her new accommodation myself."

"Did she have blonde hair?" Wren asks. "Or curls?"

"Blonde hair," says Sam, pushing up his sleeves. "Just like an angel. You're looking for Nova?"

It's then that Wren spots another large jagged scar running the length of Sam's forearm. A scar that looks far too familiar.

"It was you," says Wren. "You were in the Proving."

Sam tips back his head and laughs. "Guilty! Just taking my angel's advice, though. Needed to earn myself some pods. And she was right. Did me the world of good."

Nova hadn't mentioned that she recognized the arm

dangling through the curtain in the second test. Had she even realized that she knew who it was connected to?

"It's healed remarkably well." Wren peers at his arm and Sam proudly holds it out for her.

"I know your voice." Sam's face lights up. "You were the one who got me the sap! You saved this old man's life."

Wren nods, deciding it has to be better to have Sam feel like he owes her than the other way around.

"Seems like now I've got me two angels." Sam drops into a deep bow. "At your service. Would you like me to take you to Nova?"

"Yes, please." Wren stands as the relief slides down her spine. It seems this may not be a useless quest after all.

"Back soon." Sam winks at the other man who's somehow managing to look even less impressed. "I've got myself an angel's mission."

He leads her down the hallway and back to the stairwell.

"She's not on this floor?" asks Wren.

Sam shakes his head as he indicates for her to pass him on the stairs. "The cabins are further up."

That makes sense. Nobody could sleep over the sounds and smells on this level of the Oasis. She's surprised she hasn't heard the beating of those drums from downstairs.

"I see you got yourself five fingers on that left hand of yours," says Sam as she passes him.

"Lucky me." Wren rolls her eyes and shrugs.

Sam stops, forcing Wren to turn around and face him.

"Listen here, angel." He points a finger at her. "You *are* lucky. Not being grateful for what you have is a real slap in the face for an old Unbound like me, you understand?"

Wren swallows, aware that a flush of shame is racing up to her face. "I'm sorry."

"Nova's not in great shape. It's nice you've come to check on her. Rare for a Bound to venture into these parts, but the last thing she needs is for you not to appreciate being handed the only life Nova ever wanted."

Wren nods to show she understands. He's right. And it took an Unbound to point it out to her. "I really am sorry."

They climb two more flights of stairs and Sam begins to pant, his breath coming in sharp wheezes. It seems perhaps the pods he'd earned in the test hadn't been nearly enough. This poor old guy is in bad shape.

"It's the next floor." Sam stops at a landing and holds onto a railing to steady himself. "Fourth door on your left when you step out of the stairwell."

"You're not coming with me?" she asks.

"This old body's not built for stairs." He clutches at his chest. "Done too many of them today already. I might stop off here and get me some rest. You'll be okay from here."

"Thanks for your help," she says, hoping he's right. "I'd never have gotten this far without you."

Sam waves over his shoulder as he leaves the stairwell and Wren increases her pace, wanting to get to Nova before she runs into anyone else.

As soon as she steps onto Nova's floor, she feels an immediate sense of calm. The air is light and breezy up here. And it's quiet. It's a relief to know that Nova has somewhere peaceful to escape to.

Counting the doors as she passes them, she stops at the fourth one and knocks gently.

Her chip would open the door if she tried, but that doesn't feel right. Nova may have had most of her rights stripped from her today, but she still deserves the right to privacy.

"Nova," she calls, knocking again. "It's Wren. Can you let me in? Please?"

There's a pause, and Wren wonders what she'll do if Nova doesn't answer. The door slides open and Wren barely recognizes the girl standing before her. Her eyes are bloodshot, her normally sleek hair is a mess and her face is covered in red blotches. Yet, somehow, she still manages to look beautiful.

Nova steps back and Wren walks into the room. It's similar to her own cabin except it has a large porthole facing the forest that makes it feel less claustrophobic.

"Nice view," she says, peering out.

"Thought you were scared of heights." Nova sniffs as she sits down on her bed.

It's a relief to hear her make a joke and Wren smiles as she perches herself on the edge of the desk.

"Why did you come here?" Nova asks. "You shouldn't be wasting your time with me."

"That's not true." Wren fights the urge to sit beside Nova and wrap an arm around her, wondering since when physical comfort became her go-to. "The system is messed up. You should never have been made Unbound."

Nova crawls into her rumpled bed and covers herself with the blanket. "It's not the system. It's me. I wasn't good enough. The tests proved that."

"The tests proved nothing!" Wren leaps from the desk and paces. "All the tests proved is how stupid they are."

"Who got Selected for the High Bound?" Nova bites down on her bottom lip. "Actually, it doesn't matter. It doesn't concern me now."

Wren pauses her pacing, weighing up how much informa-tion to give Nova. Sam was right in pulling her up earlier. She needs to think before she talks.

"Kian and Dex are High Bound," she says, deciding it wouldn't be helpful at all right now to mention Shiloh.

Nova smiles through her tears as she props herself up on her pillow. "That's great."

"See, this is what I mean." Wren slams a fist down on the desk. "This! You're happy for them. Genuinely happy. Even though you're sitting there with the ass having just fallen out of our world. How can you not be Bound? This makes no sense. You're the nicest bloody person I've ever met."

Nova shakes her head, and the tears begin to not just fall, but run in streams down her cheeks. "It's not true, Wren. I'm not. I wasn't good enough."

"Well, you're more than good enough in my eyes. You're better than the whole lot of them put together."

Nova nods and this time Wren goes to her and puts her hand on her arm, patting her awkwardly.

The door slides open and Wren spins around to see Felicia standing there, her usual curls hanging limply to the sides of her broken face.

"I heard yelling," says Felicia, the whine in her voice reminding Wren why she hadn't come to check on her, too. "Are you okay, Nova? Is she threatening you?"

Wren sighs. Now isn't the time to come up against Felicia. In some ways, it's nice that Nova has someone up here to look out for her.

"Wren's here as a friend," says Nova. "She's just checking I'm okay."

Felicia nods as she folds her arms, stepping further into the room as the door closes behind her. "Well, I'm okay, too, in case you wondered."

"Look Felicia," says Wren. "I know we've had our differences, but I'm not your enemy. I'm glad you're here with Nova."

"You're glad I'm Unbound?" Felicia stares at her in horror. "Well, thanks very much."

"I didn't mean it like that," says Wren, wondering why she always manages to say the wrong thing around Felicia. It seems they're just not destined to ever get along.

Nova lets out a loud yawn and snuggles down under her blanket, leaving only the top of her head visible.

"You need some space, don't you?" asks Wren, realizing that her being here was possibly more for her own benefit. She'd needed to see Nova. It's unclear whether or not Nova needed to see her. In truth, there's only one person Nova needs to see and he's busy right now, most likely being crowned almighty ruler.

"You can stay." Nova's words are mumbled and it's obvious she'll be asleep in minutes. "I'm just tired."

"I'll stay with her." Felicia steps forward, puffing out her chest. "You don't belong here, anyway."

"I'll come back tomorrow," says Wren, although she doubts Nova is still awake to have heard. "Bye, Felicia."

Felicia gives her a tight-lipped smile.

Wren leaves the room and makes her way back toward the stairwell, determined to try to get some sleep herself. The Oasis is bigger than she'd realized from the outside. It's like a whole city in itself. So different to the sterile environment of the lab she'd grown used to over the past week. She already misses the space she made for herself on the floor underneath Dex's bunk. It'd felt safe there. Perhaps safer than she's ever felt in her life.

But it's to her lonely room she must go.

Just before she's about to turn into the stairwell, a flash of red hair catches her eye from down the end of the hallway.

"Stop!" she calls.

There's only one person in Askala she's seen with red hair. And that's the man she saw in the crowd at her Announcement. The man with the uncanny resemblance to Phoenix. It has to be the same guy.

"Stop!" she calls again. "You! Please! Hold up."

The man pauses and she runs up to him. But nothing can prepare her for what she sees when he turns to face her.

Because the man doesn't just have an uncanny resemblance to Phoenix. It's almost like he's wearing an older version of his face.

"Phoenix," she breathes, raking her eyes over him.

He shakes his head, confused. "My name's Dean."

Not being able to help herself, Wren reaches out and puts her fingers on his cheek.

He takes a step back as if she's given him an electric shock.

"You're a bit young for me, much as I'm flattered." He touches his cheek where her fingers just brushed.

She shakes her head as her eyes prick with tears. "No, not that."

"Then what?" he asks.

"You're Ronan's brother," she says. "I've heard about you."

Dean frowns. "Not this again. He was a good guy, you know. Askala made a big mistake banishing him."

"I know," she says, lowering her voice. "And that's exactly why I'm here."

It's time to set things right.

NOVA

*a*s the door slides open Nova already knows who it is. Only one person wouldn't bother knocking.

She slips further under the blanket. Not that it matters. She doesn't want to see anyone.

"I'm still sleeping."

"Don't give me that." Felicia huffs. "My bet is you've never slept this much in your life."

It also doesn't matter that she's right. Nova pulls the cover over her head, hoping the motion will be enough to tell Felicia she's wasting her time. Her throat still feels raw from all the sobbing.

The sound of something scraping across the desk grinds over Nova's nerves. "I've brought you something to eat. An apple and some greens."

No pods.

Because she no longer deserves them.

"I'm not hungry."

The edge of the bed sags as Felicia sits down. "You need more food, less sleep, Nova."

What for? To live a life with no purpose.

Without family.

Without Kian.

Felicia pauses, and Nova hopes she's deciding to give up. Knowing Felicia, she'll be back, but at least Nova will get some sort of reprieve.

"We need to go and get our hands checked. To make sure they're healing properly."

Nova's gut wrenches and she has to stop herself from curling back up into a ball. How many newly Unbound had she soothed as she checked their cauterized stump? Alongside her mother…

She buries her face in the bed. "I can't."

"Your mom's not there." Felicia's voice is soft with compassion. "I checked."

Nova looks over the edge of the sheet. "You checked?"

Felicia nods, her curls flicking against her cheeks. "I know this is hard enough as it is. Only Rose is there right now."

Nova flops onto her back, staring at the ceiling of her cabin. It's cracked and peeling like the rest of the Oasis, there's just more of it. She knows she can't stay here forever, but the thought of going out there fills her with shame.

She rolls onto her side, looking at Felicia. "How do you feel about"—she waves her left hand, pointedly not looking at her missing ring finger—"all of this?"

Felicia's gaze drops, staring at her own hand in a way Nova can't. "I wasn't surprised, but it was still a shock. All I can do is make the most of it." A smile twitches at the edge of her lips. "There are certainly advantages to being Unbound." Except it quickly disappears. "Although, it's not the same for you…"

Nova pushes herself upright, her head swimming at the motion. "This would be hard for anyone."

Felicia's hands hike on her hips. "But harder for some more than others."

Nova's brows lift up at the challenge in Felicia's tone,

deciding to change the topic. "How are you healing? Are you okay?"

Felicia rolls her eyes. "Of course you'd check on me. I'm fine. Like I said, it wasn't a surprise." She narrows her eyes, telling Nova she isn't finished. "Has he come to see you?"

Nova shrugs as she grits her teeth. Several people knocked on her door the past day, but she didn't respond. Dex called out. So did her mother. Two people left without her discovering who it was.

She doubts any of them were Kian. He knows he needs to focus on his new role. Nova understands that's far more important than her right now.

To be honest, Kian is the last person Nova wants to see, and those are words she'd never thought she'd consider.

Felicia is the only one who's ignored her wishes to be alone. Nova isn't sure whether she should be angry or grateful. It's possible she could've drowned in her own tears and pity if given enough time.

"Why are you doing this, Felicia?"

"Call me Flick," she smiles. "You were there for me when things got tough at the Proving." When Felicia realized she'd be Unbound. It was heartbreaking to watch everyone's fear being played out. "And I figured we've been through all this, whether we liked it or not. We might as well stick together."

Something warm unfurls in Nova. "Thanks...Flick."

Felicia waves the words away. "Why don't we get this hand thing over and done with? Afterwards, you might be up to checking out the party deck."

Nova has no intention of seeing the other decks anytime soon, but she doesn't tell Felicia. The girl seems to have quite the stubborn streak.

Nova pushes herself upright, feeling like her body is riddled with age. She walks over to the basin and splashes water on her

48

face. Staring at her reflection in the mirror, she notes the hollow cheeks and dark smudges beneath her eyes. She looks…broken.

"You said my mother's not there?"

Felicia stands. "She was just leaving, she said something to Rose about topping up the supplies."

Which means she was probably heading to the laundry for clean strips of hemp. She'll be gone about an hour. Long enough for Nova and Felicia to have their mandatory check. Nova glances out the porthole, surprised to see it's already late afternoon. She's been in this cabin for a full day…

Turning back to the mirror, Nova registers her hair looks like limp straw. The old Nova would've brushed and braided it.

That Nova believed she had a future to look forward to.

Her cheeks stain with pink, the only color to grace her pale complexion. How wrong she was.

Turning away from the mirror, Nova grimaces. "Let's get this over and done with."

Felicia—it's going to take some time to think of her as Flick — is by the door in a flash, swiping it open before Nova can change her mind. "We'll be in and out before you realize it."

Nova doesn't answer, knowing that's as far from the truth as it can get. Going to the infirmary will be almost as painful as seeing Kian.

As she steps through, Nova tells herself that maybe if she gets this done now, the wound it'll inflict can heal a little before she has to see the boy she's loved all her life. It's got to be the best way to do it. One torture at a time.

In the hallway, Nova pulls her shawl over her head even though they're inside. A handful of people are loitering around, a door opens and closes as someone leaves their cabin. Although these people are Unbound just like she is, for some reason she feels like she let them down, too.

"Thinks she's too good for the likes of us," sneers a voice as Nova walks past.

"The ones who thought they'd pass are always like that," scoffs another.

Nova tucks herself deeper into the shadows of her shawl. Are they right? Did she think she was better? What the second woman said is true—despite all her doubts, deep down, she actually thought she'd pass.

Felicia spins around. "Stop it. She barely failed, unlike most of us on this deck." She stalks away. "Come on, Nova. Everyone knows you should've passed."

Wincing, Nova picks up the pace. How could she think that Bound and Unbound are equal? Not when words like 'pass' and 'fail' fall off people's tongues so easily.

They reach the stairs and instinctively, Nova reaches out to grasp the rail only to stop herself. Eyes averted, she tucks her left hand in the folds of her shirt.

"Does your hand hurt?" Felicia asks in a quiet voice.

No more than my heart. "I try to ignore it."

"Which is why I think you should get it checked, even though I know this is hard. It could get infected and you wouldn't even notice."

Nova's about to object—she grew up in the infirmary, she knows the signs of infection—only to stop herself. Felicia's probably right...again. Nova can't bring herself to look at her hand, and the pain of the amputation pales compared to the anguish that slices her every time she moves. Her scar could become infected and she may not notice until it's too late.

And she refuses to be any more of a burden than she already is.

The walk to the infirmary is a short one. It was established in the center of the Oasis, so both Bound and Unbound could access it equally.

For the first time, Nova realizes what a token gesture that

was. What's the point of accessing something you're not entitled to have?

The door to the infirmary is open, allowing the voices within to trickle out.

"And where do you think that would go?"

It's her mother, her voice gentle and warm.

"Oh yes," Rose replies. "I see what you mean now."

Nova walks forward as though in a trance. Her mind is screaming for her to run the other way, but the draw is too strong. The scene is already playing out in her head. Her mother smiling as she allows Rose to bandage her arm, instructing her on how to pull so it's tight enough to hold, but not too tight that it'll restrict circulation. Asking her where she thinks the frayed end can be tucked so it won't come undone.

That's what she needed the bandages for. She's teaching Rose, in the exact same way she taught Nova.

"I'm sorry, Nova." Felicia has grabbed her arm. "I thought she'd take longer."

Nova slips out of her grasp, her focus on the door. Her heart aches, each thump a painful thud against her ribs. The thought of the comfort of her mother's arms propels her forward. She was wrong to stay away. Maybe her gentle mother, the woman who is a healer to her core, can help Nova with this agony that now lives in her chest.

She reaches the door, already feeling lighter. Seeing her mother will hurt, but it could be the beginning of her healing.

As she surveys the infirmary, so familiar it makes her eyes sting, Nova searches for her mother. She's not where she thought she'd be, over by the shelves.

"Yes, Thea," says a voice. A voice that has Nova freezing. "I'm expecting the sap will make a significant difference to what we can achieve here."

Shiloh is smiling up at her mother as she slides a layer over Rose's arm. Her mother is smiling, too, just as Nova expected, but with wonder. Shiloh lifts her hand, the gold ring on her finger unmistakable.

Shiloh is High Bound.

And Shiloh is in the infirmary with her mother, just like Nova always dreamed she would be.

The world fractures all over again, but with new intensity. The first time she lost the life she always wanted. This time she's watching someone else live it.

Nova gasps at the unexpected agony, her hand flying to her mouth as she fails to contain it.

The three women spin around. Rose's eyes widen and her face flushes bright red as if she was just caught doing something wrong. Shiloh has gone as still as Nova, looking shocked and unsure. She opens her mouth, although nothing but silence fills the room.

Her mother steps forward, her eyes moist as she extends her hand. "Nova," she whispers.

Nova steps back. "Please…no."

She wills her body to move, to run like it wanted to a moment ago. But her muscles are as shattered as the rest of her. Her entire being is no more than shards barely holding together.

Her mother stops. "I'm so glad you came. I wanted to tell you…" Her mother's voice trembles and her eyes implore her. "I want you to know you're my daughter, that hasn't changed."

"Everything has changed," Nova chokes out. She glances at Shiloh to find her staring at Nova's left hand. Nova jerks her hand behind her and Shiloh flicks her gaze back up, at least having the grace to blush.

Everything.

Has.

Changed.

Felicia pushes in front of Nova. "Leave her alone. Can't you see you're only hurting her more?" She turns to Nova. "I promise, I thought they'd be gone."

"It's okay," Nova whispers. "This was inevitable."

All she has to do is turn and leave. It's a straightforward process, but one that Nova has to focus on. Move the feet that feel like lead, tear her gaze away from the horror of seeing tears trickle down her mother's cheeks.

Her mother lost her father and it almost killed her.

Now she's lost her daughter.

Because Nova failed.

Move her feet. Look away. Run back to her cabin and curl back under the blanket. She should never have left.

"Shiloh, how much sap do you think—"

Nova slams her eyes shut. Surely the universe couldn't be so cruel.

The voice, one that used to sing happiness through her veins, stops like it was severed by a machete.

She turns slowly, suddenly conscious of her shallow cheeks and knotted hair, as if that matters considering her deformed hand.

When she opens her eyes again, she finds Kian where she knew he'd be. Only a few feet away, frozen and pale.

His earth-colored eyes muddy with anguish.

They spend long moments staring at each other, both knowing the space between them is now a chasm.

She's Unbound.

He's High Bound.

Kian swallows. "Are you..."

He trails off, and Nova knows he was going to ask if she's okay. It's instinctive for him—they looked out for each other their whole lives. But he'd know there's no way she's okay.

Nova bites her lip. She straightens her shoulders. "I will be."

Kian recognizes the lie for what it is. He takes a step forward. "We need to—"

Nova shakes her head violently. "I can't. I need...time."

She stares at his handsome face, so tight with pain. That was another lie. She doesn't need time. She needs Kian.

Taking a step back, she holds up her right hand, hiding the shame of her other hand behind her back. Kian won't be okay with seeing her in this much pain. That's why she has to leave.

It's why she hid.

"You have Askala to lead now, Kian. Just leave me to come to terms with all this."

Nova spins on her heel, desperate to hold in the sob. She stumbles down the hall.

"Hey, you heard her." Felicia sounds like a protective mother lioness. "She wants you to leave her alone."

Nova breaks into a run, realizing Kian is trying to follow her. As she reaches the upper decks she knows she can't go back to her cabin right now. It's the first place he'll look for her.

She needs to disappear for a bit. Kian will give up eventually. He'll have to. He has a colony to run.

She considers going to the gardens, but there will be others there. She can't face more curious, pitying faces. The beach won't work either. If Kian doesn't spot her walking down the gangplank, then it's the next place he'll look for her.

And she can't go to the lake. Too many memories.

She chokes. Will Kian take Shiloh there? Will their children play there like they did?

Impulsively, Nova takes a sharp left, heading to the back of the ship. A gust of wind tugs her shawl from her face, but she ignores it. No one ever goes here, there's no reason to.

This way leads nowhere but a short walk to the ocean.

She finds the ladder that extends down the side of the ship and tests it with a quick shake, finding it holds firm. It's been years since she's been down it. In fact, the last time she came here was when an Unbound died in the infirmary.

She'd wanted somewhere she could sob her heart out without having to be heard.

Without looking back, she quickly slips down it, the sound of the sea welcoming her below.

An acid ocean that destroys anything lacking the defenses to withstand it.

Defenses are one thing Nova doesn't have right now, but she doesn't intend on touching the water. There's a small beach below, a bare stretch of rocky soil between the Oasis and the sea.

Clambering down the ladder, Nova realizes it feels good to gain some distance between her and the life that's been decided for her. As she jumps down to the ground, her eyes sting. Leaving the Oasis is the first moment she's felt close to anything positive.

The sulfuric scent of the ocean fills her lungs and Nova looks out across its watery expanse. It's twilight, making the red-colored water a deep shade of blood. When humans drove their cars, flew their planes, used electricity for everything from cooling to can openers, did they ever stop to picture this?

A vital ocean desecrated until it's unrecognizable as the beautiful lifeline it should be.

None of them could've imagined the broken girl standing at the edge of it, thinking the expanse of blood looks like a drop when compared to the agony within her.

Nova's legs collapse. Curling her knees up to her chest and wrapping her arms around them, she tells herself the ocean will one day return to its former glory, the Bounds will make sure of it. Species they've never seen before are already returning, it's clear they've made a start.

Which means she'll find peace, too. One day.

Her head sinks into her arms, the sound of the waves filling her ears. She just needs to figure out how she does that alone.

Nova's head flies up at the sound of a creak.

She spins around at the sound of two feet landing on the rocky soil.

She freezes at the sound of the voice that always filled her with joy.

"Nova." Kian says her name like a prayer. "I had a feeling I'd find you here."

KIAN

*K*ian's read about deer. Seen the photos.

They were beautiful creatures, sleek and graceful. Yet they always seemed skittish. Head upright, large eyes wide and alert.

Ready to run.

Seeing Nova right now makes him think of those images.

She glances around, realizing there's nowhere to flee. Tucking her left hand behind her, she takes a few steps back. "I—I didn't think you'd find me here."

Kian shrugs, even that small movement feeling difficult under the weight of the pain growing between them. "I figured you wouldn't go to your cabin—too obvious. The beach was too public. The lake too painful." Kian winces. "Plus, this is where you came when you saw your first death in the infirmary."

He spent a good hour looking for her that time, finding her curled up as she tried to hold herself together.

Just like now.

Kian takes a step forward only for Nova to retreat.

He stops. Last time she welcomed his presence. Last time he was able to comfort her.

Nova's blue eyes, tearstained and turbulent, drink him in. Kian realizes he's doing the same.

They've become each other's source of pain, and yet neither of them has moved.

"I came here to be alone," Nova whispers.

Which is exactly what Shiloh said when she'd rushed forward and grasped his arm, stopping him as he'd gone to follow. She'd pointed out that Nova just said she needed time.

Kian had looked down at her hand. Her left hand. The one with a gold High Bound ring, not liking the way it tightened on his arm.

Her gaze had been sad, but intense. "Your father wants you to focus on harvesting the sap so we can help as many as we can. Bound and Unbound."

Which is true. His father had seen what the sap did to the two people whose arms were cut for the second test. It had sparked one of his rare smiles as he'd told Kian they needed to begin stocking up as soon as possible. Being able to help as many people of Askala as they can has always been his mission.

And now it's Kian's.

"I know it's hard, but we should respect her wishes." Shiloh's hand had squeezed his arm. "We'll look after her when she's ready."

There was no denying what Shiloh was telling him. She was reminding him of the divide that now exists between him and the girl he loves. And that Shiloh is standing with him on the side fate has chosen for him.

Except Nova has never been someone who wanted to be alone.

Her whole being is driven to connect and give to others. Nova draws her energy from those around her.

He'd pulled his arm away. "I need to say goodbye."

Shiloh had frowned as she'd looked away. "Of course. I understand."

But now that he's standing here, it doesn't feel like goodbye. It feels like he's breathing again, like his soul is coming back to life.

Nova looks like she's poised to run, probably wishing she could fly away. The only way out is past him and back up the ladder. "Please, Kian. Just go."

Kian frowns, confused. He never would've imagined a scene where Nova would ask him to leave. No matter how much she's hurting.

In the past, the more she hurt, the more she needed him.

He's never doubted she's strong enough to handle anything their harsh world could throw at her, but he'd always assumed that she wouldn't choose to do it alone.

That she needed him as much as he needed her.

A realization strikes him with such intensity, Kian jerks upright. Nova isn't pushing him away because this is what she needs to heal.

She's protecting him. Protecting him from her pain.

She's trying to let him go.

Not yet, his heart screams. Soon. But not yet.

Her eyes widen as she watches him take a few steps forward to a small patch of sand and sit down. "I can't." He looks up at her, "I don't want to leave."

Nova opens her mouth to reply and Kian holds his breath. If she insists, he doesn't know what he'll do.

Surely everything they've had can't end like this.

Nova blinks, her eyes flooding with tears. "I don't want you to leave, either."

His breath whooshing out, Kian pats the sand beside him. "Then come and watch the sunset with me."

Nova hesitates, just like Kian expected her to. In her mind, this would be a selfish decision. She should choose to walk straight past and leave him. Leave him to move on.

Leave him to lead Askala.

But if she chooses this, he'll know that coming here was the right decision.

He'll know she needs him as much as he needs her.

Her shoulders sagging, she walks over and sits beside him, although far enough that they can't touch. She pulls up her legs, resting her chin on them. "It is a beautiful sunset."

For the first time since Nova walked out onto the stage, Kian feels his lips move up.

They sit in silence for long minutes, simply staring out as the sky becomes the same shade of rust as the sea.

Kian becomes conscious of Nova's breath. Slow and steady like a heartbeat, it's a song for his soul. How is he supposed to move forward without that sound as his anchor?

Except he has to.

They both have to.

Kian clears his throat. "Mom is having problems letting the pods go."

"I'm not surprised." Kian can hear the hint of a smile in Nova's voice. "They've been her world for a long time now." She turns to look at him. "And your father?"

Glorying in her soft, perceptive gaze resting on him, Kian allows himself his first smile. "He's the one who surprised me. I've never seen him so energized. It's like he was waiting for this."

The first thing his father showed him was the ledgers. The ones where their supplies were recorded, no matter how meager. The ones that recorded their freshwater levels.

The ones where the Bound and Unbound are listed.

His father had never once acknowledged that Nova's name now sits in a different column to theirs.

Instead, he'd described Askala as an ecosystem—complex, layered...fragile.

Nova nods. "Your father's passion has been to build something great here. You were always part of that."

Kian knows what Nova says is true, he's just not sure how he feels about it. He knew his father had aspirations for him, but the joy and pride in his eyes almost seems to reach fever pitch sometimes. "I think his whole life has been geared toward passing Askala down to me."

"You'll be a wonderful leader, Kian," Nova says softly. "Like Magnus, you'll do what it takes."

Kian looks away. The greatest sacrifice that could be asked of him has already happened. His gut clenches. "Shiloh is in charge of the infirmary."

Nova doesn't move. "I saw that. I'm sure she'll be great."

At a loss for words, Kian digs his fingers into the sand. He wanted Nova to know what's been going on so she knows she's not an outsider, but he just managed to compound the pain.

Nova sighs, her chin sinking further into her knees. "Mom commented that she's a hard worker just a couple of weeks ago."

Clenching the sand in his palm, Kian stops himself from brushing back a strand of hair. He suspects Nova has no idea that her compassion is what makes her strong. He should've known coming here would just remind him why he's so in love with this girl.

Unable to stop himself, he leans in a little closer. "Wren is going to help Dex out with the labs."

Nova's eyes widen as she turns to him. "There's no way she would've put her hand up for that."

"Nope. Dex asked, saying he needed help seeing as there's only seven High Bound this time."

"Only seven?"

"Yeah...that's all that made it above the cutoff."

Nova turns to stare back out at the horizon, doing what everyone else did when they heard that—wondering what that means for Askala.

High Bound numbers are dropping.

She inhales sharply as she straightens. "Kian, look."

Kian leans to the side as he follows the line of her arm. His eyebrows hike up when he registers what she's seen.

Columns of smoke, three of them, rise into the sky on the other side of the ocean. Over in the Outlands.

"The Remn—" He stops himself, thinking of Wren. "The Outlanders. They're burning again."

"We haven't seen them do that in a long time."

"They're probably cooking a polar grizzly," Kian mutters.

The few times Askala has killed one of those massive hybrid bears, they'd limited their fires. No one likes watching those plumes of carbon spewing into the sky. Besides, drying the meat allows them to preserve it for leaner times.

"But three fires? It could be a celebration of some sort."

Nova's right, three fires is unusual. He looks at those gray, shifting pillars, wondering if he should ask Wren about it. He never would've thought someone from Outlands had enough brains and heart to pass the Proving, so who knows what other assumptions they've made about those people on the other side of the water.

Kian turns his head, instinctively going to ask Nova what she thinks, only to stop.

They'd drifted together like they always have as they'd been staring at the smoke, the movements as natural as the tide. Now their faces are only inches apart, their eyes looking nowhere but at each other.

Nova's arm drops. Her breath halts.

Kian swallows, his every muscle locked into place. He should move back, this is going to mean nothing but more torture, but he can't.

He doesn't want to.

Except Nova isn't moving either.

She's looking at him like...like she needs him as much as he needs her.

"Nova, I…" His voice is hoarse, full of confusion. He has no idea what he wants to say to her.

There's no way to make this okay. Yet there's no way to make these feelings go away.

She reaches up, her right hand cupping his cheek. "I know, Kian. There are no words."

This close, her blue eyes are mesmerizing and Kian finds himself drowning in their depths. So tender. So compassionate. So giving.

How can he walk away from her?

As he feels the emotion swell around them, Kian wonders if, maybe just for tonight, he doesn't have to.

All they've had was one fleeting, forbidden kiss. After months of hungering and yearning.

And now it's all been taken from them.

Unless they make this moment their own.

He leans forward a little more and Nova's eyes widen. "Maybe we don't need words."

Nova's breath hitches as she watches him come closer. "If we kiss, Kian…"

They won't be able to stop.

Their love doesn't know the meaning of Bound or Unbound. Their attraction has always refused to be contained.

"One night, Nova. A slice in time where it's just you and me."

Like it was supposed to be.

Nova's throat works as her hand trembles on his cheek. Her eyes flutter closed as her face tightens with pain.

Has he asked too much? Is this nothing but his own selfish need?

Her eyes open again, shimmering in the twilight. "A slice in time where you'll be mine."

He nods, his heart clenching at the fact her words were a question, not a statement. He was already hers.

He always will be.

"And you'll be mine," he promises.

His words hang in the early evening air, the sun almost gone. Time is moving forward whether they like it or not.

"Oh, Kian." Nova pushes forward, her mouth desperately seeking his.

His arms engulf her, hauling her against him, their lips melding.

Their last kiss was so restrained. They assumed there would be more.

But this time they both know this is the end.

That they need to compress every touch and taste and gasp into something that will last a lifetime

Their mouths open, hungry for more. Their tongues have barely touched when the passion explodes.

Nova climbs onto his lap, straddling him. He grips her hard, pressing her against him as his hands spear into her hair. Everything he's feeling, he's touching. It's so much more than he imagined.

Nova breathes his name, inflaming the heat inside Kian. Their passion was like a barely banked fire. And now it's consuming them both.

Their hands are desperate, their mouths insatiable. Shirts are lifted and discarded like the inconvenience they are.

As skin becomes exposed, there's a mutual understanding they should slow down. Savor the beautiful thing that's happening between them.

There are gasps, moans, the odd smile.

Nova falls back, taking Kian with her.

He holds himself above her, his heart thumping out the rhythm of their passion. "Nova."

Her name is synonymous with love. It always will be.

No matter what happens.

But he needs to know she's sure. That she wants this, too.

Nova's hands slide up his shoulders, sending a shiver down

his spine. She caresses his face, her own flushed with desire, yet soft with…love. "Be mine, Kian."

His mouth covers hers again before he makes a promise he can't keep. Part of him will always belong with Nova.

They lose themselves in a desire so powerful, so encompassing, it obliterates everything.

There are no rules.

No time.

No Askala.

Just two young hearts discovering the heights they can climb if only they're together.

Kian holds Nova throughout it all. Through scaling the peaks and troughs of their passion.

Through the gentle tumble back to Earth.

And even then, he doesn't let her go.

Lying on his back, he pulls her close, reveling in the feeling of her body curling into his as she tucks her head into his shoulder.

They lie on the sand, panting and silent.

Nova's right. There are no words.

It's when Nova's breath evens out that he realizes she's fallen asleep. Protectiveness wraps around him and his arm tightens. She'd be exhausted after everything she's been through.

Tucking his other hand behind his head, Kian stares up at the handful of early stars twinkling above.

His heart is still beating hard, his skin tingles like electrical pulses are dancing across it.

Lying here like this, with Nova, he's never felt more alive.

And yet, he has to leave.

To never feel like this again.

Nova stirs, as if she just felt his soul-deep denial, and Kian gently soothes her. With a quiet sigh, she relaxes against him.

Maybe he can carve out a little more time…

A sound from the hulking ship not far away has Kian tensing.

"Kian!" Someone is half-hissing half-shouting his name. "Kian!"

Recognizing Dex's voice, Kian glances down at Nova. Her face is peaceful with sleep, her hand curled under her chin.

"Kian!"

Not wanting her to wake, Kian slowly extricates himself. He doesn't want Dex, or anyone else for that matter, discovering they were down here together. He freezes when Nova stirs again, moving further onto her side. He pauses when he sees her other hand resting on her stomach.

Her left hand.

He reaches out to brush it, aching at the ravine it's created, but his name being called again has him stopping. Dex is starting to sound more urgent. And he's getting louder.

Finding his clothes, Kian tugs them on and clambers up the ladder.

"Kia—"

"I'm here, now keep it down."

Dex spins around, his arms flying out in exasperation. "About time! What the hell were you thinking, disappearing like that?"

Kian's brows shoot up. It seems Wren's language is wearing off on Dex. "I saw some fires over in the Outlands. I was checking them out."

Which is technically true. Kian moves away from the edge of the ship, leading Dex with him. Nova needs sleep. And privacy.

"Yeah, well, your dad saw them, too. He's been looking for you."

Kian's heart sinks. "How long?"

"Long enough that his eye started twitching, just like that time he caught us trying to spy on an Unbound party."

66

Dex starts to take a few steps only to find Kian hasn't moved. "What are you doing? We need to get you to the boardroom."

Kian hesitates. He can't leave Nova like this. Not after what they just shared. "I'll catch up in a second. I just have to take care of something."

Dex's frown is deep enough that Kian sees it despite the dark. "You can't just disappear like that. Your dad has already commented that a leader always needs to be available, Kian." Dex angles his head. "After doing nothing but tell everyone what a stellar leader you're going to be."

Kian tries to take a step, only to find he can't. "I wanted to say goodbye to Nova."

Dex returns to stand in front of him. "It looks to me like you've already said your goodbyes…"

"What?" Kian gasps. Dex acted like he just got here. "What did you see?"

"Nothing that I'll have to wash my eyeballs out in the ocean for or anything. But you were gone long enough for me to figure it was one heck of a goodbye."

"I can't do it, Dex. I can't leave her."

"You can't let your father see you're torn, Kian. That Nova has you…wishing things were different. You have to go back."

Dex's words hit him hard, as only the truth can. It would be the ultimate disappointment for his father to know that part of Kian hates being Bound.

But Nova is down at the beach, fragile and vulnerable.

Dex's arms explode out in exasperation. "What are you going to do, Kian? What's your plan? Make Nova your Unbound mistress?"

Kian reels back, horror injecting through his veins. That never crossed his mind. He would never do that to Nova.

Dex pushes his face in close. "Exactly."

Kian's shoulders slump. Dex is right. He needs to go back. He can't afford for his father to come looking for him. He can't know Kian's heart is now torn, divided between his two reasons for existing.

Askala.

And Nova.

With a last look over his shoulder, Kian accepts it's his turn to protect Nova, just like she protected him.

By walking away.

DEX

*L*eaning back in his chair, Dex scratches his chin as he stares at the bank of computers in front of him in the lab.

He's spent every chance he's had over the past two days going through the files. His father's been nowhere to be seen, which is odd, especially after he specifically told him that they had a lot to talk about after the Announcement.

Of course, the first thing Dex had looked for were the results of the Proving. His stomach had been in knots as he'd scrolled down the neatly compiled lists of numbers next to each of the nine participants' names. Points had been awarded under a wide range of criteria. *Understanding of the task. Adherence to the stated rules. Putting the needs of the greater good first. Ability to see what lies underneath the test...*

They go on and on with sixty-seven criteria under each test, some ranking almost the exact same thing.

Dex studies it again now, wondering how *Putting the needs of the greater good first* is any different to *Putting others before self* and decides that must be the whole point of it. They're check-measures to make sure the scoring is accurate. It would be nice if his father were here to explain.

It's tragic to see the columns of numbers come to a sudden stop for Jay, Fern and Thom. Two deaths and one disappearance have made it the most controversial Proving of all. With Thom still not having turned up, it seems they can almost certainly raise the death toll to three.

But it's the other columns he's more interested in. Not so much Kian's, Shiloh's or Felicia's, as the numbers were exactly as he'd expected there.

It's his own numbers he's most interested in. Followed by Nova's and Wren's.

He's looked at those three columns for so long they've become a blur.

Overall, his numbers seem generous. Nova's seem harsh.

Wren's spike up and down like the toothy grin of a leatherskin.

Isolating his report, he looks down the column once more. His father didn't score him especially high in any area, it's more that he received a slightly above average score in every one of the criteria, which add up to a high number at the end.

Clicking on Nova's name, he looks down her column. Although there are some impressive scores next to the empathy measures, her ranking on the ones more related to intelligence are a little lower. Not so low that anything in particular jumps out, but lower than he'd expect. Low enough to pull down her overall score, placing her just underneath the cutoff. He's grown up beside that girl. She's not stupid. Not even close.

Switching across to Wren's results, he decides he's never going to make sense of them. It's almost like his father pulled these numbers out of a hat. Some are generous. Some are harsh. There's no pattern to them whatsoever.

Dex jumps as the door slides open. Reflexively clicking off the screen, he spins around in his chair.

"Dad?" It's as if an imposter has entered the room. His hair is limp and greasy, his face a pale white, his forehead filled with lines. "Are you okay?"

His father walks to him and Dex reels back at the smell of this usually well-groomed man. Taking the seat beside him, his father grips the arms of the chair and Dex notices his hands are covered in scratches.

"Where have you been?" Dex asks, noticing a nasty cut on his father's leg. "You look terrible."

"I went looking for Thom."

Now, that, Dex wasn't expecting.

"And did you find him?" he asks.

His father shakes his head, turning his bloodshot eyes on Dex. "He's gone."

"You could have been killed out there!" Dex shakes his head, unable to believe what he's hearing. "We could have put a search team together. Why would you go out alone? You saw what almost happened to Nova in the final test."

"I had to." His father sits forward, resting his elbows on his knees. "Thom was my responsibility. The weight of two deaths is already enough to carry. I can't bear the burden of another."

"You didn't seem this bothered by it last time we spoke," says Dex, still trying to piece this together.

"I didn't want you to know what a burden taking on this role can be." His father's head hangs. "I needed you in that chair after the Proving."

"Why? Why me?" Dex places his palm on his chest. "It doesn't matter who does this job. We're all working for the good of Askala."

"It does matter." His father's head snaps up. "It matters a lot."

"You're worried about being found out, aren't you?" Dex points to the blank screen, but his father keeps his eyes on him. "You altered my results to make me Bound, didn't you?"

His father shakes his head.

"Admit it!" Dex is shaking now. "You changed my results. Just tell me."

His father swallows, the words seeming to be caught in his throat. "I can ex—"

"What gives you the right to mess with my life like that?" Dex stands and marches to the door, wanting to get as far away from this man as possible, but turns when he gets to the sensor, knowing he needs to stay and get answers. "This is wrong. So wrong!"

"Askala has been messing with all our lives for long enough," his father says. "It's time for things to change. I needed you here to take over my work. You're the only one I trust."

"Trust?" Dex rakes his fingers through his hair, his whole world spinning. "You trust me? You don't even know me, Dad. If it weren't for Amity taking care of me when I was little, I'd have wandered into the forest and died. Just like Thom."

His father winces at Thom's name. Dex is glad. Let him feel some of the pain he's been inflicting on others.

"No wonder I didn't score high enough to be a true Bound with your genes," Dex continues, immediately regretting the cruelty in his words.

"Sit down." His father's voice is calm as he leans over, switches the screen back on and clicks a few buttons.

Dex pulls back his chair, forcing it a little as it catches on a loose floorboard. He slides back into the seat and watches the screen, aware of the hammering of his heart.

His father selects a file and types in a password.

"It's *Mercy Forever*," his father says. "No spaces and *forever* spelled with a numeral four."

"Sappy much?" Dex crosses his arms.

His father doesn't appear to hear him. He's too busy pointing at the screen.

Dex looks across to see his results. The same numbers he's been studying so hard he knows them by heart.

His father taps on the keyboard and the numbers begin to change, several of them at once counting back like a reverse clock, the total number at the bottom of the column falling.

Dex swallows, not sure he wants to watch. He'd been such a fool when he'd stood on that stage accepting his ring, daring to believe that maybe he'd been worthy of wearing it.

"These are your results," his father says, as the numbers come to a halt. "Your true results."

Dex's brow furrows as he tries to make sense of these new numbers. "But...but I don't understand. They say I'm Bound. Are they still counting down?"

"Dex, you *are* Bound." His father sits back and waits for Dex to take this in. "You're a true Bound. I just wish your mother were here to see this. She should be here."

"Then why did you change the results?" Dex shakes his head, still not sure what to believe. "What was the point?"

His father rubs at his temples. "I needed you to be High Bound."

Dex slumps in his chair. He knew there was no way he'd have scored higher than Wren. It hadn't felt right when that box had popped open to reveal a golden ring destined for him. Of course, he's not a true High Bound.

"They don't let ordinary Bounds run the Provings," his father says.

"And why do I have to run the Provings?" he asks, feeling like they're turning in a circle.

"Because I told you, Dex. Askala is about to change." There's a spark in his father's eyes and he starts to look more like the man Dex knows. "You have to be in that chair for the right kind of change to happen."

"You want me to alter the results of the next Proving, don't you?" asks Dex. "I'm not going to do that. This whole thing just isn't right."

Shaking his head, his father draws in a breath. "I'm talking about a total overhaul of the Provings."

"No." Dex crosses his arms. "Do you understand that word? No. I'm not going to be any part of this."

"Dex, the system is flawed. There's so much wrong with the way we do things around here." His voice is pleading now. "And I'm afraid that it's all Magnus's fault. He's made things worse, not better. Kian's no different. He's just like his father."

Dex winces, not wanting to hear anything against his cousin. His father holds up his hands at his pained expression. "I love Kian. He's a good kid. But he carries the same flaw as his father. He's too loyal to the system. He believes in it too much."

It's Dex's turn to hang his head in his hands. This is all too much to take in. "Dad, you need some sleep. And a good wash. How long's it been since you ate anything?"

"Don't worry about me. It's you we need to worry about. You have a lot of work ahead of you. It's only a matter of time before everything in this place implodes. Something big is going to happen. It's inevitable."

"I haven't agreed to any of this." Dex kicks at the floor, feeling desperately like he needs to talk to someone about this. But who? There's no one he can trust with something this big. Not until he figures out exactly what his father is talking about. Hopefully after he's had some sleep he'll start to make more sense.

His father stands. "You're right. You haven't agreed. But maybe your mother can convince you."

"My mother's dead." Dex lets out a long sigh. "Please don't tell me she's alive and you have her hidden somewhere."

His father shakes his head. "Of course not. She *is* dead. But in some ways she lives on. Check the top drawer. There's a false back to it. Behind it, you'll find a device. You know the password. You'll discover you're already part of this, Dex."

Dex watches his father walk through the door, as always leaving him with more questions than answers.

His curiosity piqued, he throws open the drawer, pulling it out beyond its tracks. There's a small section at the back that's been enclosed in timber. Tipping the contents of the drawer onto the desk, he taps at the compartment, trying to get it open. It's sealed tight. Clearly, his father didn't want anyone else stumbling upon this.

Banging it with his fist, the timber walls remain in place, so he picks up a wooden cup he'd been drinking from, downs the liquid then uses it to bash at one of the edges.

Realizing it's no use, he raises the drawer above his head, preparing to throw it to the ground, then worries about breaking the device in it, so he sets it down.

He really needs something to pry it open. Whatever's in there, it must be important.

Remembering the knife he was given in the last test of the Proving, Dex carries the drawer with him and heads for the bunk room. He'd stuck that knife under the mattress of his bunk after the last test, intending to come back for it later.

Now is definitely later.

The lab is quiet as he pads down the hallway. It's late in the evening now. Most of Askala's inhabitants will be tucked up in their cabins asleep. Well, most of the Bound inhabitants. Who knows what the Unbound are up to. Who knows what Nova's up to. Although, he can't imagine she's adopted any of their carefree ways. Not yet.

Not ever.

It'd been both a surprise and no surprise at all to find Kian with her on the beach. Their naked bodies had been obscured in the fading light but there had been no doubt what they'd been doing. It was only lucky that Dex had been the one to find them.

With the impossibility of their situation tugging at his heart, he opens the door to the bunk room. Reaching for the switch, he flicks it and dim light fills the room.

It's strange being back in here. The bunks are as they left them, with no need to make them back up for anyone just yet.

He sets down the drawer on what was Kian's bunk and goes to his own. Crouching down beside it, he slides his fingers underneath the mattress and lifts it up so it's leaning against the wall.

"Bloody hell!" He jumps back several paces when he sees a pair of eyes watching him from beneath the bed slats.

"Keep your hemp panties on," says Wren, rolling out from under the bunk.

"What are you doing here?" he asks, sitting down on Kian's mattress and clutching his chest. "You nearly gave me a heart attack."

"I was sleeping, what do you think I was doing?" She sits up and hugs her knees. Her hair is mussed and she has lines on her face from resting on the blanket. It's the first time he's seen her since the Announcement and it makes his chest ache. Not just from the shock she gave him.

"You have a cabin on the Oasis." He shakes his head. "With an actual bed in there."

"I don't think much of beds." She grins at him.

"I noticed."

"I liked it better with you snoring above me, though," she says with an inscrutable expression.

He sighs. "You know what? So did I. Apart from the fact I don't snore."

"Whatever you say, oh royal High Bound." She brings her hand to her forehead and gives him a salute.

"How have you been?" he asks, quickly changing the subject away from his fraudulent High Bound status.

She shrugs. "Can I be honest?"

"I've never known you not to be."

A flicker of something passes over her face. "I liked life better in the Proving. I sort of miss it."

He chuckles. "You didn't even want to do the Proving!"

"Crazy, hey?" She shakes her head.

"Not crazy. I know what you mean. There were parts of it I enjoyed, too. Working as a team, figuring stuff out together... seeing you every day."

A silence hangs in the air. Not awkward, but not exactly comfortable either.

"I need to tell you something," he says. "I've organized a role for you. An opportunity for us to continue to work together here in the lab. You can sleep under that bunk every night if you want to. If you accept."

She tilts her head. "Go on."

"I've had approval for you to help me with the Provings," he says. "Sort of like what Lana used to do."

"What?" Wren leaps to her feet and paces.

"You don't have to accept," he says. "But I'd really like you to."

"I despised Lana and that fake smile of hers in the Proving, you know that." She pauses her pacing to stare at him.

"You don't need to be like her!" He holds up his hand. "You'd do the job your way. I could really use your input. You look at things so differently to everyone else."

Her pacing begins again as she mulls over what he just said.

"What else are you going to do?" he asks. "Hang out with the Bounds picking tomatoes in the garden. Come on, Wren. You've got a great brain for this stuff. I need you. And I promise you don't need to smile at any of the participants. But no headlocks either, okay?"

"It wasn't a headlock," she says with the hint of a smile. "I believe I strangled Felicia. And she definitely deserved it."

"Maybe." Dex watches as Wren sits back down and crosses her legs.

"Okay, I'll help you." She nods. "Besides, maybe we'll be

overrun with pesky Remnants by then and we won't even have a Proving."

"Great. I appreciate it." He studies her face carefully, trying to decide what's behind her words. There's certainly a risk that more people from the Outlands will make it here alive. But that's even more reason to have Wren helping him. Would there ever be so many of them that the Provings would fail to run at all?

"What's with the drawer?" Wren points beside him. "Your new teddy bear?"

"I was just trying to fix it," he answers a little too quickly. "One of the tracks is broken. I was looking for my knife."

Wren dives back under his bunk and comes back holding his knife by the wooden handle. "I borrowed it. In case someone holding a drawer sneaks in and wakes me up. A girl's gotta protect herself."

"I'm lucky you didn't stab me." He rolls his eyes.

"How do you know I won't?" She flicks the knife in the air, catches it, then swivels it around to hand it to him.

"There's a lot I don't know about you, Wren." He takes the knife from her and puts it in the drawer. "But I do know you're not going to stab me."

"I saw Nova," she says, leaning back on the bunks. "You seen her yet?"

Guilt punches Dex in the gut as he shakes his head. "I wanted to. I mean, I've tried to. But it hasn't worked out. How is she?"

"Exactly as you think." A sadness crosses Wren's face. "That finger thing is really awful, you know. It's like humiliation on top of her humiliation."

Dex shakes his head. "It's so hard to believe it actually happened."

"You do know that this system you're all so keen on doesn't

78

work, don't you?" Wren sits back down and leans against the bunk.

"It has some issues." She's right but this is all he's willing to admit right now. Askala has also done a lot of good.

"What did your dad want?" she asks. "He nearly caught me sneaking in here."

"Just dad stuff." He gets up and sits on the floor beside her. It's getting harder to fight the feelings he has for her. Now that they're both Bound, he wonders why he's even fighting them at all.

"Wren…" He reaches out and takes hold of her hand, stroking her fingers lightly.

"Don't, Dex." She pulls back her hand, but the way she does it tells him there was a part of her that didn't want to.

"Is there someone else?" he asks, dreading the answer, but needing to know. "In the Outlands?"

She looks at him for a long moment before nodding. "There is."

He'd suspected that was the case, but hearing her say it is a whole other thing.

A feeling he doesn't recognize hits him in the chest. Jealousy? Disappointment? Or is that the feeling of a crack appearing in his heart? Reminding himself that she made no promises to him, he pushes down his pain and does his best to sound reassuring. The last thing he wants is to lose her as a friend.

"I understand," he says. "But if you ever change your mind…"

"You don't want me." She shuffles away, folding her arms so there's no chance of him taking her hand again.

He's not sure what to say to this. Scream at her and tell her he wants nothing more than her? Get to his knees and tell her he'll never again meet anyone who's going to make him feel like this? Lie to her and say that it doesn't matter?

"Would you like me to stay with you?" he asks instead. "It can be like old times."

She shoots him a sideways look and just for a moment her tough girl face slips, revealing her vulnerable side.

Whatever's in that drawer is going to have to wait until morning. Because right now Wren needs him. She may not be able to be in his life in the way he wants her to be, but he'll take whatever he can. Because being separated from her the last couple of days sucked.

Wren crawls back under the bunk and he sets down his mattress.

"Good night, Dex," she says.

"Good night, Wren."

He turns off the light and climbs into his bunk, a sense of fatigue washing over him. In the morning he'll open the drawer to see what his father's talking about, although he doubts it's going to change his mind about anything. What his father did was wrong. He can't expect Dex to continue on with whatever it is he's started just because he's his son.

"Oh, and Wren…" he says

"What is it now?" comes her sleepy reply.

"I don't wear panties."

WREN

*W*ren wakes early and slides out from under Dex's bunk. The dim light from the exit sign is casting shadows across the room. She can see the shape of the drawer on Kian's old bed, the knife still sitting inside it.

Dex seemed to think she bought his story about fixing one of the tracks. Who would use a knife to fix a broken track? And who would carry the whole drawer around with them while they were looking for one?

Nobody.

Glancing at Dex, she listens to his deep breathing, debating whether or not she should take the drawer. She saw last night that it has some kind of secret compartment at the back. The sort that could be pried open with a knife...honestly, Dex must take her for a fool.

It's not like him to be so secretive. Whatever's inside that compartment must be important. And she came to Askala to find out as much as she could before the others join her. Just one of the reasons she agreed to help Dex even though she highly doubts there will ever be another Proving. She'd almost told him as much, instantly regretting it. Dex is a smart guy and he watches her closely. She has to be more careful.

Shaking her head, she can't believe she's even debating if she should take the drawer. The Wren who washed up on shore would already be out the door with it under her arm.

"Forgive me," she whispers, blowing Dex a kiss and picking it up, careful not to let the knife rattle inside.

Pressing her hand to the sensor, the door whooshes open. She walks into the hallway, fighting between wanting to go out to the forest to discover Dex's secret or open it in the courtyard.

Knowing the raven won't find her in the forest, she heads for the courtyard, making sure her pendant is clearly visible. The raven has to take priority, now more than ever.

Outside, the sky is bright blue without a cloud in sight. Perfect weather for ravens.

The heat of the day has already kicked in and she feels the sun's rays prickling the top of her head. They haven't had a storm since the one that came while they were collecting the pteropods. They must be due for another soon.

"Come on, sweet raven," she calls.

It's been almost a week since she sent that message to the Outlands with instructions on how to build a raft that won't fall apart. Surely, a reply must be on its way? Or were those fires on the shore some kind of message she was supposed to be able to decipher?

This is why she's been sleeping in the lab. It's not just because she likes her little space under Dex's bunk. The courtyard was where the raven found her last time. And if there's one thing she knows about ravens, it's that they're creatures of habit. This is the first place it will look for her again. Hopefully to bring her news from Phoenix. Or maybe even news from Cy.

Tilting her pendant toward the sky, she remembers the lurch in her stomach when she'd seen Dean on the upper decks. His resemblance to Phoenix had been startling, leaving no doubt in her mind about who he was.

Dean hadn't wanted to believe her at first. He'd been certain that what she'd told him was too good to be true. He'd waited almost two full decades for news on his brother, having become certain he was dead.

Finding out that Ronan is alive was a shock for him. His eyes had opened wide and his jaw had fallen as he stumbled back, trying to process the news.

To learn that Ronan had somehow survived his banishment and gone on to have children was the last thing Dean expected to hear. But Wren had convinced him. She knew too much about him to leave Dean in any doubt.

But it wasn't only Wren who had mind-blowing news. Dean also had information that had left her gasping. News that doesn't just concern Wren. It concerns the person here she trusts the most.

Dex.

Could Ronan really be his true father?

She sets the drawer down on the ground, certain it contains something important. She'd never have betrayed Dex's trust if she didn't believe that.

Picking up the knife, she eases the false wall open.

A rectangular device falls forward. Black in color, it has a screen and a round button at the bottom. She knows what this is. She's seen one in the Outlands. It's a cell phone. Except, it will be as useless here as they are anywhere. Cell phones haven't operated for decades.

Picking up the phone, she presses the round button, surprised to see the screen light up. That must be some strong battery. Unless someone's charged it recently...

Eager to see what information could be contained in such a device, she presses the button again. But her hope quickly diminishes when it asks her for a password.

"What are you doing?"

She almost drops the phone when she sees Dex walk through the door into the courtyard.

"I wanted to surprise you," she says, feeling as lame as she must sound. "I wanted to fix the drawer before you woke up. Did you know it has a secret compartment? I found this in it." She holds the phone out to him.

"Thanks." He takes it from her and puts it in his pocket, his face expressionless.

"Aren't you going to look at it?" She rocks on her heels as she waits to see how upset he is.

"I'll check it out later."

She nods and they look at each other, the secrets they both carry a ten-foot wall between them.

This is why they can never be together. Not in the way Dex wants. It'd killed her when he'd made himself vulnerable to her last night. But she couldn't go there. Not with everything she'd just learned.

"I'm sorry, Dex," she says, hating that she'd lied to him.

"Sorry that you took it?" He crosses his arms, his eyes like stone. "Or sorry you didn't know the password?"

She sighs. "I was curious. It was wrong. I shouldn't have done it. I'm sorry about everything."

A softness snakes its way across his face and she sees a familiar glint in his eyes. "Thank you, Wren, that means a lot."

"You're not upset with me?" She tilts her head, keeping her eyes on him so he can see her sincerity.

"Of course, I'm upset. If you're going to help me in the Provings, we need to learn to trust each other. This hasn't exactly been a good start."

"You're right," she agrees, not just to placate him but because he really is right. She shouldn't have broken his trust like that.

"No harm done in the end." He shakes his head. "I'm too exhausted to hold a grudge. Especially against you."

"So, you're really not going to look at what's on that thing?" she asks.

"I told you I'll look at it later." He pats his pocket.

She nods, even though the curiosity is going to kill her. But Dex didn't press her too much when he'd found her out here sending her note to Phoenix, so it's only right she returns the favor.

"Are you trying to send another message?" he asks, noticing her pendant.

"No." She bites down on her lip. "Hoping to receive one, actually."

"Seen any ravens?" There's a note of coldness in his voice. He may have said he doesn't plan to hold a grudge, but it seems it might take some time for him to forget what she'd just done.

She shakes her head. "Not yet."

"How about that one?" He points behind her.

She spins around to see a large glossy raven perched on the wall. "No way."

Leaving Dex, she rushes to the raven's side, reaching in her pocket for the dead cricket she's been carrying with her.

"Come on, sweetheart," she coos. "Look what I have for you."

The raven tilts its head, as if complaining it's not a live cricket this time.

"Look, it's breakfast," she says, waving the cricket in front of her. "Fresh from yesterday."

Swooping down, the raven lands beside her and she sees that it has a letter tied to one of its legs.

"That's it," she says, handing over the cricket and untying the note.

Her heart is racing at the thought of what information it might contain as she shoves it in her pocket.

Seeing that its job is done, the raven clicks its beak and takes off. With several flaps of its powerful wings, it's no more than a speck in the sky.

"You going to read it?" asks Dex, stepping forward.

"I'll check it out later." She pats her pocket and grins at him, expecting him to laugh at the way she's thrown his own words back at him.

But his face slips into a frown. "Wren, I'm a High Bound now. I need to know what's in that note in case it concerns Askala."

She shakes her head. The glimpse she got of the note as she'd untied it had shown it'd been written in Cy's hand, not Phoenix's. This isn't a note she can let Dex read, even if it is written in code. Codes can be broken, which means she'll protect it with her life if she has to.

Dex holds out his hand. "I'm not joking, Wren. I need to see what's in the note. Hand it over. Enough is enough."

Wren glances at the door, calculating how many seconds it will take her to get there, given she'll need to take a wide arc around Dex.

Noticing her gaze, he steps back, making it almost impossible that she'll succeed.

So, instead, she turns to the wall behind her, running at it hard in the very place she'd scouted the first time she'd stepped into this courtyard. Cy had trained her to always have an exit. Never leave yourself trapped. There's a way out of anywhere if you plan it in advance.

She connects with the wall at speed, her foot finding the small divot she'd carved out almost a week ago now, her hands grappling to find purchase on the timber panels above.

"Hey!" cries Dex, but she doesn't turn to see how close he is behind her.

Pushing with her leg, she launches upward with just enough power to grab hold of an overhanging tree that Callix really should have pruned.

With her hands on the branch, she scrambles up the

remainder of the wall, swinging herself over the top and landing with a thud on the other side, right beside the locked gate she'd exited through on the last day of the Proving.

"Get back here!" Dex calls over the wall. "Wren!"

"I'm sorry," she shouts back, before she turns and hightails it into the trees.

Knowing Dex will be right behind her once he has the gate open, she picks up her pace, concentrating on her breathing as well as where her feet are landing. She can't afford to slip.

As her lungs scream for more air, she's glad Cy trained her so hard, making her run through the burnt forests of the Outlands, pushing her harder and faster until she'd thought her heart might run out of beats.

But he'd been right to push her. Because out here, strength equals survival. It's the best asset she has.

Deciding she has enough of a head start, she ducks behind a rock and pulls the note from her pocket, decoding it quickly before stuffing it into her mouth and swallowing it.

Let Dex try to read it now.

Panting heavily, she sits down on the hard ground and repeats the note over and over, searing each word into her memory.

Rafts are on their way. Phoenix is on board. Good work. Cy.

She can't help the goofy grin that's chosen to plaster itself to her face. And it's not just because Phoenix is coming. It's because Cy has said two words that he's never said to her before.

Good work.

High praise from Cy.

High praise that makes all of this worthwhile. Even if she had to run away from Dex.

He'll forgive her when one day he opens his eyes and sees Askala for what it is.

He has to. Because like it or not, if what Dean told her is true, this involves him, too.

Dex might just be the link to both sides of this war. The one who has the power to unite them all.

He just doesn't know it yet.

NOVA

"*W*hat are you going to do, Kian? What's your plan?*"
Dex's words are caught in a loop in Nova's
head. She'd been climbing the ladder when she heard them talking. She'd almost fallen off when Dex had thrown out the last question.

"Make Nova your Unbound mistress?"

An Unbound mistress. She'd heard of the term. Rose had hinted once that she'd scored an extra pod for something that happens so freely on the upper decks. She was looking forward to keeping Dorian company now that he hadn't sired any children for several years. It seems he was in need of...companionship.

Nausea brews in Nova's gut. Is that what Kian wants? For that to be her life? She'd held on to the ladder, white knuckled and pale faced, as she'd waited for Kian to answer.

And he hadn't.

In fact, he'd walked away.

And then, like a fool, Nova had waited again. All night, she'd waited for him to come. Deny, explain, apologize...anything. He wouldn't know that she'd overheard their last words, but after what had passed between them on the beach, he couldn't just walk away.

Like she was some...Unbound mistress.

But Kian hadn't arrived.

Leaving Nova with a choice. Continue with the one-person pity party or drag herself out of bed and do what Kian's obviously done—move on.

Which is what has Nova standing at her door, hair brushed, face washed, resolve wrapped around her like armor. She needs to find something to do with her time. No matter how much that idea scares her.

The hall is empty even though it's early afternoon, although that isn't surprising. She hears the drums each night. The thumping seems to pulse through the walls, a primitive, tribal sound. The throbbing extends deep into the night and spills into the early hours of the morning.

Nova sucks in a deep breath, enjoying being outside of her cabin for a change. The sun is already bright and glary in anticipation of the new day. She pulls up her shawl, wondering where she's going to go. It seems it's time to explore her new home— the upper decks.

She reaches the stairs only to find Sam sitting on the first stair, his back against the wall. His head lolls as a soft snore drifts from his slack mouth. Nova frowns. Sam is even thinner than the last time she saw him, and his skin has taken on a gray tinge.

She squats down, brushing her fingers over his forehead. No temperature. She stills as she listens to his breathing, not liking what she's hearing. It sounds like a child's rattle is lodged in Sam's chest.

A cough wracks his body and Nova frowns deeper. What's Sam doing out here on the steps? He should be resting in bed.

The hacking motion jerks Sam awake and he looks around,

disoriented for a second. His gaze falls on Nova and he relaxes. "Hello, angel. It's good to see you out and about."

Nova sits down beside him. "What are you doing out here?" She surreptitiously sniffs the air. "Have you been drinking again?"

Another round of coughs wrench through Sam. "I wish. Been too busy."

"Doing what?" Nova glances around, wondering if they play cards wherever they can, including out in the hallways.

"Wren wanted me to check up on you."

Surprise shoots through Nova. "She what?"

"She's stopped by each day, asking about you. I told her the only two times you've rushed into your cabin, you've been crying."

Nova thinks of the night Wren visited her, after the Proving. That day, and the few after it, feel like a fog, but she knows she barely spoke to her. Guilt shifts through Nova. Wren was trying to be a good friend, and Nova didn't even say thanks.

It seems she has something she needs to do today.

Then Nova realizes why Sam was sleeping at the bottom of the steps. "You were keeping an eye on me?"

Sam grins ruefully, rubbing the back of his head. "To be honest, I was glad for something to do," he wheezes.

Nova frowns. "That's very sweet of you, but you're not well, Sam. You should be in bed, resting." Or better yet, trying to earn some pods.

"And get better for what, angel? So, I can play more cards? Drink more? Head over to the party deck and find some willing woman?"

Nova bites her lip. Not long ago, she would've argued with Sam, told him his life had purpose. But she's only been Unbound for a few days, and she already understands how wrong she was.

No children.

No future.

No reason to keep moving forward.

"Does everyone feel like this?" she asks in a whisper.

Sam slips an arm around Nova's shoulder and she registers how bony it is. "You learn to live with it. Some tell themselves this is for the best. Others drown it out with the drums." He smiles crookedly. "Others ferment berries."

Nova sighs, wondering what she'll do so she can come to accept who she is now—unwanted, incomplete…broken.

Sam's arm tightens around her, the gap where his ring finger should be feeling strange. "Promise me something, angel."

Nova looks up into his weathered face. "Yes?"

"Don't let them have you thinking you're less. When you start believing that, that's when you lose the fight."

The fight? Nova's about to ask what he means, but Sam's gaze softens.

"That's what you did for me. You showed me you didn't think I was less."

Nova's eyes sting. He's talking about when she stitched him up, even when she wasn't supposed to. There's something about Sam that tells her he would've made a good father. Her heart aches with a new wave of grief. Except his ability to have children was taken from him.

She leans over, wrapping her arms around his fragile waist. "No one is less, Sam."

Sam hugs her back, his clasp surprisingly tight. "Exactly, angel," he whispers against her hair.

Nova pulls away, drawing in a shuddering breath. Yep, Sam would've made a wonderful father. "Thank you, Sam."

Sam's grin is cut short by the next wave of coughs, and he releases her to cover his mouth as they heave through his body.

The moment he's done, Nova slips her arm around him again. "Now let's get you to bed. No more watching out for me, okay?"

She goes to help him stand, but Sam stays put. "That depends. Where you off to? Not to see that boy again, I hope."

Nova smiles despite the lancing pain the mention of Kian still brings. Although he's unwell, Sam is still looking out for her. She shakes her head. "I'm going to say thank you to another friend."

Sam's body unwinds. "That's m'girl."

As Nova walks Sam to his cabin, she keeps her frown hidden as he leans heavily on her. After seeing Wren, she's going to find out about making him some vegetable broth. He needs food and rest.

Sam is asleep before Nova has pulled the cover up over his frail shoulders. She tiptoes out of the room, wondering how many nights he slept on the steps. He was there when she arrived after the Proving, and he must've seen her run back to her room after her night with Kian.

She was a mess both times.

Well, she can't afford to be that anymore. Askala might believe Sam doesn't deserve the same level of care, but she's going to show him otherwise.

Striding through the corridors, Nova considers where Wren might be. Kian said she was helping Dex with the Provings, which means the lab is the best place to start. Tucking her shawl tightly around her head, Nova's secretly glad. Despite her newfound determination, the thought of searching the lower decks or anywhere else she could run into someone from her old life makes her gut clench.

Her mother always told her healing takes time.

Except when Nova arrives at the labs, she discovers it's hard not to think of herself as less. As she scans her hand over the sensor, the doors remain shut.

She looks down at her hand. At the four fingers. At the garish gap.

She's Unbound. Which means she doesn't have access to the labs.

Cheeks aflame, Nova knocks. It's going to be humiliating when Dex answers the door, but she's not willing to back down. She can't tell Sam she went back to her room without having found Wren.

When there's no answer, Nova knocks again. The *rap, rap, rap* seems to echo as she stands there waiting, but the door doesn't open. Either there's no one here, or they don't want Unbound visitors.

Spinning around, Nova chews her lower lip, welcoming the sting. The thought of asking around the lower decks feels overwhelming. She's about to head back down the path to the Oasis when she freezes. Two voices drift through the trees. Two voices she knows.

Two voices she can't face right now.

Darting around the building, Nova presses herself against the wall as the footsteps draw closer.

"Are you sure?" Kian asks, something about the way he says it telling Nova it's a loaded question.

There's a pause, and Nova imagines Dex rubbing his stump. "I checked and double checked. The scoring is far more comprehensive than we realized."

The door whooshes open. They must be talking about the Proving.

"There's nothing worth investigating?" Kian's voice has a hint of desperation.

Another pause, and Nova finds herself straining to hear.

"The numbers seemed a little low in places, but not enough to change the overall result. I'm sorry, I wish it were different."

The door slides closed and Nova sags against the wall, feeling like a puppet whose strings were just severed.

Kian was checking her results? For the briefest of moments, her heart soars. He's struggling to accept this as much as she is.

Only to crash again. It doesn't matter. Dex said the results were correct. Of course, they were. Nova looks at her hand. And she's infertile.

Pushing herself from the wall, Nova stumbles away. Instinctively, she turns her back on the Oasis. She can't go back there. Not yet.

As she heads to the beach, the smell of rain fills her nostrils with its earthy scent and Nova notices the dark clouds rolling in over the ocean. A storm is coming. And a big one, from the looks of things.

She clenches her hand, trying to make her disfigurement disappear. At least the weather matches her mood—agitated and bleak.

Nova's just stepped on sand when she discovers she's not the only one who's come to watch the storm. "Wren?"

Wren spins around, instantly on alert. "Nova," she relaxes. "It's just you."

Nova tries to smile. "Just me."

"You know I didn't mean it that way." She rolls her eyes. "In fact, you'll be a breath of fresh air after all those highly-strung Bounds."

"You're one of them now," Nova points out, feeling herself unwind, too.

Wren turns away. "I'll never be one of them." She grins over her shoulder. "I don't walk around looking like I just sucked on mangrove pine sap."

Nova rolls her eyes straight back at her. "They have serious stuff to deal with. Like healing Earth. You do too, now."

"Because that's the only thing worth living for, isn't it?"

Nova comes to stand beside Wren, not sure what that means, but knowing Wren intended it to be a rhetorical question. Her shawl tumbles back and she holds her face up to the wind. "I went looking for you. I wanted to say thanks for checking in on me."

Wren keeps her eyes on the incoming clouds as she raises a shoulder and lets it drop. "You would've done the same for me." She glances from the corner of her eye. "You doing okay?"

Nova's about to give some platitude when she stops herself. She realizes this is the other reason she came to see Wren—she's the one person she can be honest with. "Not really, but I'm figuring I will be at some stage."

"Damn straight, you will be, Nova." Wren throws her a measured look. "You don't need them to tell you your worth. Not Kian. Not Askala."

Nova looks away, not sure if that's even possible. Her entire life has been woven by those threads.

The sulfuric scent of the ocean is thrown at them with the next gust of wind, the trees behind rumbling as it blasts through them. The ominous clouds look like they've dropped.

Nova tucks a strand of hair behind her ear. Now isn't the time to have this talk. "We should probably head in."

Wren shakes her head. "I'm not going anywhere."

Nova frowns. "That's a pretty big storm, Wren. I get the whole I-laugh-in-the-face-of-danger thing, but those clouds look like they mean business." She grabs her sleeve. "Do it for me?"

Wren turns her large eyes toward Nova, her gaze full of foreboding. "I can't, Nova." She turns back to the roiling ocean. "They're here."

Nova's head swings back to scan the sea, wondering what Wren's talking about. At first, all she sees are dark waves and white foam. But then something catches her eye.

Rafts. Two of them.

With people on board.

Nova gasps. "Wren!"

Except she doesn't know what to say next. Wren obviously knew these people were coming. She was standing here waiting for them.

She knew Remnants were arriving.

Wren rushes forward to stand at the edge of the water, the wind yanking at her clothes. Her small body leans into the wind, telling Mother Nature she isn't going anywhere.

Nova watches, wide eyed, as several people paddle furiously on each raft. The waves toss them high before dropping them out of sight. The moment they appear again she does a quick head count. Six on each raft. Twelve people from the Outlands.

Spinning around, Nova runs to the post that holds the horn. It takes a couple of tries to wrench a sound out of it, but she manages a piercing wail of alarm. A few panting breaths and she blows out a second. Please let Kian and Dex still be at the lab. They'd be the ones most likely to hear.

Rushing back, Nova finds Wren where she left her—cemented to the spot, her gaze transfixed on the approaching rafts. Rain starts, hard and heavy, pouring down from the iron sky. It instantly soaks their hair and clothes, plastering them to their bodies.

Another gust of wind, so much stronger than the others, buffets them, whipping Nova's shawl from her shoulders. The rafts appear again, peaking on a wave, looking like cards being tossed in the swell. One of them angles high as a wave crests and the people on board scrabble to find a handhold.

"Wren, they're—"

"Going to make it," Wren finishes with grim determination.

The raft levels out again and the Remnants begin paddling furiously. Lightning streaks through the darkening sky, making Nova instinctively duck. The boom of thunder that immediately follows feels like it rocks the ground they stand on.

Wren's hands clench. "That's it. Keep rowing."

"Row!" shouts a male as if he heard her muttered words. "Hard!"

"Sweet Terra," mouths Nova, her eyes stretched wide despite the wind and rain.

Another wave, so much bigger than the last, is gaining momentum behind the rafts. Powering forward, it scoops them up, lifting them so high it looks like they could touch the violent clouds above.

The people on the rafts scramble, holding onto the edges.

"Hold on!" It's only once the words are out that Nova realizes she shouted them. Her heart lodges in her throat as she watches Mother Nature wield her might.

The wave crests and the rafts spear downward. Nova's hand flies to her mouth as Wren runs forward, the water lapping at her calves. The rafts are being propelled at an alarming speed, the faces of the people on board now visible.

They're all pale. All varying shades of terrified.

Lightning, then thunder, then Nova's scream, fill the air. They're so close! Close enough that they could make it.

The wave slams downward, taking the rafts with it and spearing them into the sea. Bodies fly forward and out, one or two screaming in alarm. They're swallowed by the crashing wall of water as the ocean becomes tumultuous pink foam.

This time, when Wren runs forward, Nova is there with her. What's left of the waves hits them, splashing them in the chest. Nova ignores the stinging in her eyes. These people need help.

And no one is less deserving.

The first head pops up and Wren grabs their arm. "Get yourself to shore!" she shouts over the wind and rain. "It's only a few yards that way."

The man stumbles as the water surges but he rights himself. Half swimming, half stumbling, he heads to the beach. When Nova sees another person, this one a female, try to right herself, she dives forward. Pulling her upright, she waits for her to find her feet. The moment she does, Nova instructs her to get to shore. Another man appears beside her, and they assist each other as the surging water tugs at them.

Scanning the black ocean, her eyes burning as waves crash

and pound her with force, isn't easy, but Nova grits her teeth. She spots another body just as Wren sees one to her left, and they repeat the steps. Help them upright. Send them to shore. Look for the next human piece of driftwood.

Nova tries her best to keep count. Twelve people were on those rafts. Twelve people need to make it to shore.

By the eighth person, she feels herself tiring. The waves yank and pull, and several times she loses her own footing on the rocky ground. Digging her feet in, she wipes the water out of her face, watching Wren help another person. Only a few more.

"Eleven," Nova shouts to Wren a few minutes later.

Just as she speaks, two strong arms appear ahead, methodically pulling through the water. Wren throws herself toward the person even though he's still several yards away.

"Look out!" screams Nova.

But the male can't hear her because he's working hard to swim through the waves. There's no way to warn him one of the rafts is coming at him. It rockets forward, heading to shore without its passengers. The man pauses and straightens, the shock of red hair apparent even in the storm as he tries to get his bearings.

"Phoenix!" screams Wren.

The crack is unmistakable a second before his body sinks into the water. The raft shoots past, its trajectory unaltered.

"No!" Wren wails, diving into the water.

Heart hammering so loud it drowns out the thunder, Nova strikes forward, too. The man hasn't resurfaced.

She's so focused on getting to Wren that Nova doesn't see the next wave until it's too late. It crashes down on her, driving her down into the ocean floor. Her body crumples as she hits the rocks below, pain slicing up her leg. A scream of agony blooms in her lungs but Nova keeps her mouth tightly shut as the water tosses about. A moment later the pressure releases and Nova kicks for the surface, shards of pain spearing through her leg.

Opening her mouth to gulp in some air, she hears Wren calling out.

"Help me, Nova. He's drowning."

Spinning around, Nova sees Wren struggling to hold the red-haired man as they bob in the angry sea. The man's head lolls, clearly unconscious, as Wren tries to keep him above water. Except Wren's small size isn't enough against the man's height and the waves.

Ignoring the sting of the acid water sweeping over her injured leg, Nova swims toward them. Within moments, she's grabbed one of the man's arms as Wren takes the other. Hooking under, they anchor him between them.

"Let's get him back," shouts Nova.

Kicking her legs, Wren starts to swim. Her look of determination is the same one Nova saw when she had the grizzly polar in the sights of her slingshot. The same one she had when they were caught in the storm during the pod harvest.

For some reason, it injects Nova with strength. Despite the growing agony in her leg, she pulls herself through the water, dragging the man between them.

Relief floods Nova when their feet touch the rocky ground, but it doesn't give her the reprieve she was hoping for. The waves feel like they're trying to yank the body out of their hands one minute, then trying to push it past them a second later.

A man appears before Nova, his arms extended. "I've got him."

Nova disentangles herself and the man takes over. She stumbles as she hits the shallows, her hands sinking into the sand. The promise of dry land drags Nova the last few yards. Panting, she drops to the ground. Her head whirls from the exertion, her throat burns from the seawater she's gulped down. Her leg feels like it's on fire.

"Phoenix!" Wren is crouched over the man, running her hands over his face and chest. "You promised!"

Nova drags herself over, ignoring the roar of pain in her leg as she takes his wrist and checks his pulse. "He's alive, Wren. Just unconscious."

"He's bleeding, Nova. We need to help him."

Wren's right. Dark red blood is seeping through the man's sodden hair.

Nova tears a strip from the hem of her shirt. "We need to get it under control." Bunching it up she presses it against his scalp, drawing a moan from his lips.

"Phoenix!" Wren's words are crowded with relief. "Thank god."

The man's eyes open and Nova notices for the first time he's not as old as she'd thought. He's probably more likely to be around the age of herself and Wren. He blinks then coughs as he struggles to sit up.

Wren falls back onto her heels. "Phoenix..." She raises a brow. "You weigh more than a leatherskin."

Nova watches in disbelief as the young man—Phoenix—pushes his hair from his eyes and grins at Wren. "You always hated that it meant I could out-run you, out-wrestle you, out—"

Wren launches herself at Phoenix as he opens his arms. They fold together, the biggest smile Nova has ever seen lighting up Wren's face.

She tucks her head in his neck. "Learn to swim better, okay?"

Phoenix chuckles. "We both know there was no way I was leaving you alone on this godforsaken island."

"If it's so awful"— a voice booms from behind Nova—"then why the hell are you here?"

KIAN

*K*ian tries to get his breathing under control as he takes in the scene before him. He'd been alarmed when he heard the horn.

He'd been terrified when he heard Nova scream.

She spins around as he throws out the question, still panting from her swim. Her hair is plastered to her skull, her clothes a sodden mess around her quivering body. She looks like a pale angel who's been tossed around by an angry sea god. He almost takes a step toward her.

Almost.

Except he can't.

When the young man doesn't bother to answer, Kian turns to Dex, who's breathing heavily from the mad run down to the beach. "We need to make sure everyone's okay."

Dex wrenches his gaze from Wren, who hasn't unwrapped herself from the one she called Phoenix. Kian's jaw tightens. Even in the bleak light, it's unmistakable. Dex looks like someone just punched him in the gut.

He nods. "We'll see if there are any injuries."

Dex and two other Bounds disperse among the Remnants.

Lightning sporadically illuminates them, scattered along the beach. They're bedraggled and drained, one or two holding each other, looking like human driftwood.

Kian looks back to Nova to find she's watching him. His chest feels too tight for his heart. Can he check if she's okay? Wouldn't a leader do that with each of the people of his colony?

Although, how can he pretend she's just another Unbound? How can he go to her and not touch her? Not take her in his arms—the place he always believed she belonged?

Nova looks away before Kian can think of what to say, her jaw tight with an emotion he can't identify. She shuffles over to check on Phoenix's bandage. "I think the bleeding's stopped. Are you feeling lightheaded, any blurred vision?"

Phoenix glances at Wren, who smiles. "It's okay. She's one of the good ones."

Phoenix grunts as he turns back to Nova. "I've had worse. Thanks for your, ah, shirt." He removes the bloodied bandage, passing it back to Nova with a rueful smile.

When the next streak of lightning catches the unmistakable orange of his hair, Kian steps forward, instantly on alert. It can't be a coincidence that this young man has the same hair color as the man who almost destroyed Askala. Or that he bears a striking resemblance to the same man's brother. "Who are you?"

Again, Phoenix glances to Wren. This time, her lips flatline. "Him, well…I thought he was one of the good ones."

Kian stiffens, his frown deepening but he doesn't take his gaze off Phoenix.

He shrugs. "Don't you guys call us Remnants? A faceless group of human leftovers?"

"Not any more." Kian's glad the flush on his cheeks isn't visible as he realizes that's exactly how he just thought of them.

Dex returns, water running in rivulets down his face. "They're tired and hungry, but no major injuries." He glances at Phoenix for the briefest of moments. "Apart from him."

"I don't think it's too deep," says Nova. "I won't be able to check until…" She straightens as she looks away. "He'll need to be checked when he goes to the infirmary."

Wren stands, about to help Phoenix do the same but he pushes himself upright. He sways and she slots under his arm, looking as if she's been there countless times before. "I'm fine," he growls.

Wren snorts. "Sure, and I'm dry."

Dex turns away, his face grim. "I'm going to bring them all in so we can get moving."

Before Kian can thank him, Dex spins on his heel and strides away. Wren seems to notice the way he avoids her gaze because she frowns ever so slightly, but then she looks back at Phoenix. Wrapping her arm around his waist, she tucks in even closer.

"I'll help," says Dorian. "It's the only way they'll hear us over the storm."

Kian nods. "Good. We need to get them to the Oasis."

Dorian pauses. "They're going to the Oasis?"

"Of course they're going to the Oasis," interjects Wren. "You guys made the rules, remember?"

They've set foot on Askala. They're entitled to refuge.

For now.

Dorian goes to speak, but Kian quickly jumps in. "Wren's right. We'll put them in the lower decks for now."

Then they need to decide what happens next.

Wren relaxes. "That's a good High Bound, Kian."

Ignoring Wren, Kian does a scan of the beach. Dex and Dorian are instructing the Remn—people of the Outlands to move toward Kian. Looking around, Kian notices Nova is the only one still sitting.

He looks a little closer, registering the way her shoulders angle a little too straight, her back a little too arched. He squats down beside her. "Are you hurt?"

Nova spins to face him, her blue eyes suddenly blazing. "Yes, I am."

Kian rocks back, realizing she's not talking about her swim in the ocean.

Pain flashes across her face before she looks away. "I waited up all night, Kian."

Kian's frozen, the rain streaking down his cheeks like tears. He shouldn't have stayed yesterday. All he did was hurt Nova more. "I—"

Nova shakes her head. "No words, Kian." She angles away from him. "Please."

Kian pushes himself upright, more words than he knows what to do with crowding in his throat.

I'm trying to protect you.

So no one knows how much I hate this.

Because I love you.

Instead, his shoulders slump as he takes a step back. Respecting Nova's wishes is the least he can do right now.

The moment he's given her some space, Nova stands, too. Except she stumbles, as if her right leg gives out. Instinctively, Kian reaches out, but she holds up her hand for him to stop. "I'm okay."

Kian shakes his head. "You're hurt."

"I'm tired." She flashes him an angry look.

Wren slips between them. "Of course she is," she glares at Kian. "Nova helped save Phoenix's life."

"And I might add"—Phoenix is right back by Wren's side—"it's quite the bonus to be eternally grateful to one heck of a good-looking girl."

Kian grinds his teeth as Wren playfully slaps Phoenix on the arm. This red-haired boy, who's now looking like he's bounced back quite well, is going to get on his nerves.

He's about to respond when a hand clamps on his shoulder.

He turns to find his father standing behind him, his frown as ferocious as the weather. "What's happened?"

"Two rafts from the Outlands arrived during the storm. They were carrying twelve people."

His father's frowning face scans the group of people standing in the rain. "Any losses?"

"All on board survived."

"All of them?" his father asks in surprise.

Wren plasters a smile to her face. "Isn't that wonderful news, Magnus?"

His father turns to Wren, registering the way she's attached to Phoenix like they're two halves of a whole. "Indeed."

Dex appears on his other side. "Let's get these poor people out of the rain."

Kian nods, turning to his father. Someone is going to have to tell them what's happening next. Except his father is looking at him expectantly.

Because Kian is now the leader of Askala.

Kian nods, turning away before his father can see that his sense of responsibility is starting to feel like a yoke.

"People of the Outlands, welcome to Askala." Kian shouts over the storm. "We will now escort you to the Oasis, the ship we call home. There, we will provide you with food and shelter."

Phoenix disentangles himself from Wren and steps forward. It seems he's the spokesperson for these people. "We thank you for your generosity." He smiles, although any warmth fails to reach his eyes. "It seems everything we've heard about Askala is true."

Kian turns away, wondering what they've heard.

And whether that's going to change, anyway.

He looks to Dex and Dorian. "Let's get them to the Oasis."

Nodding, they head toward the trees, indicating that the others follow.

Kian watches the first few walk past, noting that Nova is

holding back. Of course she'd come up the rear. She'll make sure everyone makes it there. Catching her eye, Kian decides he'll do the same. It could be an opportunity for them to talk.

Maybe, somehow, he can find some words that will make this...bearable. But Nova crosses her arms and turns her head. She doesn't want him beside her.

And then his father clamps his hand on his shoulder. "Let's walk, son."

Feeling like he has about as much control over this as the weather, Kian lets his father sweep him forward.

They've only walked a few paces before his father speaks again. "Good choice of words, Kian. You told them we'll care for them, but you made no promises."

Because he can't. "Have we ever had this many people from the Outlands arrive before?"

His father shakes his head. "Not even before the bridge was burned."

Kian didn't think so. "Then tonight's meeting will be a significant one."

His father's glance is sharp as he studies him. "You're going to call a High Bound meeting?"

"We need to decide how we respond to this." As he says the words, Kian's gut feels as stormy as the world around him. He's going to have to tell the High Bounds they have to decide these people's fate.

"I like that, son. It's exactly what I would've done."

Kian looks away from the warmth of his father's gaze. How can a person feel proud and yet lacking at the same time?

His father moves in closer. "I saw you talking to Nova."

Kian has to focus on not missing a step. "I was making sure she was okay."

"As any good leader would do," his father agrees. "But you can't afford to lose focus, Kian."

"I know." Kian has to work to keep his jaw from clenching.

His father glances at the new arrivals shuffling behind them. "This is too important."

Twelve people from the Outlands just washed up on shore. Every one of them survived.

And now Kian has to decide what to do about it.

The Oasis appears like a giant metal mountain curtained by rain. Kian hears shouts and several Bounds run down to meet them. He recognizes Tory, one of his father's closest friends.

He points to the group behind him. "People from the Outlands." Ignoring the looks of shock, Kian indicates toward the Oasis. "We need to get them inside, dry and fed."

"Got it." Tory nods. "We'll get them comfortable on the lower decks."

Kian thanks him, impressed with the unquestioning sense of duty.

Dex comes to stand before him, and Kian sees him scan the Remnants, no doubt looking for Wren. Knowing he doesn't need another kick in the guts, Kian grabs his shoulder. "Can you get all the High Bounds together? We need to have an emergency meeting."

Dex nods. "This is big, Kian."

Kian can feel exactly how big it is. It's like the weight of Askala's future has settled around his shoulders. "We'll deal with it."

"Kinda got to, don't we?" Dex slaps him on the back before jogging up the gangplank.

The group of Remnants are right behind him as Tory leads them up. Kian scans the group for Nova. He won't talk to her, but he needs to know she's okay.

He freezes when he finds her. Nova is being carried by Phoenix. Kian rushes forward, any promises he just made himself forgotten. "What are you doing?"

Phoenix doesn't stop as he strides forward. "She said she was tired."

Nova's head is resting against Phoenix's shoulder. "I'm fine, Kian. I just need to rest."

Kian frowns, not liking what he's seeing. "She needs to go to the infir—"

"No!" Nova jerks so hard Phoenix has to tighten his arms. "I'm not going there."

Helplessness has Kian's hands clenching. "But, Nova—"

Wren pushes herself up in his face. "You heard her, High Bound boy, she just wants to rest. It's like she's been through hell the past few days or something."

With a glare she pushes past him, Phoenix and Nova right behind her.

They keep walking and Kian is about to follow, concern and frustration winding through his muscles, when he hears the quiet sound of a throat clearing. It's a subtle sound, barely noticeable above the wind and rain, but it has Kian stopping before he started.

His father halts beside him. "She looks like she'll be well looked after." He pauses. "While the Remnants could pose... quite a risk."

Kian watches as they disappear into the Oasis with the others, every muscle rebelling at his lack of motion. Nova won't say it, but she needs him. He can feel it.

Just like he can feel his father's gaze on him.

Something inside him feels like shriveling up as Kian turns to his father, registering his half-smile. He has to stop himself from wincing as his father's hand drops on his shoulder. "I always knew you'd make the right decisions for Askala."

Without waiting for a response, his father strides away.

Kian stands in the soaking rain, knowing no amount of water can wash away the bitter taste in his mouth. His feet feel waterlogged as he's the last person to enter the Oasis, telling himself he made the right decision.

Just like his father, he's doing this for Askala. Its people, its future, and their promise to heal Earth.

The corridors close in on him, muting the sound of the storm. Kian works hard on pulling himself upright. He has a High Bound meeting to run.

The boardroom is already full when he arrives, making him wonder if he's moving as slowly as he feels.

Shiloh steps forward, holding something out as she blinks up at him. "I brought you a towel."

"Thanks."

She graces him with a small smile before she returns to her seat. "I knew you'd come straight here without drying yourself off."

Kian can't hold her gaze. Shiloh is making a point of knowing how he operates. He's stopped denying the invite that's so blatant in every look she passes him, but it doesn't mean he's okay with it.

Wiping his face gives Kian time to pull himself together. He's looked up to his father his whole life. Admired how he led with such unwavering commitment to Askala and everything it stands for. It's the very same society his father has helped build that will ensure Nova will be taken care of.

It's the society that he's depending on Kian to protect.

Kian clears his throat. "As you would've heard, twelve people from the Outlands arrived on our shores tonight. They're now in the lower decks being cared for."

Kian waits for the round of nods, noting the six somber faces. He takes his seat at the head of the table. "They arrived on two rafts."

Two rafts extremely similar to the ones they built in the Provings. Kian glances at Dex, whose lips are thin and white. He noticed it, too.

It seems it's a good thing Wren already had someone in her life. Because if she's helped these people arrive in some way, then whatever Dex was hoping for will be over before it could start.

Tomorrow, they'll need to go find the rafts that washed up. They could provide some answers.

Milli's palm flies to her chest. "How many more could come?"

Kian clasps his hands on the table. "Exactly, Milli. We have no idea. Which is why we're here. We need to decide what happens to them."

"What do you mean, what happens to them?" Dex frowns as he leans forward. "They touched our soil. Our laws say we must welcome them."

Trista shakes her head. "Those laws were imposed back when the bridge existed. When only handfuls of Remnants arrived."

"And we could ascertain their intent," adds Zali. "Before any Remnant could step on Askala's soil they had to show they came in peace."

If they didn't, they weren't allowed to pass. Any attempts to arrive by force were swiftly ended with the help of a trapdoor above the deadly ocean.

Shiloh's eyes widen. "Are you suggesting we're not sure what they're here for?"

Phoenix's face flashes through Kian's mind. He doesn't plan on saying anything about the resemblance to Ronan's brother until he has some proof, but it's enough to make him conscious that most Remnants didn't arrive with peaceful intent.

"Are we forgetting something?" Dex has to work to modulate his tone. "Wren arrived exactly the same way. And she's now Bound."

Kian levels his gaze at his cousin. "Which may have been a mistake."

Doesn't Dex realize what this girl could mean? At best, Wren is the first of who knows how many Remnants wanting a slice of Askala. It's impossible to guess what her worst could mean. But Dex is already shaking his head. "Wren passed those tests just like we did."

Frustration has Kian's hands clenching hard onto each other. "You might want to consider whether your heart is clouding your judgment, Dex. For a girl who's already promised herself to someone else."

The moment he says the words, Kian regrets them. Dex reels back as if he was just slapped.

Silence fills the room, awkward and uncomfortable. Kian knows he'll have to apologize to his cousin. The words may be true, but now wasn't the time to raise them. He needs to get his emotions under control.

Dex pulls his hand from the table, tucking his stump by his side. "At least someone's thinking with their heart."

Kian can't hide the flinch. If he were to think with his heart, Nova would be by his side.

"Kian's aware this is much bigger than a handful of Remnants," Shiloh offers softly but firmly. "None of us can forget this."

A few people shuffle in their seats. They're realizing they're weighing up the lives of a few against what they've been bound to protect.

Kian's heart thuds heavily as his veins fill with dread. It's time for a decision to be made. "We have two choices. We allow them to stay, or we send them back. Either way, we set a precedent we will need to honor."

Dex turns shocked eyes to Kian. "You want to send them back, don't you?"

His father's words echo through Kian's mind. I always knew you'd make the right decisions for Askala.

Kian holds Dex's gaze. "These Outlanders are too old for the Proving, and if any others arrive, it's likely to be the same. There are far more Unbound than there are Bound already. We would be taking on the care of who knows how many others. It's a strain Askala can't afford."

Dex looks away. "That's exactly what Magnus would've said."

Kian suppresses a wince. When did those words stop being a compliment?

"This storm is likely to wipe out the gardens again," says Zali in a small voice.

"And the infirmary is always short of supplies," adds Shiloh.

Dex looks around the table. "You all feel like this?" he asks incredulously.

Aarov shakes his head. "I think they should stay. Sending them back could be a death sentence."

Dex looks around only to find a table of averted gazes. His fist slams the table. "We were all selected for kindness and intelligence. Have you considered that maybe we need new blood? New ideas?" Silence is his only response. Dex turns to Kian. "How can you suggest we send them back? That's as far away from kind as you can get!"

Kian holds his gaze. "Askala comes first." He turns to the others. "Those who vote we send the people of the Outlands back to their home, please raise your hand."

Shiloh is the first to raise hers, followed by Trista, Zali, and Milli. Kian adds his hand to the ones up in the air. Only Dex and Aarov remain with their hands by their sides.

Kian nods. This is the decision his father would've wanted. He lowers his hand, glad that the loss of Nova has already deadened a part of his heart. Otherwise, the following words would be too hard to say.

"It is decided. The Outlanders will be sent back."

DEX

*A*ll Dex has wanted to do since Wren put that cell phone in his hand is find a quiet moment to look at it. From what his father said, there has to be some kind of message on it from his mom. Maybe it might even contain some answers for once. Because he sure could use some of those. He's confused about pretty much every single thing in his life right now. His father. Wren. Kian. Nova. Phoenix...nothing makes sense.

Approaching his cabin in the dimly lit corridor, he wonders if quiet moments exist when you're High Bound. There's been one thing after another getting in his way.

First, Wren running off and causing him to spend hours looking for her in the forest, before realizing there was no point. She probably tore the note into a hundred pieces and set it on fire the moment she read it. Still, leaving him had felt like a betrayal. Even more than when she'd taken the drawer while he'd been sleeping. After all that's happened between them, he hadn't expected that.

Then, Kian had wanted to talk to him about the Proving, insisting on being walked through the data line by time-consuming line, looking for something significant enough to warrant a protest.

Then, the rafts had arrived and the High Bound meeting had been called.

A meeting he really doesn't want to think about right now. Because it was a meeting that changed everything. They can't send those desperate people back. It's not right. They haven't even had the opportunity to go through a Proving.

Like Wren, these people could teach them a new way of thinking. A *better* way. They could add diversity to their declining gene pool, no different to when they'd gone out to collect pteropods in their third test of the Proving.

Dex steps into his cabin and waits for the door to slide closed behind him, breathing out a long sigh. At last.

Silence. Solitude. Serenity.

It'd taken until well after midnight but finally, he's alone.

When he'd gone to sleep the night before, he'd thought he might gather his belongings and move himself to the bunkroom to keep Wren company.

But not now.

Dex clenches his hand into a fist. As much as he might have come to love her, he needs to accept they're different, no matter how much it may have seemed their hearts follow the same beat. She's made it clear her heart belongs to someone else.

Which totally sucks.

Walking over to his bed, Dex decides the note no longer matters. It's pretty obvious now what it contained. How else had Wren known to be on the beach when the rafts had arrived? Clearly, she'd been told of their arrival.

Which means it's now also obvious what the note she'd sent out had said. The note that nobody else knows about, apart from him. The note that he'd foolishly trusted had contained nothing but news of Wren's safe arrival, yet he now knows must also have contained instructions on how to build a raft that could survive the distance across the acid of the ocean.

Pain slices through him as he realizes that she hadn't trusted him with this information, even though he's not sure what he'd have done with it.

He's already agreed to go out with the other High Bounds at first light and look for what's left of the rafts so they can see how they were made. If what he suspects is the case, then the wedge that's lodged itself between Dex and Kian is set to widen.

Which also sucks.

Kian's decision to banish the new arrivals was disappointing beyond belief. Kian knows how Dex feels about Wren. It's hard to believe his own cousin could be so brutal. Was this how his father had felt when Magnus decided to burn the bridge?

Cursing, he reminds himself that he wasn't going to think about the meeting. He came here to see what message his mother might have left him. If he doesn't look at it now then who knows when he'll next get the chance.

Dex settles down on the bed and props himself up on a pillow. His heart is beating fast, almost as if he's holding a bomb instead of a phone. Perhaps it isn't so different. All depending on what it contains…

Resting the phone on his lap, he presses the round button, staring at the screen when it asks for the password.

His father's voice is clear in his mind.

Mercy Forever. No spaces and forever spelled with a numeral four.

Typing in the password, he watches as the screen unlocks.

Numerous icons light up, but one in particular catches his attention. It's an image of a woman's face. She has brown hair, fair skin, dark eyes and a smattering of freckles across her nose. He squints, daring to believe it's an image of his mother, aware this is the first time he's seen her face with anything except the eyes of an infant.

Photos don't exist in Askala. It's a waste of resources to

capture a moment in the present when all eyes should be turned to the future.

Dex has had to build an image of his mother using the snippets he's gathered from people who knew her. Nobody has told him that she wasn't beautiful, but that's the impression he got. Words like 'beautiful heart' are often mentioned, but never 'beautiful' all on its own. The picture he's had painted is that she was plain to look at, neither ugly nor especially attractive. Which is fine with him. No child loves his mother for her face.

There are two words underneath the image.

For Dex.

When he taps the icon and the photo comes to life, the woman he sees isn't plain at all. There's kindness in her eyes. A love that's shining out from her face that's lighting up the goodness in her soul.

"Mom," he breathes. "You *are* beautiful."

"Hello, my darling, Dex," she says.

Something splashes on the screen and he realizes it's a tear. Wiping at his cheeks, he brings the phone closer, taking in every detail of his mother's face.

"I'm hoping that you'll never need to watch this video. But if you are, it means I'm no longer here to tell you these things myself, so please, listen closely."

The camera moves away from her face and points at a crib. There's a baby asleep. Dark hair, a scrunched-up face... two hands.

"This is you, Dexy," she says. "Asleep for once, you little terror."

She laughs and the sound floats across his cabin as Dex stares at his former self, wishing he could shout at the screen and warn himself of the devastation that's about to hit that innocent child's life.

"You're gorgeous, Dex," his mom says. "The most beautiful

little baby. You're my whole world. My most treasured person. I didn't even know what love was until I met you, my darling."

Dex's eyes are drawn to the image of his left hand. The hand that should have stayed with him. Just like the woman holding the camera.

His mother's face fills the screen once more. "I'm making this video because you need to know a few things. About who you are. Who you *really* are."

Dex's stomach drops, just as his mother's face turns serious. Who he is? What the hell does that mean?

"The truth is, Dex"—her voice lowers to little more than a whisper—"you're the child of an Unbound. Me. I'm Unbound, Dex. It's a secret that I've had to keep from everyone here. Except your father, of course. My protector. Your protector."

Dex hits the pause button and draws in a deep breath as he feels his whole world breaking apart. This can't be true! Unbound can't have children. That's the whole point of this system in Askala. If someone doesn't have the heart and intelligence needed to care for this planet, then it's extremely unlikely their offspring will either.

And that offspring is Dex.

Thoughts of the Proving race back into his mind. His father had to have altered the results more than he's admitted to. It's not possible he could be Bound. Not with a mother as an Unbound.

Staring at his mom's paused face on the screen, he realizes this news hasn't changed the way he feels about her. He loves her just as much now as he always has. Is that what it feels like for Kian and Nova? A title handed out to someone you love is never going to change the strength of your feelings.

He hits play again, wanting to hear more. *Needing* to hear more.

"Let me explain," his mother says, keeping her voice hushed. "My Proving didn't go as I'd hoped. I was so nervous which led me to make some silly mistakes. I was certain I was destined to become Unbound. The only thing I ever wanted to do was be a mother and I could see that chance slipping away. The thought of my fertility being taken away was killing me."

Dex swallows, not having ever really given too much thought to the impact of the sterilization on the emotional state of the Unbounds before. He'd always thought more about the loss of their finger. But the loss of the chance to become a parent must hurt so much worse. Especially for someone as maternal as his mother.

"I had a friend in the Proving," his mother says. "His name was Ronan. I suspect you may know his name for all the wrong reasons. He had his flaws, that's for sure, but he wasn't as bad as everyone would like to believe. He was impetuous. Hungry for recognition and power. And not exactly a team player. But he was also loyal. Well, he was loyal to me. For reasons I never really understood, he loved me. Fiercely. And he protected me right up until the end."

Rubbing at the back of his neck, Dex winces. This isn't easy to listen to. He'd been told that Ronan had been in love with his mother. Ronan's own brother had even accused Dex of being Ronan's son. His father had denied this, but could it be true?

"Ronan cut out the chips from two dead Bounds." She shakes her head, her eyes spilling with sadness. "He kept one for himself and gave me the other. We switched them with the chips we were given in the Proving. And we were able to pass ourselves off as Bound. You have to understand that this was before...well, you know what they do to Unbound in more recent times. We'd never have gotten away with it now."

This is even worse than Dex had thought. His mother was not only Unbound, but she played a key role in the events that led to all the recent changes made in Askala.

"Ronan went on to make some other questionable decisions that I'm sure you've heard all about. He wanted to increase the population of the pteropods and he turned up the temperature in the tank. It killed them all. As terrible as this was, I believe that he was genuinely trying to do the right thing. But he got banished for it. Sent across the bridge just before it was burned. It was the worst night of my life. I hope never to have another like it."

Dex's heart breaks at these words, knowing she's about to have a night far, far worse.

"I didn't love Ronan." Her voice hardens. "Not in the way he loved me. Mainly because I was in love with someone else. Your father. And Callix has kept my secret. A secret that's now become yours. The truth of who you are. The child of an Unbound."

The camera pans back to sleeping baby Dex, and he wishes he could become that baby once more. Sleeping calmly, totally unaware of the tornado of lies he was born into. Oblivious to the traumas and loneliness that lie ahead.

"I worry every day, Dex. I worry about being discovered. About being banished. About being separated from you—my reason for living. That's why I'm making this video. In case I'm not here to tell you this in person. It's not something you should learn from anyone else."

Her face fills the screen once more.

"I want you to know that none of this was done with any ill intent. I didn't think about the consequences of having a child until you were here. But now that you are, I'm certain you'll be Bound. You have to be. I can tell already how bright you are. You're always looking around and figuring out the world, more interested in staring at faces than sleeping. But there's part of me that worries. I'm ashamed to say, I asked your father to make sure you're Bound, but he said he can't alter the results. Further proof that he's a good man."

Dex snorts. Ha! Just how well did his mother know his

father? If indeed he really is his father. What other lies have been told that she'd decided to keep out of this video?

"Dex, the fact that you're watching this is because your father honored my wish and passed it to you. Which proves he's trustworthy. He wouldn't have given it to you otherwise. I want you to do everything he tells you to do. He's a smart man. The smartest I've ever met. He'd have made a wonderful leader of Askala. The best we've ever had. But, sadly, his father put Magnus in the job instead."

Dex grimaces. There was a time he'd have disagreed strongly with this. But now…he's not so sure. Perhaps his father would have done a better job than Magnus? He'd told Dex he hadn't agreed with burning the bridge. Or the taking of the finger. His father had broken rules so he could be with the Unbound he loved instead of treating her like his mistress…

"Do what your father asks of you." His mother's eyes fill with tears and Dex touches the screen, wishing he could comfort her. "Please, Dex. In this world, it's hard to know who you can trust, but trust him. And always remember that I love you."

She blows him a kiss and Dex chokes on his sobs. He can't remember ever having those words said to him. He'd do anything to be able to say them back.

The screen goes blank and Dex immediately watches the video a second time. Then a third. Each time he hears something different, sees something different, as he builds a new picture of his mother in his mind.

Mercy. The woman who wanted nothing more than a child. The woman who wanted *him*. In fact, she wanted him so much that she'd lied about being Bound. And his father had covered it up. No wonder he'd spent so many hours in the lab as Dex was growing up. No doubt, he was trying to make sure that his mother's secrets remained exactly that.

Secrets.

His whole life has been built on lies.

He understands now why his father went to such lengths to make sure Dex took over the Provings. With access to all the previous years' results, the truth of his birth was just sitting there waiting to be discovered.

And then what would happen to him? They've never had to deal with the child of an Unbound before. Would Kian put him on a raft and send him to the Outlands alongside the twelve who only just arrived?

Swinging his legs down to the floor, he sits on the edge of the bed and hangs his head in his hands.

That video hadn't just altered Dex's image of his mother. It had altered his image of his father.

And most of all, it'd altered his image of himself.

Why has everyone been so blindly following the rules set by the High Bound? Surely his father can't be the only one to see how wrong they are? The Unbound must know. Nova must certainly know.

Wren. Her face comes to his mind with such force it's almost like she demanded his attention.

Wren knows how wrong it is. She's been telling them ever since she arrived, determined to prove their system is flawed. Begging them to treat everyone with the same compassion, instead of pretending that some lives are worth more than others.

Is it really so wrong that she'd sent a message to her people, letting them know what they needed to do to join her? It's not like Kian's going to rebuild the bridge and welcome them across anytime soon.

Wren had been desperate. He'd seen it in her eyes that she'd hated running from him. She's not a bad person. He'd meant what he'd said in the High Bound meeting. She's exactly what Askala needs. A new way of looking at things.

Because Askala is broken. It can't continue the way it is.

These twelve new citizens of Askala haven't even been given a chance. And that includes Phoenix.

Hating the jealous pull of his stomach when he thinks of Phoenix, Dex acknowledges that he also has a right to stay.

Wren clearly loves him. That much had been clear by the way she'd launched herself at him on the beach.

But there's something about him that's unsettling. Like the way he'd openly flirted with Nova in front of Wren. Even more concerning was the way Wren hadn't seemed to mind. Is that how men behave in the Outlands?

There's something even more concerning than that, though. And it has nothing to do with his relationship with Wren.

It's why Phoenix looks so much like Dean.

Who apparently looks a lot like Ronan.

Could Ronan have survived after his banishment and gone on to have a son? And if Dean is right and Ronan is Dex's father, does that make Phoenix his brother?

He sighs deeply, lifting his head from his hands. Askala does seem to have a tradition of brothers falling in love with the same girl. A tradition he hadn't wanted to mess with when it came to Nova, deciding from a young age that Nova wasn't the girl for him. Not that Kian is his brother. Right now, he doesn't even feel like his cousin.

He's a stranger. A stranger making dangerous decisions.

Shoving the cell phone under his pillow, Dex leaps to his feet. He has to warn Wren about Kian's decision. If there's even the slightest possible chance that Phoenix is his brother, then he can't let him be sent away. He needs a chance to figure things out first.

Winding his way down the corridor of the Oasis, Dex finds Wren's door and taps on it, uncertain if this is where he'll find her, or if she'll be with the rest of the new arrivals. Surely, she wouldn't be stupid enough to take Phoenix to the lab? She's on thin ice with the High Bounds as it is.

He knocks once more, deciding he should leave her a note in case she returns. He has to find her before sunrise.

Pressing his hand to the sensor, the door slides open to reveal Wren fast asleep on the bed, her head resting on Phoenix's bare chest. He has an arm draped around her in what looks like a possessive gesture. Like he's afraid she might run away in the night if he doesn't hold onto her.

Dex steps back, his gut churning, a deep flush racing to his cheeks. How often has he imagined Wren sleeping beside him just like this? Too often. But never again.

This had been a mistake. Big time.

"Getting a good look?" asks Phoenix, his eyes springing open.

"I need to...I need to talk to Wren." He takes another step back and the door starts to slide closed, hitting him on the arm and bouncing back. "It's important."

Wren's eyes snap open. "Dex! What are you doing here?"

He steps into the room, rubbing at his arm. "Sorry to interrupt the reunion, but I need to talk to you."

Wren sits up and stretches her back. "I still have no idea how you people sleep on something so soft."

"Matches their brains," says Phoenix, laughing. "That leader of theirs certainly looks a bit soft in the head."

"Some of them have soft hearts, too, you know." Wren looks at Dex and he swears just for a moment he sees something in her eyes that tells him she's missed him.

Phoenix props himself up on the pillow and Dex openly stares at him, searching for any kind of brotherly resemblance. He's taller than Dex, with muscles layered on top of his muscles. His leather pants are clinging tightly to his powerful legs and his red hair has been cropped short. He has a pendant around his neck identical to the one Wren wears, and there are a series of black lines down one of his arms, like some sort of strange permanent artwork. He's annoyingly good looking in an overly obvious masculine kind of way. Not the sort of guy anyone wants to have to compete with. And he certainly has no resemblance to Dex. Could their different mothers have made that much difference? Not all siblings look alike.

Or perhaps they're unrelated at all.

"Interesting," says Phoenix, noticing his gaze. "I thought you were more interested in Wren, but whatever floats your boat."

"Leave him alone," says Wren swatting at Phoenix.

Dex feels the color continuing to stain his cheeks. Phoenix couldn't be more wrong.

"What's wrong, Dex?" Wren asks. "Is this about yesterday?"

"It's not that," he says, waving his hand. "You need to hide Phoenix. Kian's going to send your people back in the morning. If you want him to stay, you need to find somewhere to keep him. This is the first place Kian will look."

Wren's eyes open wide and her jaw falls. She leaps from the bed and paces. "We need to hide all of them."

Dex shakes his head. "No. Not all. Just Phoenix. If you hide all of them, the search will be wider. If Phoenix is the one you want to stay, then keep it at him for now."

"You can't let him do this, Dex." Wren goes to him and puts her hand on his arm. He steps back, not sure what to do with her familiarity. "You have to stop him."

"I can't." He shakes his head. "I already tried. There was a vote. It didn't go my way."

"But they could die!" Wren lets her hand fall and resumes her pacing. "It's too dangerous. How could Kian be so cruel? How could I have been so wrong to think I could trust him?"

"Don't trust any of them," grunts Phoenix. "Including this one."

"I trust Dex," says Wren without hesitation. "I trust him more than anyone else here."

"Kian wants to send a message," says Dex, ignoring Phoenix's comment. "He thinks if he lets this lot stay, then more rafts will arrive. He's drawing the line."

"Does he want to send me back?" Wren looks at Dex with dark eyes.

"No," he says, hoping he's right. "You've been through the Proving. People know who you are. It would be too controversial."

She harrumphs. "The leaders of Askala haven't seemed too afraid of controversy before."

Dex nods, with no choice but to agree. If Kian decides to send Wren away, there's no way he's going to stand idly by. Perhaps that's the reason it hasn't been suggested already.

"Where will we hide him?" Wren asks, picking up her pacing again.

"That's easy," says Phoenix, folding his hands behind his head, a move that makes his biceps double in size. "I can hide in Blondie's cabin."

"Nova?" Wren looks aghast.

"Actually," says Dex. "That's not as crazy as it sounds. Kian will never look for him there."

Wren nods, her trust in Dex obvious. "Come on, Phee. We need to get you upstairs."

Phee? Dex really isn't sure how much more of this he can take.

"You coming?" Wren asks, tilting her head at Dex.

"I'll be in my cabin if you need me," he says.

Phoenix gets up with a groan.

"Oh, and Phee," says Dex. "If you lay one finger on Nova, I will kill you. Just so you know."

Phoenix throws back his head and laughs. "I'd like to see you try."

Dex follows them from the room and after waving them off, heads back to his cabin

Only this time when the door slides closed, the solitude feels like a weight on his shoulders.

Lying down, he rests his hand on the cell phone under his pillow.

"Thanks, Mom," he whispers.

At least someone in this world chose him first. And he's determined to make her sacrifices mean something.

He's going to make her proud.

WREN

*W*ren drags Phoenix down the corridors of the Oasis by the hand, urging him to keep quiet.

"You need to take this seriously," she hisses.

"Sorry, Cy." He grins at her.

She rolls her eyes, knowing she's nothing like Cy with his my-way-or-the-highway approach. "This is for your own good. Do you want to be sent back?"

"Of course not," he says, falling serious as he squeezes her hand. "We've only just been reunited."

"I really missed you, Phee."

"Missed you, too, little bird," he says.

She smiles. That's how he tells her he loves her. Not with an endless procession of hugs, not with words, but with the name he made up for her when they were kids and he hit a growth spurt and she stayed the same.

It was the nickname that spurred her on to train even harder with Cy. To add muscles to her small frame to make up in strength what she lacked in height. In time, she'd grown to like her nickname. Because even the strongest girl in the world needs to be looked after sometimes. It's a reminder that Phoenix has her back.

Always.

"I forgot to ask you," he says. "Did you see my message?"

"What message?"

"The fires. I lit three of them on the shore before I came, just in case you didn't get the raven. I wanted to let you know I was on my way. They were big. I found some old car tires that let off a hell of a lot of smoke."

"Oh, I did see them!" She doesn't add what a stir they caused in Askala. "But I wasn't sure what they meant."

"Well that was a waste of time then." He laughs. "But at least it was fun."

"It's just here," she whispers, knocking gently on Nova's door.

"Can't you just use that thing in your wrist?" he asks.

Wren shakes her head at him as the door slides open.

Nova's standing there with her hair mussed and her face pale. She lurches forward, grabbing for Wren, who for a split-second thinks Nova is going to attack her. Then she realizes that this girl who's never attacked anyone in her life, is fainting.

Wren breaks her fall, cradling Nova's dead weight.

"I've got her," says Phoenix, lifting her from Wren's arms and carrying her to the bed.

The door slides closed behind them and Wren rushes to the bed, placing her palm on Nova's forehead. "She's really hot."

"And she's bleeding," says Phoenix, inspecting Nova's leg. "Holy hell, that's one heck of a flesh wound. When did she do that?"

"She must have cut it on the rocks," says Wren. "When she was saving your life..."

"Where do they keep the sap around here?" he asks.

Wren shakes her head. "They don't. Would you believe they didn't even know about the sap until I told them?"

Phoenix lets out a whistle. "Wow. Primitive."

"There might be some in the infirmary, though," she says. "Shiloh was going to start using it there."

"Shiloh?" he asks. "What kind of a name is that?"

She shrugs. "Just a name."

"Is she cute?" He raises his eyebrows, then his open palms when he sees the stern look on her face. "Just kidding!"

"You have to stop joking like that," she warns. "They don't know you like I do. They think you're serious. Kian was ready to kill you when you carried Nova up the gangplank. It probably played into his decision to send you away. He hated seeing your hands on her."

"They're an item?" Phoenix's eyes sweep up to Nova's face. "Blondie and the Almighty Leader? What the hell am I doing hiding in her room then?"

"They're not together," says Wren. "Not any more. It's...complicated."

Phoenix nods and she knows he's trusting her on this. Which is smart. He's the one person on this godforsaken planet she'd never double cross.

"I'm going to get some sap." She wipes her hands down her pants. "If Nova wakes up, tell her I'm not far."

"I've got this."

She watches as Phoenix picks up a hemp cloth next to Nova's washbasin and dampens it, pressing it to Nova's forehead. He has got this. He knows what to do. Despite what the others here might think, Nova's in safe hands. He might come across as rough and crass and full of bravado, but really he's a total soft touch.

Wren's halfway to the infirmary when she realizes she doesn't have to creep around. She's Bound now. She can pretty much go wherever she likes without having to explain herself. Shiloh will give her mangrove pine sap if she needs it.

Although, maybe she needs to have a cut to heal first.

Dragging her arm along the rusted bannister of the stairwell, she presses down until it stings.

She pauses and inspects the damage, happy with the series of superficial cuts it's produced. Pinching the skin, she forces out some blood, making the wound look worse than it is.

That should do it.

If Shiloh's even in the infirmary at this late hour.

Making her way down the corridor, she taps her wrist against the sensor at the infirmary door and it slides open. There's a flurry of color and movement inside. Shiloh is working alongside Nova's mother as they move between cots, tending to the new arrivals from the Outlands.

Kian's there, too, keeping watch over them.

"Wren," he says, looking up at her. "I'm glad you're here."

"What's going on?" she asks. "They don't look sick to me. They hardly touched the water."

"We decided to move them here," he says. "Just to be sure. They need fluids and their skin's irritated."

Wren nods, understanding a whole lot more than Kian would like her to. They're here so he can make sure they don't run off. And he wants them in good health so he can send them back in the morning with a clear conscience, telling himself he did all he could to help them.

"We're missing one," says Kian. "Your friend. Have you seen him? It's important he gets a proper check-up."

"He decided to sleep in my cabin." Wren's policy when lying is to always tell as much truth as possible. It's far more convincing that way. Kian could use a few lessons. She supposes that being deceptive must be something that's new to him. He'll get better in time.

"He's there now?" asks Kian.

"He was using the washbasin when I left him," she says, still not technically having told any lies. "I just came here for some sap, if that's okay."

She holds out her bleeding arm.

"It's over there," says Shiloh, nodding toward several full jars on the workbench. "I'll be with you in a moment."

Kian heads for the door and Wren realizes she needs to be quick. As soon as Kian sees Phoenix isn't in her cabin, he'll be on her tail.

"It's okay," Wren says to Shiloh, opening a jar and rubbing some sap on her arm. "I can do it."

Shiloh turns back to the woman on the cot in front of her at the same time Kian presses his wrist to the sensor at the door. Wren sees her opportunity and tucks the jar into her pocket.

"Hey!"

She spins around, heart beating, mind already racing with explanations she can provide.

But it's not Shiloh calling out to her. It's the woman lying on the cot, and the pitch of her voice has all eyes in the room turning on Wren. Including Kian, who's paused at the door.

"I know who you are," the woman says to Wren. "You're Cy's girl, aren't you?"

Wren's stomach lurches and she has to remind herself that it's okay. Kian doesn't know who Cy is.

But the other patients have all turned their heads and are staring at her like she's turned into a leatherskin. There's a mixture of awe and fear in their eyes.

Wren shoots them a nervous smile as she shakes her head and tries to still the beating of her heart. "I think you're mistaken."

"No, it is you." The woman pushes away Shiloh's hands and sits up. "I've seen you with him."

"I've seen her, too," says a man, glancing at Kian as if seeking his approval. "She's definitely Cy's girl."

"Who's Cy?" asks Kian, stepping back into the room.

"Nobody." Wren shoots him a smile. "Don't you have something to do?"

"Who's Cy?" he asks again.

"Her father," says the woman.

Great! Wren puts her hands on her hips and glares at the woman. So much for Outlander solidarity. She's been thrown to the sharks at the first opportunity.

"And who's her father?" he asks.

"The Commander of the Outlands," the woman says, proudly.

"Your leader?" Kian's eyes are wide, all thoughts of finding Phoenix have clearly vanished.

The woman nods.

"And this here is your Commander's daughter?" Kian points at Wren and she flinches, her mind reeling with ways to get out of this.

"It's no big deal," says Wren, feebly.

"No big deal?" Kian's face is pale. "You don't mention that you're the Commander's daughter and that's no big deal? This is a huge deal!"

Wren's eyes dart around the room, looking for a way out. But there's no wall here that she can launch herself over. There's one door. And a guy twice her size blocking it.

And he's shaking his head at her, disappointed and angry. "You lied to me. To all of us."

"I didn't lie!" Wren holds out her palms. "I just hadn't had the chance to tell you yet."

"You leave me no choice." He turns away. "Thea, press the button."

Nova's mother gives him a quick nod and crosses the room to hold down a large red button on the wall.

An alarm immediately pierces the air and Wren claps her hands to her ears.

Wren looks to Kian but his eyes are glued to the door. An alarm like that can only mean one thing. It was a call for help. And on a place like the Oasis, help is never far away.

The door slides open to reveal several people gathering in the corridor, all looking to Kian for instruction.

Something in Kian's face changes. He's no longer the boy in the Proving who Wren had grown to admire.

He's the leader of an army of people. An army who are set to destroy everything Wren's trying to achieve. Which means that once more, Kian's her enemy.

Kian shouts over the sound of the alarm, ordering his people to take hold of the *Remnants*.

His use of that word says all it needs to. It's proof that everything Wren's done to prove her worth has been undone. Feeling all the fight draining out of her, for a fleeting moment, Wren thinks about how easy it would be to give in. She's fought so hard. She can't possibly start all over again.

But that's not how Cy raised her. She *is* his daughter and she knows better than that. She can never give up. The moment she gives up is the moment she dies, and she's nowhere near ready for that.

She takes a step toward the door. Maybe it's possible to slip out while chaos reigns and sabotage the rafts. She has to buy some time.

"Including her!" shouts Kian, destroying her hope in an instant.

Two sets of strong hands grip her by the arms. She squirms and struggles but it's no use.

She's dragged from the infirmary.

Through the corridors.

Down the gangplank.

Across the sand.

Onto the beach.

To a future she's determined to fight against.

The full moon lights the sky, casting eerie shadows on the sand.

"No!" she screams, when she sees a group of Bounds

working furiously to repair the rafts her people had arrived on. "You can't do this!"

She kicks at the shins of one of the men holding her, then the other. They weaken their grip and she wrenches herself free. But another pair of hands take hold of her and these ones are even tighter.

Turning, she's not surprised to see it's Kian.

"Bring me Dex!" she says, struggling against him. "I need to speak with him."

"You've already said more than enough." Kian hauls her across the sand, his face like steel. "It's time for you to go home."

There's a scream behind them and Wren turns to see the woman who revealed Wren's identity.

"See what you've done!" Wren shouts. The rage is boiling in her stomach like a soup made from fire. "This is your fault. What were you thinking?"

"I'm sorry," the woman cries, seeming to be fully aware of the huge mistake she made. "I didn't know."

Wren shakes her head and looks away. There's nothing more she can say.

One of the rafts has been readied and Wren digs her feet in the sand. She hasn't been through everything she has over the last few weeks only to end up like this.

Struggling against Kian isn't working, so she decides to try another tactic.

Using Nova as her inspiration, Wren lets her body fall limp and closes her eyes.

"What the Terra?" Kian lets go of one of her arms to catch her, scooping her up to carry her.

Wren lies still, relaxing every muscle, waiting for her moment.

Kian shifts his hold on her to better support her weight.

"What's wrong with the Remnant?" someone asks.

"She fain—"

Wren leaps forward, slamming the hard part of her forehead into the soft part of Kian's nose.

With a twist and a leap, she launches herself out of his arms and heads across the sand, weaving between outstretched hands that are trying to stop her momentum. She's never going to get away. Not with this many people working against her. But she has to try.

Then she sees him.

Dex.

He's running down the sand, the anguish on his face mirroring her own.

Changing her course, she heads directly for him, throwing herself into his arms and pressing her face to his chest.

"Help, Dex," she cries, feeling so much like the little bird she was named after. "You have to help me. They're trying to send me away."

"I won't let them." She hears the break in his voice as he presses his lips to the top of her head. "You're not going anywhere."

Even though she knows she's far from safe, this is what she feels. This is how she always feels when she's with Dex. He may not have Phoenix's muscles, but she knows he'd lay down his life for her if it came to that.

And if that's not the definition of love, she doesn't know what is.

Breaking free of his embrace, she reaches into her pocket for the jar of sap and hands it to him. "Take this. Nova needs it. She's not well. You have to check on her."

"Where's Phoenix?" he asks, slipping the jar into his pocket.

"He's with her. He knows what to do. You can trust him." She's talking quickly, knowing she doesn't have much time. If she gets sent out on a raft tonight, she needs to know Nova and Phoenix are safe.

For now.

"And take this." She slips her pendant from around her neck and presses it into his hand.

"Wren, I'm not letting them take you," he says, putting the pendant around his neck and tucking it into his shirt.

"I'm not sure you have a say." She flinches as a sharp pain grips her around the arm.

It's Kian. He has blood running down his face, and a determined expression on his face.

"She has to go, Dex," he says. "We have no choice."

Dex grabs her by the other arm. "She's not going anywhere."

"Has she told you who she is?" Kian asks.

Dex looks at Wren, the moonlight making his brow seem even more furrowed than it is.

"She's the daughter of the Commander of the Outlands," says Kian.

The hurt on Dex's face is instant. He shakes his head and she can feel his trust slipping away from her.

"I can explain!" says Wren. "If only you let me. Please. Dex, you have to let me explain."

"Let go of her, Dex." Kian pulls at her arm.

"A little foolish to let someone so valuable go, don't you think?" asks Dex.

"We don't have time for this," says Kian, motioning to the rafts with his head.

Wren sees the others are already being loaded. They're struggling to break free, but they're outnumbered. By a lot. It's like every Bound in Askala is making sure they're sent back.

One of the rafts has been pushed out into the waves with half a dozen screaming people on board.

"Think about it, Kian," says Dex. "If they got hold of you in the Outlands, they'd never let you go. They'd get all your secrets out of you first. Don't do anything rash. Put her in the brig until you find out what she knows."

Wren's not too sure what a brig is, but decides she likes it far better than the idea of being cast back out to sea.

Kian pauses, bringing his sleeve to his nose to mop up the blood that's still seeping from it.

"Did she do that?" Dex asks.

"Who else." Kian's voice seems resigned.

"It's the right decision to keep her here," urges Dex. "Always keep your enemies close."

"Okay," Kian says, shaking his head, the contradictory movement betraying the uncertainty in his decision. "But one more false move from her and she's going in the water. Without a raft."

"Let me stay and I'll tell you everything you need to know," Wren says, even though she's never going to reveal Cy's secrets. Kian can torture her if he likes. Not that she expects torture is a signature move in Askala.

"She stays with me," says Kian, dragging her back down the sand to the water's edge.

Dex follows closely behind.

"*Nova*," Wren mouths at Dex, but he ignores her request, no doubt concerned she'll be sent away the moment his back is turned.

The second raft is loaded and the people pushed out to sea.

"This is cruel," Wren calls out. "You're sending these innocent people to their death."

Kian glares at her.

"I'm sorry." She falls silent, remembering she'd promised to behave.

"I know this is painful. I know this feels harsh," Kian shouts over the sound of the waves. "But this is necessary for the survival not just of Askala, but our whole planet. Our level of sacrifice is the measure of our commitment." Kian pauses, seeming to need to pull in a breath. "The Remnants must be sent away. It's for the greater good."

"The greater good!" shouts Shiloh, who's appeared from nowhere beside Kian. "For Earth!"

Shiloh punches her left hand into the air, her palm facing the crowd as her High Bound ring flashes in the moonlight.

One by one the people in the crowd lift their left hands, just like they did at Wren's Proving ceremony.

Except with their solemn faces shadowed in the moonlight, this looks nothing like the same thing.

This is a salute that says their lives are worth more than those of the desperate people being pulled out to sea by the relentless currents of an ocean leached with acid.

Wren can only hope they live long enough to deliver a message to Cy.

Because when he finds out what they've done…

Askala is going to fall.

NOVA

*A*s Nova begins to wake, she senses she's been out for quite a while. How long, she can't tell, all she knows is that trying to climb back to consciousness is like trying to climb through sap.

She registers the sound of rustling somewhere to her right, but her head feels too heavy to move. The smells of her room filter in—the slightly stale air, the coppery tang of the ocean, a hint of pine that shouldn't be there. Then light seems to jab through her closed eyelids, making her frown.

The last thing she remembers is the storm. It was dark then. There were people in the rain...

Opening her eyes takes effort, and she blinks groggily. Someone is in her room with her, their blurred shape moving closer.

"Kian?" she croaks.

"The insults don't get much bigger than that," chuckles a male voice.

Nova rubs her hand over her face, trying to bring the room into focus. She opens her eyes again, seeing a face coming into her field of vision.

She scuttles back in the bed, gasping at the pain in her leg and the person across from her. "Dean!"

The young man shrugs. "No idea who that is, but he's got to be better than Kian."

Nova tucks herself up against the wall. "Get out of my room!"

"If I could do that, I would've gotten out of this overgrown tin can two days ago."

Two days? Nova shakes her head. "You're not making sense. But I want you out of my room, Dean. You have no right to be here."

This is the brother of the man who led to her father's death. What the Terra is he doing in her room? While she was asleep!

Dean ignores her words and takes a seat on the other end of Nova's bed. He holds up a finger. "One, my name's Phoenix." He holds up a second finger. "Two, saving your life has got to give me some sort of allowances when it comes to being in here."

Confusion has Nova's mind whirling. Phoenix. She's heard that name. During the storm. She peers closely at him, trying to place him.

The red hair. The cocky grin. The way he doesn't look away like he has anything to be ashamed of. They're all Dean. Except...he looks younger somehow. And what are those black inked patterns snaking their way up his arm?

Nova goes to climb out of bed, needing a bit of space to process this. Maybe some fresh air—

She gasps as she puts weight on her right leg, pain firing so bright she squeezes her eyes tightly shut. Agony engulfs the whole limb.

Phoenix is instantly by her side. He grasps her by the elbow, supporting her weight as she collapses back onto the bed. "Easy there, Blondie. That cut on your leg was pretty impressive."

It takes a few seconds for Nova to swallow back the pain and nausea. They swirl around until she can't tell where one starts and the other finishes.

"Just go slow, and you'll be fine. You've been pretty out of it with a fever for two days."

Flashes of the storm are starting to return. Two rafts. Violent waves. Remnants battling to get to shore. A red-haired young man wrapping his arms around Wren...

Nova rubs her temples, feeling the pain slowly abate. "Two days. I've never slept for that long."

Phoenix points at Nova's leg. "I bet you've never had one of those before."

Looking down, Nova's eyes widen. Sticky sap is lathered down the side of her calf, but what's underneath is unmistakable. A thick, red gash zigzags from her knee almost to her ankle.

"Just take it easy and you won't reopen it." Phoenix leans forward, his hands on his knees. "It's gonna leave one hell of a scar though."

The movement to hide her deformed hand is reflexive. More ugliness marring her body. But then Nova remembers more.

Heat and pain searing through every cell. Gentle hands holding a cool cloth to her head. Water trickling into her mouth when she called for it.

This young man cared for her while she was sick. Very sick. He's seen her hand and who knows what else.

"You're not Dean."

"Nope."

Realization dawns through Nova. The red hair. The uncanny resemblance. "You're Ronan's son."

Phoenix grins. "Chip off the old block, huh?"

Nova blinks, trying to assimilate all this.

Ronan almost destroyed Askala. And standing before her is pretty clear evidence that he made it out alive. He might still be.

142

She clasps her hands together, running her fingers over the gap in her hand. It was because of him that she's now like this.

Yet she helped save his son's life.

And it seems he saved hers.

Her head swims again and she holds a hand to her forehead, as if to steady it. She closes her eyes as the room whirls.

"Here."

Nova opens her eyes to find a cup of water pushed close to her face. She takes it, realizing how parched her throat is. She downs the content in three fast gulps.

Phoenix takes a seat on the end of the bed again. "Much more efficient than when I did it."

As he nursed her through the fever. "I...I suppose I should thank you."

Phoenix shrugs. "Just returning the favor." He looks away, glaring at the door. "Plus, it's not like I can leave."

"You can't?"

"Not with your boyfriend running a ship-wide manhunt for me."

Kian? "He's not my boyfriend." Not any more. Was never going to be, as it turned out.

Alarm shoots through Nova's body. "What have you done? Why does he want you?"

Phoenix snorts. "I'm guilty of being born on the wrong side of the ocean."

Nova scoots forward, placing her feet on the floor. There's a flash of pain through her calf, but it's bearable. Maybe Phoenix is right. She just needs to go easy. "I think you need to let me know what's been happening."

"Well, you were there for our arrival. But then that little cut of yours got infected and you were out for the next two days. In that time, your High Bound friends"—Phoenix spits the words out— "decided we needed to be sent back."

"Sent back?" Nova gasps. "How could they do that?"

"Wren asked them the same thing. They almost sent her, too, except Dex talked Kian into throwing her in the brig."

Nova shakes her head, causing the room to spin again. "No. Kian would never do that."

"It's for the good of Askala," sneers Phoenix.

Any words Nova had ready to defend him die in her throat. For the good of Askala. So many Remnants. One the son of Ronan.

Of course they wouldn't be allowed to stay.

"But you're here," she points out.

"Not for long, I'd say. Dex brought you the sap. He's been checking up on you. He reckons they've combed the rest of this rotting ship. I doubt even the sacred space that is your cabin will be safe for long." Phoenix's hands flex. "But I'm not leaving Wren."

His final words are laced with steel.

Nova recognizes his determination for what it is. "You love her."

Phoenix's eyes blaze. "We're two halves of a whole."

Nova nods. She remembers how that felt.

And how it felt for that whole to be shredded into more pieces than she thought possible.

Nova glances around the cabin. "Well, we're going to need a plan then."

"We?" Phoenix couldn't inject more surprise into one word.

Pushing herself upright, Nova tests her weight on her injured leg. It objects, sending an ache straight through to the bone, but she ignores it. "You heard me. Wren is my friend, and although your father may have almost destroyed Askala, you saved my life."

Phoenix's eyes narrow. "My father tried to help Askala. He wanted to make it as great as any one of you. But you were threatened by him, so you banished him. Sent him to the

Outlands, away from his family and the girl he loved, and left him to die."

That's what he's been told? Ronan almost killed an entire generation through malnutrition and starvation. But now's not the time to set the record straight. Grabbing her sheet, Nova quickly shreds several strips off it and wraps them around the sap on her leg. "We need somewhere to hide you."

Phoenix leans forward, arching a brow suggestively. "I could hide in your bed."

Nova's mouth pops open. This cocky young man just said he loved Wren like she was his other half. And now he's suggesting *that*?

Stepping away, she glares at him in disgust. "I don't know how things work in the Outlands, but that's not an option here."

Phoenix shrugs. "There are a lot of things you don't know about the Outlands," he purrs. "I could teach you quite a few tricks."

Gingerly taking a few steps, Nova's relieved to discover she can almost walk without a limp. "If they've searched the other Unbound cabins, then maybe…" She inhales sharply as the solution hits her. "You're Ronan's son."

"Yep. We've covered that." Phoenix rolls his eyes.

"Which makes Dean your uncle."

Phoenix sits up straight. "Are you saying my uncle is still alive?"

Nova nods. "Ronan's brother is also an Unbound."

Just like Ronan was supposed to be, except he lied and pretended otherwise, but Nova doesn't add that. She doesn't know whether Phoenix belongs in Askala, but she won't be a part of sending him back to the Outlands, treating him like his life isn't important.

She clenches her fists. No one is less.

"My father mentioned he had a brother. Said he was just like him—someone who would do anything for family."

145

That doesn't sound like the Dean Nova knows, but she keeps her mouth closed. "Sounds like just the cabin you can hide in, then."

She heads to the door, testing her leg over the few steps. Shards of pain splice up her calf with each movement, but it's bearable if she grits her teeth. All she needs to do is find Dean and she can rest it again.

"I'll be back as soon as I can," she offers over her shoulder. A thought strikes her and she straightens in alarm. "Has Felicia been here?"

Where would Felicia's loyalties lie? With the Bound or Unbound? Nova almost gasps. Since when did she start thinking in terms like us and them?

"Who's Felicia?"

Nova allows herself to relax. "Never mind. You'd know if you met her." Rubbing her temples, she wonders if she bumped her head while the waves were throwing her about. Everything that's happening is giving her a headache.

"Nova?"

She pauses as she's about to scan the sensor. "Yeah?"

Phoenix glances at her raised hand. "What they do here—it isn't okay."

For once, Nova doesn't hide her missing finger. "The problem is, Phoenix, that I'm guessing what you do over there isn't either."

She steps through and the door slides closed behind her. Leaning back against it for a moment, she pulls in a steadying breath. Her head is spinning again, probably her body objecting to so much movement, so soon.

Or everything her mind is refusing to process jostling for attention.

Wren is in the brig.

The people of the Outlands have been sent back. Some or all of them could be dead already.

Phoenix, Ronan's son and Dean's nephew, is hiding in her cabin or he'll suffer the same fate.

Kian, the boy she's loved all her life, is making each one of those decisions.

Voices trickle over, and Nova's only taken a few halting steps when she sees why. Sam is where she found him last time, sitting guard at the base of the stairs.

Except he's not alone.

Nova's brows hike up as she approaches them. "You've brought friends?" Not only that, he's brought a small table and chairs.

Sam sets down his cards with a smile. "Ah, angel. It's good to see you up again." He indicates to the two people across from him. "I'd like you to meet my sister, Beatrice, and her partner, Vern."

Nova smiles in welcome, noting the use of the word 'partner.' Of course the Unbounds would find mates.

Even though they can't have children.

Sam squints at her. "How's the leg?"

Nova shifts her weight. "How do you know about my leg?"

"Everyone on the upper levels knows about you hurting yourself, Nova," Beatrice offers. "How you were trying to save that Remnant."

Sam nods. "It's why they're here." He grins. "They insisted, and when they arrived with the cards, I couldn't turn them back. It would've been rude."

"We wanted to be part of what you're trying to achieve."

What she's trying to achieve? "Ah, well. Thank you. But really, it wasn't necessary."

"Sam reckoned you'd say that," chuckles Vern. "Another reason why we're here. He said you were a good one."

Beatrice nods. "And we look out for our own."

Sam coughs, his whole body hacking and shuddering. Nova notices the glance Beatrice and Vern pass each other.

Nova narrows her eyes at Sam. That cough is starting to sound worse. "I hope you're looking out for this one. He doesn't know when to stop."

"We tried telling him we'd take shifts, but he wouldn't hear of it," scowls his sister.

Nova moves closer, taking in the gray skin that's hanging off Sam's bones. "You should be in bed. You won't get better if you keep doing this."

Sam shrugs, picking up his cards with trembling hands. "We're all wasting away up here, angel. It's what we're sent here to do."

Nova's mouth slams into a flatline. How can she argue with that? It's the truth.

Beatrice places a hand on Nova's, the gaps where their fingers are missing overlapping. "He said he'd go once he knows you're okay."

"I'm feeling much better. In fact, I'm off to find Dean."

Sam straightens. "That piece of double-crossing filth?"

Vern's lip curls. "That cheater gives us a bad name. My guess is he's on the level below. Probably tired after taking part in the search all day."

Nova isn't surprised Dean's been involved in the search for Phoenix. Wren would've found a way to let him know his nephew is the one they're all looking for. "He'd be the first person to want to find him."

"Of course he would," scoffs Vern. "The High Bound have offered five pods to anyone who brings in the runaway."

Nova blinks. Kian has offered pods in exchange for Phoenix? That's a significant reward in Askala. One she's never heard being offered before.

"You don't want to be around the likes of him, angel," warns Sam.

"It's just a quick message. It has to do with the people who came in on the rafts."

148

Beatrice wraps her arms around herself. "The ones they sent right back."

"You watch—we'll be next," growls Vern, glaring at the cards in his hands.

"They'd never do th—" The realization that's exactly what she said about sending the Remnants back stops Nova. She shakes her head. "Bound are kind and empathetic. They wouldn't."

Sam shakes his head, glancing at Nova's left hand. "Sending those poor souls back wasn't so kind."

"What's best for Askala is the question we should all be asking ourselves." Vern slaps his cards on the table. "Sacrifices have to be made."

Beatrice grimaces. "We just get to be the ones who make them."

Something on Nova's face has Sam shifting in his seat. "They're not all bad," he assures. "Like that Dex. He came twice a day to check on you and give us updates." His gaze sharpens. "He brought you a pod."

Dex brought her a pod? One which Phoenix must've made sure she ate. Nova shakes her head. "He shouldn't have done that."

Sam arches a brow. "Because you don't deserve one?"

"He should've given it to you," Nova shoots back.

Sam's face blooms into a grin which quickly morphs into a chuckle...and then deteriorates into another round of coughs.

Nova wraps her arm around his frail shoulders. "I want you to go to bed. Please."

Sam hesitates. "But—"

Beatrice stands. "I'll take him. You've got important stuff to do."

Nova works not to frown. How much do they know about who's hiding in her cabin? And why does it feel like she's being painted as some sort of protector? Like a guardian angel she's not.

She's about to object but she can see that Sam likes the idea. She sighs. "I'll come to check on you, okay? I don't want you back here before that."

Sam smiles tiredly. "Looking forward to it."

Nova watches as Vern helps Beatrice half-support, half-carry Sam down the hall. Twice, she tries to assist, but both times her hands are firmly slapped away.

"Go do what needs to be done, Nova," Sam wheezes.

Nova watches them leave, unsure what that means. She's Unbound just like them. Powerless.

She turns to head the other way, the movement prompting another head spin, this one closely followed by a wave of nausea. Gritting her teeth, she starts walking. These people don't realize she's doing this because she owes Phoenix. Nothing more, nothing less.

The sound of the drums grows louder as she descends the stairs. Hopefully Dean will be playing cards and she won't have to navigate that room. Her entire life she was told such a place was little more than a den of frivolity, a reckless waste of time.

Except a quick scan of the games room tells Nova he isn't there. The walls vibrate with the rhythmic beat next door. Please don't let her have to go in there.

She taps a young man on the shoulder. "Excuse me, I'm looking for Dean."

He turns to her with a frown, obviously unhappy at being interrupted. But then his gaze meets hers and his face clears. "Oh, hey Nova. Good to see you up and about."

"I...ah, sorry. I hadn't realized we'd met."

The man waves away her apology. "We haven't. I play cards with Sam most evenings. He's told me all about what you did for him."

The man across the table points in her direction with his cards. "And what she did for those Remnants."

Nova flushes. "I'm looking for Dean," she repeats. "Have you seen him?"

The first man snorts. "He lost so he went into the room next door."

"More like we got tired of his cheating," scoffs the second man.

Nova steps back. "Ah, thank you."

"No, thank you for helping Sam. I can't think of a person in this room he hasn't been there for."

Nova ducks through the door before she has to respond. The way these people seem to see her is making her uncomfortable.

The moment the door slides closed behind her, Nova is swallowed by the new world she finds herself in. It's dark, only a few pale lights along the walls, and the whole room is moving in time to the drums.

They line the back walls, several shirtless men perched up on a bar. Their arms swing batons down, booming out a tempo that seems to climb straight into her chest. Everywhere, barely dressed people twist and grind, a heaving mass of smiles and heavy breathing. As the drums work as one, so do the people.

"Welcome!" someone shouts and Nova finds herself being inhaled into the mass of people.

Moving in time with them isn't optional. As she presses between the moving bodies, she feels their wanton exhilaration. Nova suddenly finds herself feeling very…Unbound.

Reminding herself of Phoenix sitting vulnerable in her room, she scans faces as she works her way through. She finds Dean in the center, arms up high in the air, one hand holding a wooden cup. He's writhing and twisting next to a dark-skinned woman.

The moment he sees her, he stops. Turning to face her, his

smile changes. He glances down at her left hand, confirming she's Unbound. "Well, hello."

Nova's glad the dark room can't show the shame that reflexively heats her cheeks. "I wanted to talk to you."

Dean leers. "Not a lot of talking happens in this room."

Nova suppresses a shudder. "It's about the Remnant they're searching for." Nova's about to tell him the truth but Sam's words have her pausing. "I think he's related to you."

"Ah, the nephew I've been told about." Dean gyrates closer. "It'll make it harder to turn him in, but not impossible."

"But, he's family!"

Dean pushes his face close to hers, his breath moist on her face. "Don't you even start to judge me, Nova. Unlike you, I've never even seen something as wondrous as five pods all at once."

Nova reels back, watching as Dean pulses his hips from side to side, his grin back. "What did you want to tell me?"

So much like Phoenix. And yet nothing like him.

There's something different about Dean. A hardness in his eyes. A harshness.

Did Askala create that? Or would he always have been like that?

"That was it." Nova steps back, letting the crowd swallow her.

She stands still, arms and hips bumping against her. She can't tell Dean where Phoenix is. She may as well put him on the raft herself. But where does that leave her? Nova can't be the one to harbor him, it would betray everything she's grown up to believe.

But she can't let him be found. Just like the decision to stitch up Sam, just like the decision to help Wren save Phoenix, she can't bring herself to treat someone as...less.

She puts her hand to her head, the stifling room sparking

152

another wave of nausea. She needs to get back to her room. Rest her aching leg.

Something gets shoved into her other hand. "Here, it helps."

A woman, not much older than her smiles kindly. "It'll make it all go away, for a little while at least."

Nova's first reaction is to refuse the brimming cup she's now holding. Except the drums are throbbing. The room is pulsing. Each pound of wood on leather feels like it's pushing all this further away. Like all the uncertainty and pain doesn't exist beyond these walls.

In that moment, she feels it. What the other people in this room have given into.

The draw of oblivion.

Impulsively, Nova takes a sip, only to grimace. How could sweet, soft berries be transformed into something that packs that much punch? It burns the back of Nova's throat, making her wheeze.

"That a girl!" The woman whoops. "Enjoying the time we have left is all we've got."

The woman twirls away, falling into the arms of a man nearby. He laughs. "No point counting those sad minutes, is it?"

They kiss passionately and Nova looks away, suddenly understanding.

Wondering if that will be her soon...

"You gonna finish that?" asks an older man beside her.

Nova shakes her head, passing the cup. The man's gone before he can see her grasp her head. The wine is far more potent than Nova realized.

She needs to get out of here.

Slipping her way through the gyrating bodies, Nova makes it to the edge of the crowd. Maybe Phoenix will have to hide in the forest. Surely it's no more dangerous than the Outlands, but even as she thinks it, Nova knows that's a lie. In the Outlands,

Phoenix would've had some sort of shelter to protect him. And family.

Seeing the door isn't far away, Nova ducks her head down, pushing forward. She's so focused on her escape that she slams straight into a solid wall of chest. It's only when her hands fly out to steady herself that she recognizes the muscles her fingers wrap around.

"Kian!"

His own hands grasp her forearms. "Thank Terra! I've been looking everywhere for you."

"You came here? To find me?" Nova asks incredulously.

"Dex said you were resting. I got tired of him saying I couldn't go in. So I went back to your cabin."

Nova's heart thumps. Phoenix is still there.

"But Sam told me you'd come down here. Said you were looking for someone."

"Oh."

Kian came looking for her. Nova becomes hyper-conscious that her hands are still holding him. That he's still holding her.

Kian's fingers tighten. "I was...worried."

Nova's about to tell him she's fine, but she stops. She's as far away from fine as she could be. Her gut is still lurching. Her leg aches. Her head feels like it's going to burst with all the decisions waiting to be made.

And her broken heart is screaming for her to heal it.

Someone jostles Nova from behind, pushing her flush against Kian. "That's the idea!" It's the woman who gave her the cup of wine, still wrapped around her man. "You work fast, love." She nods toward Kian. "He's under your spell already."

Nova's about to object, but she looks up. Kian is looking down with such...yearning. His arms come around her, as if acting of their own volition. Warmth envelops Nova. It feels so...good. So right.

The woman was wrong.

154

Nova is under Kian's spell.

The drums feel like they've taken over her pulse. They surge, picking up tempo, and so does her heart rate.

The wine. The relentless beat. Her traitorous heart remembering what it was like to touch Kian. To love him with every inch of her body.

They begin to sway, the movement instinctive…practically primal. It's just them and the drums throbbing through their bodies, their hearts wanting to touch again. Kian's mouth parts, drawing Nova's attention to it. She flicks her tongue over her lips.

One more taste. One more moment where she can pretend.

The drums intensify and they draw closer. Their need hangs in the air between them, the pounding amplifying it.

Someone shouts beside Nova. "Unbound forever!"

A roar lifts through the crowd as bodies jump high and fists punch into the air. "Unbound forever!"

The hoarse voices shatter the moment. That's exactly what Nova will be. Unbound forever.

Her fists clench. Free to make her own choices. Free to be who she really is.

Nova steps back, her arms falling to her side. "You sent them back."

"I had to, Nova." Kian's voice is pained, heavy with the choice he's made. "I had to protect what we have here. What we're working toward."

"And Wren?"

"Her father is the leader of the Outlands. They call him the Commander."

Nova gasps. No wonder Wren didn't want to talk about her life before Askala. She had more to hide than any one of them realized.

Kian steps forward, trying to close the divide that just grew between them. "Don't you see? Each and every one of them is a threat to Askala."

Nova shakes her head. What exactly are they protecting?

"We voted," Kian states angrily. "The majority agreed this is what needed to happen."

Anger flashes through Nova. "And Shiloh voted for this too, didn't she?"

Kian looks away, that one motion giving Nova her answer.

They both stand there, breathing heavily. The drums have abated, waiting to build up to their next crescendo. Now, they're little more than a countdown to the moment Nova and Kian are going to have to say goodbye once more.

Nova takes another step back, letting the humid air rush between them. They've run out of words again. The emotion, the wishing this was all so different, have swallowed them.

But as she raises her eyes to meet Kian's, she finds them. She finds the words that need to be said. The words that will make the break complete.

"I don't believe what you believe any more, Kian."

Kian looks like she just sliced him. He flinches. His eyes flash with pain. His mouth opens only to find silence.

It hurts to see him like that, but Nova still turns away. Right now, she's almost glad she's not Bound. How could she live with the choices he's made?

"Nova..."

She turns back, not wanting to see the agony her name just carried but knowing there's one last thing she needs to do. "Phoenix, the guy you're looking for. He died this morning."

"What? How do you know that?"

"I was nursing him back to health in my cabin." Nova doesn't like the flash of satisfaction at the hurt that streaks across Kian's face, but it flares nonetheless. "His cut was quite deep. I thought the sap would be enough." She shrugs. "You'll be relieved to hear it wasn't, the Unbound threw his body into the ocean this morning."

Kian shakes his head, his whole face pained. "I'd never be glad to hear that."

"And Kian."

Nova's glad he braces himself. These last words are the final ones that need to be spoken.

"You should choose Shiloh. She's High Bound. She agrees with all"—Nova waves her arm to encompass the crowd beside them—"this." Two more steps and Nova is at the door. She mouths the last words, ignoring the pain the truth causes her. "And she loves you."

KIAN

a nger powers Kian as he strides to the labs. It bubbles hot and low in his gut and he has no idea what to do with it. He's never felt such virulent emotion. It's like a disease, eager to spread.

It wants out. It wants someone to consume.

Kian reaches the door of the squat building and draws in a steadying breath. The leader of the High Bound can't feel like this.

Even if the girl he's loved all his life just turned her back on him.

His hand is a fist as he scans the sensor and he has to work to unclench it, knowing he needs to make this feeling go away. Somehow.

Everything Nova just said to him in the upper decks is clinging to his consciousness. It's like the words grew barbs and have sunk into his gray matter.

In the past, talking to Dex has always helped. It's more than his ability to make anyone smile, no matter how impossible it may feel. Dex has always been able to see a problem from multiple perspectives. It's why he was the natural choice to run the Provings.

Except Dex hasn't been around the past two days. Not since the Remnants were sent back. And Wren was put in the brig. He gingerly presses his nose, glad there's no ongoing damage from Wren's headbutt. A part of him is glad she did it.

Except for brief corridor conversations, his cousin has been avoiding him, and Kian doesn't blame him.

He probably has some anger of his own simmering in his gut.

Kian can't help the frown, wishing he were here. He's a fellow High Bound. If anyone can understand what Kian's going through, it's him.

Heading for the computer room, Kian expects to find it empty. He'll check and then he'll leave. He needs to keep moving. If he stops, the awful, hot feeling in his gut seethes and festers. It seems to need movement to rock it to sleep.

But as the door whooshes shut, Dex spins his chair around. They stare at each other for long moments. Something flashes in Dex's eyes but he looks away. "You're later than usual."

Kian started his afternoon rounds the day after he was named leader of Askala. His father suggested it, being the most logical way for him to learn all the parts that make up the colony he's now responsible for.

"I stopped off at Nova's cabin."

Dex straightens. "I told you she was fine."

"I needed to see for myself. She wasn't there, she was on the party deck."

"Go Nova." Dex whistles.

Nova, a sheen of sweat gilding her skin. Those drums seeming to make the air throb. Her lithe body so close to his. It was…intoxicating.

"She told me…" That I should be with someone else. "That Phoenix died this morning."

"What?"

"Yeah, she said she'd been nursing him in her cabin. He died of the injury he sustained in the storm. The Unbounds sent his body out to the ocean."

Dex relaxes back into his chair. "Well, one less thing to have to worry about, isn't it?"

Kian's whole body contracts. Nova said something similar. Does everyone think he's so heartless? Doesn't Dex realize that's another death he now has to carry? "I never wanted him, or anyone else, dead."

Dex sighs, rubbing a hand over his face. "How are you feeling, Kian?"

Angry. But he doesn't know who at. "Like it's been a big few days." Kian glances at his cousin, noting the weariness around his eyes. "You look tired."

Dex half-smiles. "It *has* been a big few days."

The decision that was made down on the beach hangs between them, waiting to be discussed. But Kian needs Dex to understand.

He needs *someone* to understand.

Kian grabs a chair beside Dex, gripping the back as it catches on a loose floorboard. "You know I didn't like making that call."

Dex looks away, staring at the screen. "I know."

"And you know I wish it were different."

That Kian doesn't have to keep thinking of their frightened faces as the rafts were pushed back out, that he doesn't get to keep hearing their screams as they begged for mercy.

Dex sighs. "I know."

Something unwinds inside Kian. The heat in his gut dials down to a simmer. Finally, someone who understands. "Have you spoken to Wren?"

"Every day." Dex keeps his focus on the screen. "She says there's nothing to tell. The Outlanders have a leader, just like you. Why would we expect that to be any different?"

Kian frowns. Wren has done nothing but lie since she arrived. "Does he know that his people are building rafts to come to Askala? Does he know that his daughter is here?"

"She said they're not that coordinated." Dex frowns. "I don't know the answer to the second question."

"What *do* we know about him?"

Dex shrugs. "Just that his name is Cy. They call him their Commander."

"Is *he* trying to make his way to Askala?"

Dex shakes his head. "She says he isn't."

"Is she lying?"

A muscle ticks in Dex's jaw. "I don't know."

Kian's hands are white knuckled on the back of the chair. "We need to know if he's a threat, Dex."

Dex finally turns to face Kian. "Because we protect Askala at all costs, right?"

Kian stiffens, surprised he has to make this explicit. "When we protect Askala, we protect Earth."

"Whatever that means," Dex mutters.

"What did you say?" Kian asks, even though the room is too small to have missed those murmured words.

Dex waves the question away. "It doesn't matter." When Kian goes to object, Dex continues. "Have you considered what needs to happen next?"

Kian nods sharply, willing to go with the change of subject for now. He expected some animosity from Dex. "We'll need to establish patrols. In case they don't get the message." Kian swallows, knowing he's talking about those people dying before they had a chance to reach shore. "And more come."

"And if they do get the memo?"

Kian frowns. "What do you mean?"

"What message do you think you sent when you shipped those people back?"

"That they're not welcome here."

161

"Or"—Dex pins him with a glare— "that they can't come peacefully."

Alarm shoots down Kian's spine. There's no way people of the Outlands would understand why it was necessary to do what they did. "We need to know what the Remnants want with Askala. We need the truth from Wren."

"I've tried, Kian. Have you considered she's telling the truth?"

Not for a moment. "And if she isn't?" Dex doesn't answer, but Kian didn't expect him to. "You need to talk to her. Tell her she needs to tell us whether her father or the others are planning anything."

Dex stills, his gaze narrowing. "And if she doesn't?"

Heat sears the back of Kian's throat. Some part of him doesn't want to say the next words.

But he knows he has to. It's what his father would do.

"Then she'll be sent back to the Outlands, just like the others."

Dex's intake of breath spears through the stillness Kian's words pierced.

Dex studies him for long moments before stepping away. "No matter the price, huh, Kian?" He heads for the door with long strides.

Kian steps away from the chair. "Where are you going?"

Dex angrily swipes his stump over the sensor. "To see Wren."

Kian watches another person he loves walk away from him. Pain arches through his chest, but it's quickly swallowed by the anger. It bubbles up like hot lava, scalding him from the inside out. Kian doesn't know which is preferable—he's powerless to make either go away.

Unable to stay still in the silent lab, Kian follows Dex out the door, knowing he'll be long gone. He has a feeling Dex would've run like a polar grizzly was on his tail rather than keep talking to him.

Striking left down the path, Kian sets off to finish his rounds before heading back to the boardroom to make notes. His father kept meticulous records during his time as leader, and Kian's determined to maintain that.

He's already seen Milli, the High Bound tasked with overseeing the Unbound, before he'd decided to visit Nova. When Milli told him one of the Unbounds was gravely ill, his heart had almost stopped in his chest. Something about Nova had been off, like she was in pain, as she'd stood in the storm. But as Milli had listed those who were sick, Nova wasn't among the names.

Kian finds Aarov as he's leaving the water treatment system. He reports it's operating well, the shells of the raven eggs continuing to work their benefits. Kian makes a mental note of the water quality reading for when he returns to the boardroom. He thanks Aarov, wishing the good news had some impact on his mood.

Next is the gardens, where Kian knows Zali is still probably working with a few others on the fencing. The storm that brought the Remnants also damaged the timber designed to keep hungry animals out.

Zali wipes the sweat from her face and smiles when she sees Kian approach. "Almost finished."

Kian admires the row of fresh timber enclosing the gardens. "You've done well to have it repaired so quickly."

"Well, we can't afford to lose this lot to a polar grizzly."

"Were we able to salvage anything from after the storm?"

Zali's face is tight with tension. "Some. We're hoping we can graft new tomatoes onto the remaining root stocks. We dug up what was left of the yams. If we use them to make soup it might be enough to feed those who need it the most."

Kian nods, making a mental note to cross yams off the ledgers for this season. He rests a hand on Zali's shoulder. "Thank you for your tireless work."

Zali holds his gaze. "Together, we'll make sure there are future generations to do our work, Kian."

With a quick smile, Kian turns away. This is why they're doing this. Why he's making difficult choices. It's only a matter of time before Dex sees that, too.

But as Kian returns to the path, something strikes him.

When Zali was talking about feeding the yams to those who need it most, he was thinking of the Unbound. They have a responsibility to care for them. But did she mean the Bound? Those who will continue what they're working so hard to preserve?

Kian lengthens his stride, too much energy firing through his muscles. His gut feels like it's filled with lava again. He's going to need to go for another lengthy swim in the lake tonight if he wants any chance of sleeping.

One more stop.

Except the last one is the infirmary.

The entire space is littered with memories of Nova. Nova carefully folding bandages, treating them like the precious commodity they are. Nova never losing her calm, gentle façade, no matter how much blood she was trying to staunch. Nova smiling when she'd look up and find him standing at the door.

Thea feels it, too. Kian can tell by the way her smile seems heavier.

By the way she's spending less and less time in the infirmary.

The door slides open to reveal an empty room and Kian lets out a breath. All he needs to do is look at the records of who was here today and he can leave. The less time in here the better.

A chair scrapes behind him and Kian spins around to find Shiloh standing beside the desk in the corner, a smile spreading across her face.

"Hey." Kian forces his muscles to unwind. "I thought the place was empty."

"I was just doing some paperwork…while I was waiting for you." Shiloh moves toward him and Kian is suddenly conscious of how alone they are. "I have great news. There was a birth today."

"That is great news." Kian finds himself unwinding a little.

Shiloh's glowing. "It was a beautiful thing to watch, Kian. She was so proud. She refused to stay here, she wanted to take her little boy home to show her family." Shiloh rolls her eyes. "Actually, to show anyone who's within a twenty-foot radius."

Kian's about to comment that's understandable, a baby is something that's widely celebrated in Askala, but he registers that Shiloh hasn't stopped.

She doesn't halt until she's right before him, her face ablaze with something he's only seen hints of. "I can't wait for that to be me."

Everything in Kian freezes. His muscles, his mind, his breath. Shiloh has made it clearer and clearer what she wants over these past days. Sometimes she acts like it's an inevitability.

But he's made enough difficult decisions for now.

"Shiloh—"

She places her hand on his arm. "I know things have been tough lately, I just want you to know that I'm here. That I'm looking forward to fulfilling my duty as a Bound…"

Shiloh doesn't finish, but two words hang in the air.

With you.

Kian doesn't realize he's stepped back until he sees the flinch on Shiloh's face. "Shiloh, you're beautiful, kind, and a committed High Bound." Everything a leader would be looking for in a partner. She must think the same because a rosy glow creeps up her cheeks. "It's just that…"

Nova.

Shiloh's eyes soften. "You went and saw her again, didn't you?"

165

Some days it takes every fiber of self-control to stay away. "I wanted to make sure she was okay after the storm."

"I know you two have history." Shiloh smiles, her face full of understanding. "And I know it will take time for you to let go."

Kian has to concentrate not to double over from the sucker punch those two words wield. *Let go.*

Nova already has.

"And I want you to know that's okay, Kian. My father had an Unbound mistress. We can still be together." She swallows. "You could visit Nova whenever you need to."

Kian's eyes widen, not sure which part of that suggestion his mind rejects more. "You'd do that?"

Shiloh's eyes are shining as she slowly nods. "The two of us, leading the Bound to heal Earth would be a dream come true. I love you, Kian."

Her words leave Kian paralyzed.

That was a dream he built with someone else. Those are the words Nova was supposed to say to him.

Those words aren't supposed to make him want to run.

Shiloh closes the distance between them, her hand sliding up his arm. Her intention is clear as her blue gaze flickers to his lips.

Every part of him wants to step back, to stop her trajectory.

But he doesn't. This is what's expected of him.

This is what he needs to do.

Even Nova realized it.

You should choose Shiloh.

Shiloh pushes up on her tiptoes and presses her mouth to his. Her lips are soft and warm and willing.

His are shocked and overwhelmed and still.

Trying to work himself into the moment, he kisses her back, squeezing his eyes closed, telling himself this is supposed to be right.

The kiss is short. Pleasant.

Wrong.

Pulling back, Shiloh smiles up at him. "You don't have to do this alone."

Kian tries to smile back, but it feels like his muscles have turned to stone. "You have a generous heart, Shiloh."

Her eyes sparkle. "It's in my genes."

Shaking his head with a rueful twist of his lips, Kian steps away. "I need to go. I'll see you tomorrow."

He strides to the door, glad to be creating some space.

Shiloh calls out just as he steps through. "I'll be here, Kian." Her last word hits him between the shoulder blades. "Waiting."

Kian practically runs the whole way to the boardroom, regretting that it's so close. Although, right now he could run to the edge of Askala and it wouldn't be enough to work off the energy pounding through his system.

He pauses at the door, knowing there's one more meeting waiting to be had. One where he can't afford to show the war going on inside him right now.

His father turns around as Kian steps through, a smile blooming across his face. "That took longer than usual."

Kian takes the seat beside his father, noting that he was going through the ledgers again. He wonders how much of it is difficulty letting go, and how much is mentoring his son. "A few things needed to be discussed."

"Oh?"

Kian points to the open page. "A child was born today."

His father beams. "Wonderful news." He pushes the book toward Kian. "It will be your first entry showing our colony continuing to prosper."

Picking up the pen, Kian looks at the columns. This boy will be listed among the Bounds, hoping that's where his name will remain.

He stares at the black line between the Bound and Unbound. That line decides so much. Whether you're entitled to yam soup. Stitches. Children.

And this is the system he now advocates. The system he's doing everything he can to protect.

Kian pauses. "Dex doesn't agree with what I've done."

His father leans back, understanding dawning across his face. "There was dissent when it was decided we needed to burn the bridge. My own brother didn't agree with it. But people realized it was necessary. That this is about something bigger than us."

"He thinks more Remnants might arrive. That by sending them back we've shown them they can't come in peace."

His father's lips flatten. "They've never come in peace, Kian. They are the humanity who created the world we live in now. The ones who plundered and pillaged until it was too late. They'll do the same to Askala."

Kian thinks of Wren. She's one of the brightest minds he's ever met. But is she just as selfish as the people she was born of? Will she honor what Askala stands for now that she's Bound?

His father's hand covers Kian's. "This is why the High Bound are only those with the highest levels of intelligence and kindness, son. We can't let what happened before happen again."

Kian scans the Unbound column. There's so many of them. It's not just Nova's name there, but Felicia's and others he knows. "It just seems so..." Kian can't bring himself to say it.

Heartless.

"Don't you see? Eventually the Unbound will die off. Their numbers are already dropping. There will be fewer and fewer of them, until Bound outnumber Unbound. Then we will have the leaders of our future, a new humanity who will inherit this Earth."

Except his father is talking about people. About Nova.

Kian nods, and the fire in his belly screams an objection.

His father sighs. "I wish things were different, Kian. If all this had happened a year earlier, you wouldn't have to be weighed down with these choices."

His father would've made the call to send the Remnants back, without all this debilitating agonizing. What would he have done with Wren?

Sent her back there and then.

And yet Kian wasn't strong enough to do that.

Just like he's not strong enough to let Nova go.

What will he do if Wren refuses to talk? Will he be strong enough if more Remnants arrive?

His father levels his dark gaze at him. "It's a good sign you're torn."

Kian's brows shoot up. "It is?"

"Of course. It shows you care. It shows you know how much is riding on your decisions." He clamps a hand on Kian's shoulder. "Right isn't always easy. Especially when right can only be achieved through sacrifice." He squeezes tighter. "You've got this, son. I know you do."

"It's hard, Dad." Kian whispers the words as if they're a confession. "Really hard."

"Yes, it is." His father's face is somber. His eyes are dark with understanding. "But every choice you've made so far has shown you'll be the leader I knew you would be."

Except he feels nothing like the leader he imagined. He doesn't feel kind. He doesn't feel wise.

And he's never felt more alone.

He looks at his father. "When you had to make the tough calls, at least you had Mom."

"Shiloh has feelings for you, Kian. She's a good woman. Caring, yet strong in her convictions. And you care for her. It wouldn't be an unhappy union." He smiles. "She's the right choice for you."

Because Shiloh passed the Proving. Shiloh's High Bound.

And Nova's not.

He straightens. It's time to take charge of the festering mess that's inside him. It's time to make it go away.

Kian picks up the pen and adds the newest arrival to Askala in the Bound column. "One day, I'll list my own child's name in this ledger."

The smile that graces his father's face as he leans back is the biggest he's ever seen. He pushes up, pride filling his chest. "Those will be your most memorable moments as the leader of Askala, son. I know they were for me."

Kian nods as he puts down the pen. This is the life he's meant to lead.

His father turns to leave, only to stop at the door. "We can't let any more Remnants set foot in Askala, Kian. They are why I burned the bridge. We can't lose it all now."

Kian knows what his father is waiting for. As he turns and stands, he realizes he needs to make a decision.

It's time to be strong.

He holds his father's gaze. "We won't, Dad. I'll make sure Askala becomes everything it's meant to be."

His father nods once, the motion acknowledging the promise Kian just made. "That has always been your destiny, Kian."

The door slides shut with a click. Kian falls back into his chair, sure that now he's chosen his future, the burning feeling in his gut will be gone. Now that he's committed himself to leading Askala the way he should, the other decisions will fall into place.

Like Wren. And Shiloh.

There's no need to be angry anymore. Not with Nova, not with Dex, and not with fate for forcing his hand.

Except the anger isn't gone.

Kian's hands clench as it assaults him from the inside.

In fact, it's roaring to be acknowledged. To be released. To be appeased.

It's furious with the one person he can't escape.

The one person who just made a promise he's not sure he can keep.

Himself.

DEX

*T*hrowing a rock as far as he can into the ocean, Dex knows what he has to do. The chat with Kian only confirmed it. How dare he threaten Wren like that!

Kian knows how Dex feels about her. Even if the feelings aren't reciprocated. It doesn't matter. She's still his best friend.

It'd taken all of Dex's self-control not to react, opting instead to put as much space between them as he could. It's important that Kian continues to trust him. Wren would already have been sent back if he didn't.

There's no way he'll stand by and watch her be sent to the Outlands. She's the best thing that's happened to Askala in a long while. Her unique way of looking at the world will help all the work they've done to heal the Earth, not hinder it.

Which is why he needs to break her out of the brig and find somewhere safe to hide her. Maybe wherever it is that Phoenix has been moved to, because there's no way Dex is buying that story about him being dead. Kian might know the old Nova better than anyone else—the Nova who wouldn't dream of telling a lie—but Dex knows who she's become. *Who she was forced to become.* And the new Nova is lying to protect Phoenix. He'd bet his right hand on it.

Phoenix had looked perfectly fine when Dex had brought him fresh food and water last night. And doing a surprisingly good job of caring for Nova, telling Dex that he was certain she was about to wake up. And it seems she did. And headed straight for the party deck.

Dex smiles as he turns from the beach, imagining the look on Kian's face when he saw the girl Askala cast aside, dancing with her fellow Unbound.

Enjoying the way Wren's pendant bounces on his chest as he walks, he takes the path to the Oasis, keeping an eye out for Kian. He's used to looking for his cousin, although it's an unfamiliar feeling to be hoping *not* to see him. A feeling that's becoming more normal as each day passes.

He understands now how his dad felt when Magnus decided to burn the bridge. Why he withdrew from the world, rather than face the outcome of a devastating action he was unable to stop.

But Dex isn't his father. He's not going to spend the next twenty years in that lab trying to change things. He's going to change them now. His father had told him that something big is about to happen in Askala. And he's more right than he possibly even knows.

It's changing.

Now.

Marching up the gangplank, Dex heads to the bow of the ship toward the brig. He'd never been inside it before he'd visited Wren for the first time. It's a small room with padded walls, a bed, and a tiny bathroom. There's a sensor on the door to get in, but nothing on the inside to get out.

Wren is being guarded by a group of Bounds who Kian has put on some kind of roster.

Dex is going to need to distract them.

Or outsmart them.

Winding his way through the maze of corridors, he arrives to find two Bounds seated outside the door to the brig. One is Tory, a friend of Magnus. The other is Aarov, a fellow High Bound. Kian's taken no chances with who he's put on his roster.

"Hey guys," says Dex, trying to keep his tone casual.

"You here to talk to Wren?" Aarov tilts his head toward the door.

"Kian wants to talk to her, actually," says Dex, smiling. "He asked me to collect her and bring her to the boardroom."

"We haven't been told anything about that." Tory glances at Aarov.

"Yes, you have." Dex forces out a laugh. "I just told you."

"Our orders are not to let her leave with anyone," says Aarov. "Perhaps you should come back later."

"She can't even leave with a High Bound?" Dex's brows shoot up.

Tory nods solemnly.

"Dex." Aarov shuffles his feet. "We were sp—"

Tory puts a hand on Aarov's arm. "Don't."

"Don't what?" Dex asks. "What's going on?"

Aarov sighs, shaking his head at Tory. "Dex, we were specifically told not to let Wren go with you if you asked. Kian was very clear about that."

Dex takes a step back, feeling like he's been punched in the gut.

Kian *doesn't* trust him. He knew Dex might try to do this and was one step ahead.

"Then let me visit her," he says, hoping Wren might have a better plan. He doesn't mind admitting she's smarter than him. That much was obvious in the Proving. She was smarter than them all.

"That, we can do." Tory nods.

"Why don't you come back later?" Aarov is looking at him strangely, almost as if he's trying to tell him something.

But Tory has already pressed his wrist against the sensor and the door slides open.

"Thanks," says Dex, standing right behind him.

"What the Terra?" Tory steps back like he's been hit by lightning, crashing into Dex.

Dex steps around him and looks in the room, blinking as he tries to take in what he's looking at.

Wren is nowhere to be seen. Instead, Nova is sitting on the neatly made bed.

"Surprise," she says, smiling sheepishly.

"Sound the alarm!" cries Tory, his face pale.

Aarov seems to hesitate, then hits the red button and the screech of a siren bounces off the walls.

Dex rushes to Nova, crouching down in front of her, his heart leaping out of his chest as he tries to work out what all this means.

"Where is she?" he asks over the high-pitched noise. "What happened?"

She leans forward, pressing the warmth of her cheek to his so she can speak directly into his ear. "She's safe. She's with your dad."

Dex rolls back on his heels, almost toppling to the floor. His father has Wren! How is that possible? How had he even known that Wren was in danger and needed to be broken out?

But there's no time for questions now. Bounds are crowding into the hallway outside the room and Dex knows he has to leave before Kian arrives.

"Go!" says Nova. "I'm okay."

Dex nods as he gets to his feet. Nova *will* be okay. Askala may have underestimated her, but he's not going to make that same mistake.

Racing from the room, he weaves his way through the chaos

in the corridors, ducking around the corner when he spots Kian's dark mop of hair. Not now! Not even later. He needs to find his father.

He needs to find Wren.

Hearing footsteps behind him, he picks up his pace, taking a chance by scanning his chip on one of the cabins, hoping to find it empty.

Stepping inside, he lets the door close behind him and presses himself against it as he waits.

Damn it! There's a small girl in here. She sits up in the bed, wide-eyed.

"Want Mommy!" she wails.

"It's okay." Dex smiles at her. "I'm leaving."

Pressing his eye to the peephole, he sees Tory running down the corridor.

"In a minute," he says to the girl, aware that his hands have started shaking.

"Mommy!" she cries.

Dex counts to ten then taking a deep breath, he opens the door and takes off in the opposite direction.

Making his way to the stairwell, he heads up instead of down. Past groups of Unbounds lounging on the stairs in a drunken haze and to the very top. Racing across the upper deck he gets to the ladder and scurries down it so fast he loses his grip right near the bottom and lands on the dirt with a thud.

He rubs his backside as he stands, aware that he needs to get to the lab before Tory gives up waiting at the gangplank and gets there before him. Surely, that's where his father and Wren will be waiting for him?

With his heart pounding and his breath coming in short gasps, he winds his way through the trees, the sound of the siren dying with each step he takes.

The sight of the squat building of the lab in the distance is such a relief, it almost feels like a mirage. He heads for the entrance, his stump held in the air ready to press against the sensor. If his father and Wren are in there, he needs to warn them. They don't have much time to get Wren into hiding.

But once inside the lab, it becomes quickly apparent he's alone. There's an eerie silence as the door slides closed behind him.

"Dad?" His voice bounces back at him from the thick walls.

He does a quick check, going from room to room, even looking underneath his old bunk, half expecting Wren to roll out and make some kind of joke.

But there's nobody here.

Where else can he possibly look? Where could his father have taken her?

Going to the computer room, he sinks down into his chair and puts his head in his hands, trying to steady himself while he thinks this through.

A noise underneath his chair startles. A tapping.

Leaping to his feet, he moves his chair, his eyes bugging as he sees part of the floor beneath him lifting up. The floorboard that always seems to catch underneath his chair.

A hatch? The whole time he's spent sitting in this room and there's been some kind of secret hideout beneath him? This is unbelievable!

"Dex!" His father's head appears at the opening. "Get down here. Quickly!"

"What the Terra?" Dex squats down to get a better look.

The hatch opens further and Dex sees his father is standing on a ladder.

He moves to the side. "Get down here," he hisses. "Hurry!"

Dex hesitates, still trying to process what's going on.

"Dex!" calls the unmistakable voice of Wren from down below.

That's enough to convince him. He climbs down the ladder and his father closes the hatch behind him.

Blinking in the dim light, he lets his eyes adjust as he takes in where he is. With walls made from crudely dug out soil, it's not a large space, but by no means small. It's around the size of his cabin on the Oasis.

Wren throws herself at him and wraps her arms around his waist. "I knew you'd come looking for me."

"You sure know how to worry a guy." He locks his arms around her, aware of how his heart has slowed down knowing that she's safe. Then he notices Phoenix sitting on a mattress in the corner and releases his grip.

"Hey, Dex." Phoenix gives him a wave. "Fancy meeting you here."

"Knew you weren't dead," Dex says.

"They think I'm dead?" Phoenix's eyes are wide. "That's so cool."

"Not sure this is much of an upgrade from the brig," Dex says to Wren, glancing around the dimly lit room, his nose wrinkling at the musty smell.

She shakes her head. "That's where you're wrong. Because I'm here by choice. I was in the brig as a prisoner. Massive upgrade if you ask me."

Dex nods, accepting the truth in her words. Just like the birds Wren so keenly watches out for, she isn't a creature who likes to be held captive. She was born to be free. But is this strange underground room freedom? It doesn't feel much like it.

"Keep your voices down." His father steps off the ladder. "I've soundproofed it as much as possible, but we could still be heard."

"Are you going to tell me what's going on?" Dex keeps his voice low. "How Nova ended up in the brig in place of Wren?"

"God, I love that girl," says Wren, sitting down on the mattress beside Phoenix.

"You and me both," says Phoenix, wrapping an arm around her.

Dex ignores the comment. They're not here to have a competition as to who loves Nova the most. A competition that Kian would once have won, although now Dex isn't so certain.

"I heard you and Kian talking in the lab," says his father, going to a device on a shelf that looks like some kind of radio and passing it to Dex.

Dex takes it from him and studies it. "You've been down here listening in to my conversations?"

"Only some of them," his father says.

Dex thinks back over everything he's said in the lab. He's only spoken with his father and Kian... and Wren. Although, that was in the bunkroom and it doesn't look like his father had any devices in there. He hasn't said anything in the computer room that he wouldn't want his father to have heard.

"What is this place anyway?" Dex scans the room noticing it has jars of preserves stacked in a corner next to a barrel of water. A person could survive for weeks down here if they had to. "Did you build it?"

His father nods. "You never know when you're going to need to disappear for a bit. Or keep someone hidden."

A realization crosses Dex's mind. "When did you build it?"

"A long time ago." His father waves his question away, taking back the listening device and returning it to the shelf.

"You built it for Mom, didn't you?" Dex asks. "And me. In case they ever found out."

His father turns back to him, Wren and Phoenix watching on in silence. "I did. I couldn't risk Magnus sending you away. I needed a place I could hide you in an emergency."

"Were you digging this out the night Mom died?" The irony of the situation hits Dex in the chest—his father in the lab building a place to keep them safe, rendering him unable to protect them when they'd needed him most.

179

Phoenix lets out a long whistle. "Whoa. Heavy father and son talk."

Wren puts a hand on his arm, silencing him. "Leave them."

"I...I...I..." His father kneads his hands as if he can squeeze out the words he needs.

"You don't have to answer that question," says Dex. The sadness spilling from his father's eyes is enough. "It's in the past. Tell me what happened just now after you heard me talking to Kian."

Letting out a sigh, his father finds his voice. "It was obvious you were going to try to get Wren out of the brig. I may not be the world's best father, but even I could figure that out."

Dex glances at Wren, trying not to notice the possessive way Phoenix has his arm around her. He thought Wren had said they weren't big on physical affection in the Outlands.

He turns his attention back to his father. "And you didn't think I could get her out by myself? So, you did it for me?" Dex crosses his arms, hating that he feels the sudden need to hide his stump again.

"Kian's watching you too closely," his father says. "It would've been impossible for you to do it."

"He's right, Dex," says Wren. "There was no other way."

"And how exactly did you do it?" Dex keeps his arms crossed, turning to face his father.

"I saw Nova on my way to the Oasis." His father crosses his own arms, mirroring Dex's body language, whether intentionally or not. "She had her hair covered by a veil to keep the sun off her and I realized that underneath it, she could be anyone. If they were distracted, of course. So, I asked her for help."

Dex shakes his head, not surprised that Nova had agreed, but amazed that such a plan had actually worked.

"I had my doubts, too," says Wren, noticing his look of confusion. "But it worked. Callix and Nova came in. Nova gave me her veil and I walked out with Callix. After he tripped in the doorway and pretended to twist his ankle, of course."

"And Aarov and Tory still didn't notice?" This still sounds a little far-fetched to Dex.

"Aarov stood between Tory and Wren," says Callix. "He's one of us."

"One of us?" Dex uncrosses his arms and throws his arms in the air. "What does that even mean? One of who?"

"Quiet!" Callix hisses, picking up his listening device and turning a dial.

There's the sound of footsteps overhead and a voice crackles to life.

"He's not in here, Tory. This place is empty."

Dex's father looks relieved. "It's okay," he whispers. "That's Aarov."

"I'm sure I saw him come in," says Tory's voice over the radio.

"Then he must have left through another exit," says Aarov. "There's nobody here. Let's go."

Dex holds his breath and waits, still shocked that Aarov has been somehow working with his father and he had no idea. Had his father altered Aarov's results to make him a High Bound, too?

The footsteps get louder before they retreat, then disappear. It seems Aarov has successfully steered Tory away.

"So, what happens next?" whispers Dex. "Wren and Phoenix can't stay down here forever."

"We can stay as long as we need to," says Wren.

"And how long is that?" Dex fixes his gaze on her, daring her to tell him exactly what's going on. There has to be a reason the daughter of the Commander of the Outlands is here. And why the guy she loves has followed her. "What exactly are you up to?"

"Our goal is no different to Callix's," says Wren. "All we want is for our people to be able to come here in peace. Like they used to be able to before the bridge was burned."

"But before that can happen, certain changes need to be made," adds Phoenix. "Changes that it turns out Callix has been working on long before we arrived."

Dex's father nods. "Phoenix is right. Our goals align. Askala's rules are flawed. You're walking proof of that, Dex."

"Me?" His brows shoot up. "In what way?"

"You've watched your mother's video, haven't you?"

Dex nods.

"Then think about it." His father comes closer. "Your mother was Unbound and you're Bound. A true Bound. You're proof that the Unbound shouldn't be sterilized. It's possible for the Unbound to give birth to children who have the smarts and heart needed to make this world a better place, just like it's possible for a Bound to give birth to an Unbound."

Dex thinks about this. His father's right. Being Bound or Unbound might contribute to what someone's child turns out to be, but it's definitely not set in stone.

"You want to put a stop to the sterilization?" he asks.

His father nods vigorously, a new energy shining in his eyes. "And the cutting of the finger. And I want to rebuild the bridge. Askala will become the place it was supposed to be. The place it would have been had my father chosen me to lead instead of Magnus."

"And how are you going to do any of that with Kian in charge?" Dex asks. "You know he's keen to follow in Magnus's footsteps."

"The Proving's where the true power lies." His father claps him on the arm. "Not in being the so-called leader."

That doesn't make a whole lot of sense to Dex. He doesn't have half as much power as his cousin has.

"But Kian has the people on his side," he says. "They're loyal to him. We saw that when Kian sent back the rafts. Nobody stood up to him."

Except Aarov. His vote makes total sense now. It seems Aarov truly is aligned with his father.

"Who were the people helping on the beach, Dex?" his father asks. "The ones pushing the rafts out."

"Bounds." Dex shrugs, not sure what he's getting at.

"And the Unbound outnumber the Bound."

"But the Unbound don't care!" Dex sighs. "You've seen how they behave on the upper decks, living for the moment. They won't fight for you."

"Not all of them are like that." His father paces, reminding him of Wren, who's sitting unusually still beside Phoenix. "I've been building a league of Unbounds. One recruit at a time. Our numbers are getting stronger every day. Momentum is building. And I have two new members now." He tilts his head at Wren and Phoenix, who nod their agreement.

"We've pledged your father our full support," says Phoenix. "We're willing to work with him in an alliance."

"And what will your father think about that?" Dex asks, directing his question at Wren.

"We'll have his support," says Wren. "Part of sending me ahead was to identify if there were any like-minded people here. I didn't expect to find any, but it appears I have."

"How many did you say that you have in your army?" asks Phoenix.

"Hard to say." His father chews on his bottom lip. "Our last meeting had about fifty show up. Not sure I'd call us an army just yet."

"You have meetings?" asks Dex, wondering how it's possible he didn't know about this.

"On the upper deck." His father nods. "The one with the ladder to the beach. We meet at midnight every new moon. Extreme caution has to be taken."

"And what happens at these meetings?"

"We prepare. We talk about the injustice of the system." His father clenches his hands into fists. "And we try to figure out the best time to strike."

"And when is that?" asks Dex, shaking his head. "Now?"

"Soon," his father says. "Any civilization is at its weakest when the leadership transfers. At first, I was concerned about the timing of Wren's arrival, but then I realized it was perfect. If we align with the Remnants, we'll be unbeatable."

Dex glances at Wren to see her reaction to the use of that word, but she doesn't flinch.

"We'll be the Unbound Remnants," she says, grinning. "We'll show the world what a bunch of rejects can do."

Dex is unable to help himself from returning her smile. She's come so far in letting her defenses down since she first arrived here. Not that she needed to change, but it's like she's become an even better version of herself.

"I need you to do something for me," says Wren, leaping up and reaching for her pendant hanging around his neck.

"Oh, of course," he says, bringing his hand to his throat, aware of their fingertips brushing. "You want it back."

Wren shakes her head. "No, I need you to send a message. You've seen how it's done. We need to tell Cy to wait until we're ready."

"Wait for what?" he asks.

"Wait before he sends more people." She lets go of the pendant but doesn't step back. "We'll need to recruit more Unbounds to our side first. The timing is crucial."

Dex weighs this up. There can't be any harm in sending a message telling this mysterious Cy to wait, can there? If anything, that's being cautious.

"She's right," says his father. "We're not ready. We need to spread the word. When we have the numbers, we'll send another message. Then it begins."

Wren pushes a note into his hand.

"Please, Dex," she says. "It's important. If Cy sends more people across now it could ruin everything. Callix knows what he's doing. We have to strike at the right time."

Dex's father is already climbing the ladder, motioning for Dex to follow.

Shoving the note in his pocket, Dex takes one last look at Wren, fighting the urge to brush his fingers down her face. Aware that Phoenix is watching them closely, he turns and climbs the ladder.

"Do you need anything?" he asks Wren just before his father opens the hatch.

"I have everything I need," says Wren, just as Phoenix hauls himself to his feet and stands beside her.

"I can see that," Dex says, pushing down the wave of envy that sweeps over him.

Phoenix has a history with that girl. They were friends when they were children, just like Kian and Nova. He can't compete with that. He can build new memories with Wren, but he can't erase the old ones she has with this guy she seems to love so much.

Following his father up through the hatch to the computer lab, he squints, adjusting to the brightness he never noticed before. How is Wren going to cope staying down there for who knows how long?

"I know it's a lot to take in," his father says, sliding the chairs back over the hatch.

Dex nods. He's done with talking for now. His head feels like it might explode with everything he just learned.

"I'm going to try to send this note," he says, heading for the door.

His father follows and Dex holds up his hand. "Let me do it alone."

"Okay." His father slides into a chair, looking as exhausted as

Dex feels.

Dex steps out of the room, turning at the last moment.

"Thanks for getting her out," he says.

His father nods and opens his mouth to say something, but his words are swallowed by the door sliding closed.

Dex scurries along the hallway, making his way out to the yard. It's sweet relief to step out into the fresh air. He adjusts Wren's pendant so it catches the sun, aware that if this takes too long, he's likely to change his mind.

Taking the note from his pocket, he unfolds it, feeling like he's betraying Wren's trust, but knowing he can't possibly send out a note when he has no idea of what it really says.

As he lifts the last fold of paper, it's with dread that he realizes the note has been written in code.

Well, that's just great! Now what?

"I'm so sick of this!" he shouts to the sky.

A raven swoops down as if it'd been waiting for him to call and stands in front of him, its beady black eyes drinking in the sight of him.

"I don't have any food for you," he says, wondering how it's possible this bird knew it would find him out here. He'd expected to have to wait for hours. Days perhaps.

The raven lifts a foot and tilts its head. How on earth do you train a bird to do that?

Dex remains perfectly still. Everything that's happened to him over the last few weeks comes down to this one moment. This one decision.

Does he trust Wren and send the note? Or does he take the note to Kian and tell him everything?

The raven hops closer and Dex lets out a deep sigh, thinking of his mother.

She told him to trust his father. His father seems to want him to trust Wren. His heart wants to trust her, too.

But...

Working quickly, he uses a small piece of string already attached to the corner of the note and ties it to the raven's leg.

Giving him a disgusted look for his lack of dead crickets, the bird takes off into the sky, leaving Dex wondering if he just made the best decision of his life.

Or the worst.

WREN

*W*ren knows she's dreaming but it doesn't feel any less real than when she's awake. Her heart's pounding, her eyes darting from left to right, her feet pushing her through the burnt-out forest.

Cy is timing her. She has to get back to him faster than her last attempt. If she fails, he'll be disappointed. And when he's disappointed, he lets her know. You don't become the Commander of the Outlands by accepting mediocrity. Cy expects the best. And as his daughter, that's what she needs to deliver.

Increasing her pace, she drives herself forward, her feet moving so fast it feels like she's flying. Then her feet lift from the ground and she *is* flying. But flying isn't possible. She can't fly. This is a dream.

The moment she has this thought, she crashes to the ground, landing at the base of a mangrove pine. The roots rise up from underneath the soil and grab hold of her, tangling themselves around her wrists and her ankles, pinning her down so she can't move.

"Dex!" she screams, fighting to break free. "Dex!"

She sits up with a gasp, eyes open and chest heaving as she tries to figure out where she is.

"Bad dream, huh?" Phoenix is lying beside her, watching her with his arms folded behind his head.

A bare lightbulb hanging above their head is flickering.

The secret room. That's where she is. With Phoenix beside her, not Dex. Strange that Dex had been the one she'd called for when she needed help.

"Thanks for waking me up." She lets the sarcasm drip from her voice as she reaches over for the cup of water she'd left beside the mattress and drains it. She'd kill for some fresh air right now.

"Better not to wake you," says Phoenix. "Dreams are our way of processing our thoughts. Seemed to me like you had some serious processing to do."

She raises an eyebrow at him. "Next time wake me up, okay?"

"Sorry." He extends a hand and trails his fingertips down her arm. "What was it about?"

"Cy was making me run." She lifts the cup to her lips again, checking for any last drops of water.

"And you needed Dex's help with that?" He withdraws his hand and tucks it behind his head once more, the lines of his tattoo expanding as his bicep flexes.

"A tree grabbed hold of me. I couldn't get away."

"Interesting." Phoenix nods. "What is it with you and Dex, anyway? He's clearly got it bad for you."

"He saved my life. He's my friend, that's all."

"Again, interesting."

"There's a rumor that Callix isn't his father." Wren leans back on the uneven wall of this cave-like room.

"Not so interesting." Phoenix yawns loudly. "Do I care who his father is?"

"Dex's mother was Mercy," she says, waiting for Phoenix to react.

Phoenix lets out a whistle as he pieces together what she's trying to tell him. "I've always wanted a brother."

Wren shrugs. "We don't know if it's true."

"Looks like Dad got busy before they banished him," says Phoenix. "Who told you this?"

"I heard it from Dean. I'm not sure how reliable a source he is. I was so excited to meet him. He looks so much like you, but..."

"Well, I know Dad loved Mercy," he says. "He has her name tattooed across his chest, for God's sake. It's not like we're going to forget her name in a hurry. Always going on about her like she was some kind of saint. It's all very possible. The timing works."

"You should hear the way they talk about him." Wren sighs. "Ronan this and Ronan that. Blaming him for all the troubles here. You'd think he was the devil."

"Fools." Phoenix shakes his head. "If they'd listened to him and let him help with the pods, there'd be enough for everyone by now. So shortsighted to send one of your best minds away out of nothing but pure jealousy. If Magnus is anything like his son, I can see why he felt threatened."

Wren weighs up what she should tell Phoenix. The stories she's heard are quite different to the ones they've been told in the Outlands.

"What is it?" asks Phoenix, his ability to read her mind not seeming to have diminished with their separation. "You're not telling me something."

She sighs. "The story here is that Ronan-the-evil turned up the temperature in the pteropod tank without permission and wiped them all out. That's why he was banished. The colony here almost starved. It's also why they take a finger from the

Unbound now. They say that Ronan had posed as Bound when really he was Unbound."

Phoenix leaps to his feet and paces the small room, a habit she's aware she has herself.

"Bloody liars!" he punches the air. "Rewriting history! How dare they! Are you sure we want to align with people like that?"

"Phee." Wren gets to her feet and goes to him. "What if they're not rewriting history? What if that's what really happened?"

"No way." Phoenix directs a look at her that she's never seen before. It's like he's wondering who she is.

"What's that noise?" Wren tilts her head when a sliding sound drifts into the room.

She looks up at the hatch, but it remains firmly closed.

"It's this." Phoenix takes Callix's radio from the shelf. "Someone's up there."

"What time is it?" She stands beside him, ready to listen.

"Can't tell down here." He keeps his voice low as he holds the radio between them.

There's the sound of tapping and the scraping of a chair.

"Not sure if you're listening," Dex's voice comes through the radio. "But just in case, it's only me. I can't check on you just yet. Apparently Magnus wants a word with me. I'll wait until he's gone. We don't want to take any chances."

There's the sound of more tapping and Wren imagines Dex at his desk staring up at the computer screens in front of him. It's nice knowing he's right there above them.

"This could be our opportunity," Phoenix whispers in her ear.

"For what?" Wren paces the room.

"To ambush Magnus." Phoenix looks up at the hatch. "We could lock him down here. Nobody would ever know."

"We're not ambushing anyone, Phee." Wren sits back down

on the mattress and wraps her arms around her legs. "We've just told Cy to hold off on sending reinforcements."

"That's if Brother Dex sent the note."

"Don't call him that!" She waves a hand at him.

"Reckon he sent it?"

She shrugs. "I think so. If he could find a raven."

"Yep, he's got it bad." Phoenix sits down on the mattress beside her, still holding the radio. "Sending a note to his enemy when he has no idea what it said."

"He trusts me," says Wren.

"I'd say that feeling's pretty mutual."

She studies him, wondering why that felt more like an accusation than an observation.

"I didn't want to trust anyone here," she says. "You know that. But you didn't live through what I did with the Proving. Some of these people are good. Like *really* good. It's not like what we've been led to believe growing up."

"You mean you're a fan of the system?" The accusation is still written across his face. But there's no point lying to him. He's the one person who could always see straight through her.

"I'm a fan of some aspects of it," she says cautiously. "They don't have the answers. But neither do we. The balance lies somewhere in the middle. That's why this alliance makes sense. It's our best chance of finding the right solution to fix this planet."

"The planet?" Phoenix is looking at her like he doesn't know who she is. "Since when have you cared about the planet? It's the people who matter."

"People who can't exist without air to breathe and food to eat." She knows it's going to take more than one conversation to convince him but she has to start somewhere. "We have to protect the Earth if the human race has any chance of survival."

"It's gone too far for that." He shakes his head.

"You haven't seen what I have." She looks up at him, trying to find the words to explain. "During the Proving we went up a cliff. The view went for miles and all I could see was trees and wildlife. It was breathtaking. I wish you could have seen it. I hope you will see it one day. It's possible to restore the environment. I know that now."

"You went up a cliff?" He frowns at her. "But you hate heights!"

"Don't worry, I still hate them. Maybe even more now..." Thoughts of Fern's final scream as she fell off the edge echoes in her ears. She doesn't think she'll ever forget that terrified sound.

"Remember that time you climbed the tree and I had to come and get you down?" He laughs. "There was nothing breathtaking about that, except when the wind was knocked out of my lungs when we fell the last few feet."

"I was five years old!" she complains, rolling her eyes. "Give me a break."

There's a noise and Dex's voice comes through the radio. "Dad, what are you doing here?"

Wren and Phoenix hold still, listening intently.

"Heard you were meeting Magnus," says Callix. "Thought you might want some support."

"Would be nice if you stopped treating me like a kid," says Dex.

"Sorry. I can leave if you like."

Wren huffs, not believing for a moment that Callix would leave.

"It's okay," says Dex, probably coming to the same conclusion. "Stay if you want."

"You checked on our guests yet?" Callix asks.

"Not yet. Too risky. Been checking on some numbers instead."

"Oh. And?"

"You changed Aarov's results, didn't you? To make him a High Bound."

There's a muffling and Wren can only imagine that Callix is either nodding or shaking his head.

"And you made sure a few other Bounds didn't make the cut," says Dex. "That's why we had such a low number this year."

"I did what had to be done," says Callix. "The numbers have been falling for years anyway."

Wren smiles to herself as she shakes her head. She'd completely underestimated Callix during the Proving, thinking he was some Askalan die hard. And a terrible father. When as it turns out, he's neither of those things.

"He's here," says Dex, his voice lowering.

"Magnus!" The false joy in Callix's voice is obvious even through the radio. "Nice to see you, my brother."

"What are you doing here?" asks Magnus. "This isn't your job anymore."

"And nor is it your job to keep track of the High Bound," says Callix. "But here we both are."

Wren can imagine the grin on Callix's face. He makes an excellent point.

"It's not too late," hisses Phoenix. "There's four of us. We could overpower him easily."

Wren puts a steadying hand on his arm and shakes her head. "We have to be smarter than that. Magnus is no fool. He has a lot of supporters."

"What did you need to see me about?" asks Dex.

"I'd rather talk to you alone if you don't mind." Magnus's deep voice filters through the radio.

"Anything you need to say can be said in front of my father."

Good for Dex! Magnus is no longer the leader. He can't tell Dex what to do.

"It's about the missing Remnant," says Magnus.

Wren snatches the radio from Phoenix's hands and holds it closer to her ear.

"I'm sorry, but we don't use that term around here anymore," says Dex. "Do you mean Wren, the girl you approved as a Bound?"

"She's no longer Bound." Magnus's voice has a hard edge to it that Wren hasn't heard before. "She lost that privilege when we discovered her father is the Commander of the Outlands. I'm also told that her friend who died in Nova's cabin was the son of Ronan. I need to know how Ronan and the Commander are connected. Because it seems to me that if their children are friends that it's likely they're working closely together. Goodness knows how many of our secrets Ronan has revealed to him. What do you know about this?"

"I know nothing about it!" says Dex.

Wren imagines the confusion on his face. He's telling the truth. He really doesn't know anything about how anyone in the Outlands is connected.

"But you know that Ronan's alive?" Magnus asks.

"No idea. But he must have made it over the bridge if Phoenix is his son," says Dex.

"*Is?*" asks Magnus. "Don't you mean *was?*"

There's a pause.

"Just because someone is dead doesn't mean they're no longer someone's son," says Callix.

"You went to the brig to get her out, didn't you?" Magnus is cutting to the chase now. Wren just hopes Dex has thought up some answers to satisfy him.

"I went to visit her," says Dex.

"Tory told me that you lied to him. You said Kian asked for her. Then you disappeared the moment you realized she'd escaped." There's a threat in Magnus's voice. It's the kind of voice that's used to being obeyed. But Wren holds no fear that Dex will give her up.

"I thought that's what Kian wanted," says Dex, feebly. "I was mistaken."

"Tory also told me that you and Nova visited the brig earlier

195

in the day." Magnus must be directing his question at Callix this time. If only Callix had installed a camera instead of this device. She'd love to see Magnus's face right now. "Strange that somehow Nova ended up in the brig and Wren disappeared, isn't it?"

"Very strange," says Callix. "But I can assure you that Nova left with me. I have no idea how she got back in there. Have you asked her?"

Callix is a far more accomplished liar than his son. Which is no surprise.

"Nova says she can't remember how she got there," says Magnus. "Apparently she's been sick and it's affected her memory. Very convenient, don't you think?"

Wren suppresses a laugh.

"Good one, Blondie." Phoenix shakes his head and Wren presses her finger to his lips, afraid he spoke too loudly.

"How unfortunate," says Callix. "I do hope she's feeling better soon and can solve the mystery for us."

"Listen here, Callix." There's the scraping noise of the chair both through the radio and echoing down from the floor above. "I don't know what you're up to. Either of you. But I'm watching you. Kian needs your full support. The entire planet is depending on it."

"How does it feel to be so sure of yourself?" asks Callix over the sound of more chairs being pushed back. "Because the only thing I'm sure of is that appointing you leader was the worst mistake our father ever made."

"Settle down!" cries Dex as the radio crackles with a confusion of grunting and cursing and banging noises.

"Are they having a fight?" Wren raises her eyebrows at Phoenix.

"Sounds like it. Is Magnus a big dude?"

"Bigger than Callix," says Wren.

"Time to go up and help?" Phoenix leaps to his feet.

196

"No! Dex is there." Wren stands and goes to his side. "He'll sort them out."

"With his one hand?"

"You don't know anything about Dex." Her knuckles turn white as she clutches the radio to her chest. "Maybe he lost that hand fighting off a leatherskin."

"Maybe," says Phoenix. "But I bet he didn't."

"Enough!" screams Dex. There's no need for the radio to hear his cry, the shout filtering down through the floorboards. "You're behaving like children. What would your father think if he could see you now? This isn't helping anyone."

The radio falls so silent that Wren taps it to check it's still working.

Somebody sighs loudly and footsteps retreat from the room.

It has to be Magnus.

"That went well," says Dex.

"Yeah, real well," Callix agrees.

"You might need to get that looked at in the infirmary," says Dex.

Phoenix nudges Wren. "Black eye or broken nose? I'm taking bets."

"Both," says Wren.

"I'll take you over there," says Dex. "No excuses. That needs to be stitched up."

There are more footsteps overhead and then silence.

"Reckon Dex will come back?" Wren asks.

"I'm not taking bets on that one," says Phoenix.

"Why not?" She replaces the radio on the shelf.

Phoenix rolls his eyes. "Because of course he's coming back. That guy can't keep away from you."

Wren lies down on the mattress and turns her back to Phoenix, not wanting him to see her face. Because the truth is that as much as Dex can't keep away, she also doesn't want him to.

NOVA

The knock on Nova's door interrupts her heaving. "Coming!" she calls out, glaring in displeasure at the meagre contents of her stomach. She leans against the wall of the small bathroom, wiping a trembling hand across her brow. She thought yesterday's nausea had passed.

She quickly rinses her mouth out, frowning as she inspects the wound on her leg. The thick, purple gash looks as if a streak of the berry wine she sipped in the party room has zig-zagged down her calf. It's still raw and angry and she needs to be careful it won't reopen, but there's no puffiness, no tell-tale signs of infection. The vomiting is probably due to the stress of the past weeks.

The knock sounds again, this time rapping with more urgency. Nova opens the door to find the woman she saw dancing in the party room standing there. "Magnus is on his way."

Nova sighs. Again. "Thanks, Eilish."

"You'd better get going, he looked like he was doing his rounds then suddenly made a turn for the upper decks."

Which means this was a snap decision, or Magnus suspects

he's being watched and that the moment he heads toward Nova's cabin she'll be alerted.

Exactly like she is now.

"I meant to leave earlier, anyway." Nova doesn't mention the vomiting. She doesn't have time for being sick right now. "I'd like to check up on Sam."

He looked so weak when Nova saw him yesterday. She would've been more worried except he was still talking of going to the level below to play cards.

Eilish grins. "You've got time. We'll keep our kind and generous leader busy."

Nova shakes her head with a smile. The support of her fellow Unbound has been touching. She hadn't thought as far ahead as to what she'd say about helping Wren escape. When Callix told her of his plan she'd agreed without hesitation. Wren had been the one who showed them the sap in the second test of the Proving. She'd treated Bound and Unbound the same. It was a perspective Nova hadn't understood back then.

She glances down at her left hand. She sees the world differently now. No matter her heritage, or why she came here, Wren deserves to be treated better than that.

But Magnus had wanted answers. Nova isn't surprised he came calling rather than Kian. Magnus knows how close they are.

They were.

Nova's glad. She'd already lied to Kian about Phoenix being dead. And although she agrees with Kian's choices less and less, she didn't like lying to him. The divide between them already feels wider than just the existence of their nine or ten fingers.

And the story she gave Magnus when she was found in the brig was totally implausible—that she was unwell and had no idea how she ended up there. Nova gave hazy answers about going to visit Wren, finding Callix there, lying down on Wren's cot because her leg needed a rest and the next thing she knew, Dex was standing at the door.

She'd blinked innocently as she'd looked up at him. "I had a welcome party last night." She'd frowned in confusion. "Or was it this morning?"

Nova's not sure whether she was relieved that Magnus looked as if he believed her or whether she was hurt. Did he really think that just because she was judged as Unbound she would do something like that?

Magnus had gone to ask more questions, but Nova had rushed to the bathroom. By the time she finished vomiting, he'd gone. At least the surprise wave of nausea had helped to back up her story.

Nova shakes her head again. "Thanks, Eilish. I'll get going now."

Eilish doesn't move. "You still sick?"

"Almost back to normal." Nova smiles, ignoring the seesawing of her gut. There are few secrets on the upper decks, in part thanks to the thin walls, but largely due to the strong sense of community among the Unbound. Everyone here has no one to care for but each other.

Eilish nods. "Good to see it's not your leg causing you trouble. We all get it from time to time." Her face puckers. "No one has a great immune system up here."

Nova's lips flatten. Growing up in the infirmary, she noticed the cuts that seemed to take longer to heal, the way a cold could hang onto an Unbound and not let go. She assumed it was a product of their hedonistic lifestyle. But now that she's lived here, she knows otherwise.

How would her cut have healed without the sap? And she's seen how the Unbound seem older than their years...because they have no hope...and because they age faster. No wonder they lose themselves in anything they can find.

Straightening, Nova steps out and the door slides shut

behind her. She may have failed these people when she was in the infirmary, but she's not going to now. "Can you give me five minutes? I want to check on Felicia."

Eilish's eyes glitter as she sashays away. "I'll work my magic."

Nova almost blushes as she hopes those swaying hips don't mean what they seem to. Poor Magnus won't know what to do with an Unbound who won't take no for an answer. "You're the best," she calls out after her.

Eilish throws an arched look over her shoulder. "Apparently not."

Not sure whether she should frown or smile at the retort, Nova steps to the neighboring door and knocks. She's barely seen Felicia since the Proving, and it's time to fix that. Flick was one of the few people who insisted on being there for her in the early days, no matter what she said.

Just like Wren.

When there's no answer, Nova knocks again. She could've sworn she heard Flick moving around in there this morning.

The door slides open with a whoosh and Felicia comes barreling out, causing Nova to quickly step back. She pauses, thinking Felicia is about to rush off somewhere.

But she stands outside her door, smiling brightly in a scrappy hemp slip. "Hey, Nova. You feeling better?"

Nova blinks. "Almost back to normal," she replies automatically. In fact, her stomach has settled. Maybe Eilish was right. She peers a little closer. "Are you okay, Flick?"

Felicia's smile does the impossible and brightens even more as she tries to pat her wayward curls into order. "Sure. Just enjoying the peace and quiet in my cabin."

"Sorry I woke you. I can't stay." Nova glances over her shoulder as if she can feel Magnus homing in on her. "But I wanted to see if you needed anything."

Without warning, Flick throws her arms around Nova and

hugs her. "You're so beautiful, Nova." She pulls back. "I'm doing fine. Never better in some respects."

Nova sniffs surreptitiously, wondering if Flick has had an early sip of berry wine, but she can't smell anything. "Okay, if you say so..."

Flick nods vigorously, her messy curls bouncing in agreement. "I say so. Seriously, I'm fine, Nova." She giggles. "I just need a little more sleep."

Nova turns toward the hall. If she had time, she'd ask to come in so they could have a chat—Flick is acting odd. She makes a mental check to stop off on her way back, maybe becoming Unbound has impacted Felicia in ways she's not letting on.

She turns back to say goodbye to find Flick gone, the door sliding shut with a click. It seems she really was tired...

Not having time to wonder if she has a mystery on her hands, Nova heads down the hall. She needs to disappear for an hour or so.

Sam's cabin is only a few turns away, but she doesn't take the halls most people use. Although her injured leg objects at the extra steps, she knows the discomfort is preferable to talking to Magnus.

The man who had been a surrogate uncle as she was growing up. A fellow High Bound like her mother. In all the time she'd visited Kian, she'd been able to forget he was the leader of Askala. Down in their cabins, he'd been a caring father and husband who was tirelessly committed to healing their planet. Nova had sat by his feet just like Kian and his siblings as he told stories of the beautiful creatures that used to live on Earth. Some days they'd laughed at his fantastical stories, scarcely believing things such as ferocious tigers, delicate butterflies, and silvery tuna had ever existed. Nova had always loved the stories of the mythical deer that had once roamed the forest.

But when he'd questioned her in the brig, that Magnus was gone. Actually, it'd felt like that man was dead. With each piercing glare and sharp question, he'd made her feel...Unbound.

Not even Kian had done that.

It had only cemented her decision even further.

Nova notices the crowd several doors before she reaches Sam's cabin. At first she's not surprised—many Unbound come to visit Sam, seeking help with their problems. He's become a father to many. But then she registers that no one is playing cards, no one is laughing. No one is smiling.

Nova slips through, looking for Beatrice or Vern. She finds them both outside Sam's door. Vern has his arm around Beatrice's shoulder as they cling to each other, their faces drawn with lines of worry.

Nova rushes over. "What is it? Where's Sam?"

Beatrice glances at Vern before her concerned gaze returns to Nova. "He's sick, Nova."

"Yes, I know. But he was talking of going down to play cards last night."

Beatrice shakes her head. "He never went. I doubt he ever intended to—he could barely walk."

"And now he's not letting anyone in," growls Vern. "Gets himself all worked up every time someone steps foot in there."

Nova stares at the door, worry tangling through her. "He needs help."

Beatrice wrings her hands. "Sam has always been everyone else's rock. He doesn't want to be a burden."

Nova stills. No one wants to be a burden.

And yet that's what the Unbound are.

She lifts her hand to scan the sensor. "Sam is no one's burden."

Beatrice's eyes widen but Nova steps through before she can

say anything. The room is gloomy, the curtains closed against the morning sun. The place feels like a...tomb.

There's a shuffling sound from the bed. "I don't need"—coughing so fierce it makes Nova wince, fills the room—"anything."

The door slides shut behind Nova and she waits as more coughing hammers the air. "Well, *I* need something—to talk to you."

There's a pause and Nova holds her breath. This is why everyone left. Sam can't afford to get worked up right now.

"Ah, angel. It's you."

The bed creaks as Sam leans back and Nova relaxes. "I'm here so I can have a word with you." She walks to the bed and kneels beside it, tucking his covers in. "You lied to me about going out last night."

Sam begins to chuckle but the sound quickly deteriorates to another round of coughs. "Would you have left this old man in peace if I told you the truth?"

"Of course not! I would've stayed here to take care of you."

Sam sighs as he settles back into the bed, the sound rough and choppy. "Exactly." He pauses to take a few shallows breaths. "But I'm glad you're here. I want to talk to you."

"Just let me open the curtains, it's so—"

Sam's hand shoots out and clamps onto Nova's. "No."

The coughing starts again, sounding like it's going to shake Sam apart, so Nova quickly kneels back down. "Okay, okay. I won't." She grips Sam's hand back, shocked at its warmth. "For now."

Sam's teeth glint in the gloom as he smiles. "You're just what Askala needs, angel."

Nova frowns. "What are you talking about?" Sam is holding her left hand. He'd be able to feel the gap where her ring finger should be. "I'm Unbound, remember?"

"When those bastards took your finger, they also freed you."

He grips her hand tighter. "You're no longer bound by the way they think."

Sam's hand is dry and hot, making Nova frown deeper. "That doesn't mean—"

"It means far more than you realize!" Sam arches from the bed, triggering more wracking coughs. Nova tries to release his hand, but Sam holds tight. "The time is coming, angel. And you'll be part of it."

"Shh," Nova soothes, wondering what Sam's talking about. She brushes her free hand over his forehead and almost gasps at the heat. "You need to take it easy."

"Then listen, will you?" Sam growls.

Any worries that Sam's becoming delirious with fever fall away. Nova finds herself smiling. "I am listening."

"No, you're not. You're fussing."

Nova retracts her hand and wraps it around their clasped ones. "You're right. I can't help it. I care about you, Sam."

And Beatrice wasn't exaggerating. Sam is sick. Really sick.

"Which is why you're going to be such an integral part of the changes. You don't pick and choose who you care about. Your empathy isn't defined by labels. That's what Askala needs."

"Changes? Sam, what are you talking about?"

When the next rounds of coughing starts Nova sits back and waits, keeping her worry hidden. But they don't stop. They jerk Sam's body, yanking at their clasped hands. Sam releases her, his hand coming to his mouth as he rises up in the bed, powered by the wracking coughs.

"Sam…" But Nova can't see much in the gloom. She rises and moves to the window, opening the curtains.

She turns around to rush back, only to stop with a gasp. She just discovered why Sam insisted she keep the curtains closed.

He's struggling to sit up in bed, his skin is dry and ashen, seeming to mold to his bones. The color is a direct contrast to the glistening blood spattering the hand he's moving away from his mouth.

Nova's no longer worried. She's scared.

She strides back to Sam's bed, placing her hands on her hips. "Are you decent under that sheet?"

Sam's eyes widen through the coughing as he jerks the rumpled, dirty sheet further up his chest. "It's my chest that's giving me troubles, nowhere else, if you don't mind." He glares at her. "I don't want no wash down."

Nova smiles, glad Sam has enough energy to be cantankerous. He's going to need it. "You're going to the infirmary."

"Like hell I am."

Nova waves the objection away. "You're far sicker than you've let anyone know, Sam. You need help."

Sam wipes his chin, leaving a smear of coppery red through his stubble. "And what help are they going to give me, angel? Some bandages for my aching lungs? A cool compress for my burning bones?"

"My mother works there. I'm going to get you a pod."

Sam snorts. "I'm not sure if I should admire or scold you for believing that."

Nova ignores his retort, scanning her chip at the door and stepping through.

Beatrice's face lights up when she sees her. "You managed to talk to him."

Nova waits for the door to slide closed. "I'm taking him to the infirmary."

Beatrice's eyes widen. "You're a miracle worker, girl!" She pauses. "Are you okay to do that on your own?"

Nova waves away the question. Her leg will hold up. It has to. "But I need everyone gone for that to happen."

Beatrice nods, understanding instantly. Sam has too much pride to be seen in his current state. She turns to Vern, who's already moved to the nearest person.

"Show's over, people. Sam needs his beauty sleep."

Concerned glances are passed around but no one objects. Nova returns to the room as they leave.

She finds Sam sitting up in bed, his back curled as he breathes noisily. "I'm not going."

"The coast is clear," Nova says gently. "I've sent them all away."

Sam's bushy brows arch in surprise. "How did you do that?"

Nova smiles sweetly. "I asked them nicely." She takes a step closer and holds out her hand. "We'll go together."

The room fills with the sound of soft wheezing as Sam stares at her hand. "You know there's a storm coming?"

Nova glances to the window, surprised to find a few heavy clouds crowding the blue sky. "It was clear when I came."

"I can feel it in me bones." Sam pushes himself upright. "I'll go, but we go via the upper deck. It would be good to see a storm."

Sam sways as he tries to straighten himself and Nova quickly tucks herself under his arm. If that's what it takes to get Sam to the infirmary, she's happy to agree. "Unfortunately, they come far too frequently. There will be plenty more for you to watch."

When Sam leans on Nova, she knows she was right to insist. Someone as proud and strong-willed as Sam wouldn't take this offer of help easily. He doesn't object as they shuffle to the door, Nova supporting his fragile, too-hot body.

Nova's relieved to find the hallway empty as they make their way to the stairs. They ascend the single flight slowly, Sam's breathing rattling around the close confines. With each step, he leans more heavily against Nova, and soon her leg is screaming with enough pain to make her light-headed.

She grits her teeth. Sam needs help. He needs pods.

As they reach the top of the stairs Sam begins to cough and Nova feels the waves of pain as they wrench through him. He pulls his hand away from his mouth and it's blood splattered again.

Sam sighs as the spasms abate. "I don't think I'll get to see the storm," he says quietly.

Nova pulls him closer. He's right. There's no way he can make it up another flight of stairs to the upper deck. They'll have to head straight to the infirmary. "There'll be more, Sam."

"I got to see you." Sam smiles down at her. "And that's even more beautiful."

Nova takes a step forward, leading them down the hall. "Yep, the fever is melting your brain. We need to get to the infirmary ASAP."

Sam begins to chuckle only to cut it off abruptly, no doubt avoiding anything that could trigger more coughing.

Nova grits her teeth, ignoring the pain lashing up her leg and the agony of worry slicing through her chest. "Not long now."

They make slow but steady progress and Nova's glad the infirmary isn't far. Sam's breathing becomes labored, even his sporadic coughs sound like they're losing their will to wreak havoc.

They reach their final turn and Nova closes her eyes in relief. "Good thing you're the toughest person I know, Sam. We're almost there."

"Angel..." Sam slows and Nova adjusts her pace but doesn't stop their momentum. "Callix is the one you want to speak to." Nova has no idea what he's talking about, so she focuses on getting to the infirmary. "Remember, though, Callix wants revenge as much as he wants change. It could make him—"

Nova cries out as Sam collapses against her. She grapples with his unconscious body but it's like trying to hold melting wax. His arms slip down, his legs buckling. Nova slams into the wall as his weight overwhelms her, the corner colliding with her injured leg.

Pain explodes, screaming for her to buckle, but Nova holds fast onto Sam. She feels the moment the cut tears open under the pressure of two bodies as she slows their implosion. Black points of pain swim in her vision as she crumples, holding Sam to her. They slide down the wall in a slow, painful descent.

"Sam!" Nova slips from beneath him. "Sam, you need to wake up!"

Sam's head lolls, his mouth slack. Nova checks his pulse, finding it weak and thready. Her leg feels like someone has thrown salt on the tear, so she favors her right leg. She'll rest it when she gets them to the infirmary.

"Help! Someone!" she calls out desperately.

Slipping her hands under his arms, Nova tugs. But he's too heavy, there's too much pain. Panting, Nova pulls again only to slip on her sticky, red blood.

"Help! Please!"

Footsteps echo down the hall like a ripple of hope. Thank Terra, someone is coming.

"Nova! Are you okay?" It's Shiloh, her face tight with concern.

Nova moves to Sam's shoulder. "It's Sam. He's fallen unconscious. We need to get him to the infirmary."

The first thing Shiloh does is glance at Sam's left hand. Her eyes flicker as she registers he's Unbound.

Then she gasps. "He's bleeding."

Nova doesn't bother to clarify that it's her blood beneath Sam. "We'll deal with that when we get him into a cot."

Together, each clamped onto one arm, Nova and Shiloh drag Sam to the infirmary. Lifting his comatose body onto the cot takes every fiber of Nova's strength as her leg feels like it's about to explode, but she does it. Sam comes first.

The moment he's lying on the cot, Nova looks around the room frantically. "Where's my mother?"

Shiloh pulls a blanket over Sam. "She went to get more bandages. But it's fine, I can—"

Nova's hands spear into her hair. Her mother always sent other people to do those errands. She hated leaving the infirmary. "I need my mother."

"I can do this, Nova. Thea has tutored me well."

Light-headedness hits Nova with the force of a tidal wave. She stumbles to the nearest chair, clinging with all she has onto consciousness. She needs her mother. Shiloh would never consider giving Sam a pod.

"Nova?" Her mother's startled voice fills her with relief. She rushes to Nova's side, but Nova shakes her head. "It's Sam. He needs help."

Her mother nods, an expression of calm competence sliding over her face. Nova relaxes. That's the look she needs right now. Her mother will fix Sam.

She moves over to him, hands fluttering gently but with purpose. She checks his pulse, places her palm on his forehead, presses her hand to his chest. She frowns, no doubt feeling the fever and the rattles trying to break Sam's chest apart.

Nova's mother turns to Shiloh. "He'll need fluids. Get him some weak broth."

Nova straightens. "What? He needs a pod!" She struggles to moderate her tone. "Please, just one."

Shiloh's eyes widen as she turns to look at Nova's mother. "Thea?"

Her mother straightens slowly, as if she's worried the truth is weighing her down. "Nova, he's—"

Nova spears her hand up, palm out. The world spins again as she tries desperately to make this right. "Don't say it. I know he's Unbound. But you need to help him."

Her mother's eyes swim with sadness. "We can't."

Shooting to her feet, Nova goes to take a step only to collapse with a cry. Her arms grab her leg as every cell explodes with agony. The edges of her sight blacken, narrowing her world and slowing it down.

She watches her mother rushing toward her. Sees Sam lying on the cot beside her. She hates how pain is painting everything with a haze.

"Her leg!" her mother cries out. "She's injured."

Firm hands push Nova backward and she crumples onto the cot, tightening her throat against the scream that wants to escape.

"Shiloh, go get me some bandages."

There's a pause. "You just came back with some. I'll stay and—"

"No arguments—this cut is deep and long. Go!"

Shiloh leaves. Her mother moves away and Nova clings to the relief in the maelstrom of agony. She just wants to be alone with Sam. She'll regain some strength and find a way to get him back to his cabin. She should never have brought him here.

He was right. They won't do anything to help him.

There's pressure on Nova's leg, then a prick of pain like a bright star in the galaxy of agony she's floating in, but Nova doesn't turn to look. Sam's eyes are fluttering open.

He blinks at the ceiling for a few moments then turns his head. As his gaze finds her a slow smile spreads across his face. "Angel."

Nova reaches out and grasps his hand. "I'm so sorry, Sam."

He shakes his head. "Thank you for fighting for me," His gaze sweeps down, blinking when he looks at her leg, then looks back up. "I'm glad we came."

Another prick of pain and Nova blinks away the tears. "I didn't fight hard enough."

Sam won't be getting a pod, and now her leg...

"You fought in the only way that matters. With your heart"— he pauses as his eyelids grow heavy—"and sweet Terra, we need more of that."

Sam's hand relaxes in Nova's and she sits up with a start. *Please, no…*

But then a rattly breath passes his lips.

"Stay still, I'm almost done."

Confused, Nova turns to find her mother beside the end of the cot. Her eyes widen.

She's dragging a needle up into the air, a thread pulling tight.

Nova jerks her leg away. "What are you doing?"

Her mother raises moist eyes to her. "That cut was deep, Nova. I couldn't leave it."

Looking down, Nova registers the row of stitches climbing like a ladder up her bloodied leg. All that's left is a small, fleshy gap in the top. One or two more and her mother would've been done. "You stitched me up?"

"Please, let me finish, then we can talk."

Nova jerks her leg back. "You wouldn't give Sam a pod, but you stitched me up?" Nova has to work not to screech the final words.

Her mother extends her hand, her eyes pleading. "You're my daughter, Nova. What was I supposed to do? Let you bleed out and die? Watch it become infected knowing there's no way I can help you?"

The pain in Nova's chest dwarfs the agony in her leg. "You broke the rules for me, but not for Sam. If he had been your son, and I some Unbound, you'd leave me to die."

Although tears spill down her mother's cheeks as she shakes her head, she doesn't speak.

Because Nova spoke the truth. Her mind whirls at the injustice, taking the world with it. Nova clamps a hand to her forehead, trying to make it stop. She closes her eyes, only to find it makes the spinning worse.

"Take it easy, daughter. The blood loss is going to take its toll."

Nova grabs a nearby basin and empties the contents of her

stomach. Little more than yellow-green bile retches into the metal container. Her mother moves closer, reaching her arm out, but Nova pulls away.

Her mother can't comfort her now. She doesn't think she ever can again…

Pulling in a steadying breath, Nova looks up to find a cup of water extended toward her. She hesitates, but the need to wash her mouth out wins.

Her mother is looking at her carefully. "You never throw up, Nova."

Nova glares at her, putting the cup on a table beside her. "Well, I've done it several times in the past days. It seems being Unbound will do that to you."

Her mother shakes her head. "But the cut, it wasn't infected."

"Getting sick easily seems to be one of the many blessings of being Unbound."

"Except—" Her mother stands and begins to pace. "We're the same. We have stomachs of steel, it's one reason you were such a natural in the infirmary." Her mother stops, looking at Nova with eyes the size of portholes. "The only time I ever vomited was when…"

Nova pushes herself up on the cot, uneasiness adding to the unsettled feeling in her gut. "When?"

Her mother shoots to the cot, grasping Nova's arms. "When was the last time you bled, with your cycle?"

Too shocked to push her mother away, Nova blinks at her. "I'm not sure. Be—before the Proving, I think."

"Nova," her mother breathes. "I think you're pregnant."

"What?" Nova shoves her mother's arms away. "No. That's impossible!"

"Is it? Have you been intimate with anyone?" Her mother's eyes sharpen. "With Kian?"

Nova wraps her arms around her middle. She and Kian… down on the beach… She shakes her head. "I'm Unbound."

"What if your chip was faulty?"

Nova glances at the back of her hand. Is that even possible?

"Nova." Her mother's voice is full of urgency. "Until you know for sure, you can't tell anyone. It's too dangerous."

Nova stares at her hands. One with five fingers. The other with four. "And if I am?"

"Then..." Her mother straightens, her face hardening with determination. "Then we keep you and your baby safe."

Your baby...

A groan splinters the confusion that was starting to feel bigger than Nova. "Angel?"

Nova shuffles to Sam, wincing as pain shrieks up her leg. "I'm here, Sam. I'm not going anywhere."

A sigh wheezes past Sam's lips. "Good. Remember—fight... with...heart."

"Shh." Nova brushes his hair back, startled at the spike in heat. "I'll remember."

A soft smile flickers across Sam's face as he drifts back into unconsciousness. The room fills with the sound of his breathing. Shallow, harsh. Rattling from deep within his chest.

"Nova..." Her mother's voice is full of anguish.

"Stay away from me," Nova whispers.

Her mother knows just like she does what this means. She was the one who taught Nova what that crackly, sickly sound is called.

Death rattles.

As tears wet the cot, just as she discovered she may be carrying life, Nova faces what every part of her wishes was untrue. It's what she knew the moment she opened the curtains in Sam's cabin. What she's been denying since the moment she discovered she wouldn't be able to secure a pod for him.

Sam is dying.

KIAN

The gust of wind tugs on the net Kian is trying to stretch over the pod pool, almost yanking it from his hand. He tightens his grip, wondering if insisting he do this on his own was a smart decision.

As he clips the second corner into place, he acknowledges he wanted to show he could do this. Looking after the pods is something he knows. Their rhythm became his rhythm long ago. Being here gives him a sense of control he hasn't experienced since before the Proving.

As it turns out, it hadn't taken much to convince his mother to leave him to cover the pods as the storm approaches. She's worried about his younger sister. At eight years old, a cold usually isn't something to worry about, but Willow's cough has intensified. His mother wanted to get an extra pod to her sooner rather than later.

Kian shoves his hair out of his face as he grabs the third clip. The fact that his mother left him to do this on his own shows she's starting to hand over the reins. She'd hesitated but then she'd smiled a little and nodded. A flapping, luminescent pod in her hand, she'd brushed her lips over his forehead. "You've got this, Kian."

The same words his father had said to him.

Squatting, Kian pulls hard on the net. How odd that his mother's faith feels like it lifts him while his father's feels like a dead weight.

Click. He secures the third clip. The net is now stretched over most of the pool. Standing, he glances at the last corner, secured by a rope to the railing so he can still reach it once the other three clips were attached.

How long ago was it that he and Nova caught that one together? Him holding her hand, her reaching out over the water as it flapped and splashed in the wind.

She'd looked so beautiful. He'd been so full of confidence. They'd been so... Kian's hands clench as one word slams through him.

Naïve.

A drop of water strikes Kian's cheek, trickling down like a tear. Striding to the rope, he quickly unties the knot. His father had pointed out that a strong stance was more important than ever before.

Their world is under threat.

Remnants can't be allowed to stay, especially after their soft hearts had welcomed a spy into their fragile lives.

Especially when Wren was freed by those closest to them all.

Including Nova.

His father's gaze had settled on Kian. "I was right and the testing only supported that. Shiloh is the best person for you."

As he secures the final clip, Kian straightens, twisting the rope around his hand. It was strange. The pain of his impossible love for Nova is still there, but he didn't feel betrayed by her choice.

He was almost relieved.

Nova is forging her own fate. She's learning she's strong, just like he always knew she was.

In some ways, she's making the decisions he wishes he could.

With a crack of thunder the skies open, making Kian instinctively duck. Heavy raindrops fall, splattering around the pool and peppering the surface of the water. Wind lashes at him, just like his guilt.

Guilt for all the choices he's made.

Guilt for the choices he's going to have to make.

With the pool as prepared as it can be, Kian heads for the door. The storm, so soon after the last one, is unsettling. The gardens haven't had a chance to recover, and he doesn't want to have to cross another food source off his ledgers. Hopefully these winds and rain don't become more than a rumble and a downpour.

But he'll check them just like he does the pods. Deciding what to do if they lose the gardens isn't something Kian wants to face.

He's about to scan the sensor when he hears a splash behind him. He pauses, angling his head. Has something blown into the pod pool?

There's another splash, then another, telling Kian one of the clips must've come undone. With a sigh, he turns around.

He was supposed to at least do this well.

The rain saturates him as he heads back to the pool, squinting through the water. The corner that he secured with Nova so long ago has unclipped and is being tossed about by the wind. It cracks the surface of the water over and over.

Cursing, Kian wonders how he's going to catch it without calling his mother back when he stops in his tracks.

An older woman, bedraggled and wet, is crouching by the pool, her arm extended into the water.

"Hey!" Kian calls out as he runs toward her.

She looks up in alarm but doesn't remove her arm. "Stay away from me!"

"Get away from there! You can't take those!"

The woman frantically grapples beneath the surface as she watches him approach. "I'm telling ya, don't come near me," she shouts over the wind and rain.

Behind her, the net flicks like an angry eel, the heavy clip on the end sailing down to hit the water again. Kian stops. "You need to move," he calls urgently.

"Because of your precious pods?" the woman sneers. "So precious that you can't even spare one for my brother? No matter how sick he is?"

Kian shakes his head, water droplets flying out like a fan. "It's not safe. Please, move away from the pool."

Staying where he is, Kian tries to figure out who she is. She's got to be Unbound. He doesn't recognize her...and a Bound would never steal a pod.

Instead, the woman crouches lower, her arm sinking further into the water. "This is why the league was formed, you selfish bastards! Just you wait!"

She scrabbles desperately in the water, her face suddenly lighting up.

He takes a step forward, knowing she just caught a pod. "I don't know what you're talking about, but you need to move. It's not safe!"

The metal clip strikes the water again but the woman doesn't seem to hear. "Or what? You'll banish me? Send me to the Outlands like you did those poor Remnants?"

She jerks her hand out of the water, peering down at it in victory. She clutches the pod to her chest, looking up into the sky as the rain pours down on her. "I've got one, Sam!" she shouts just as the clip slices down through the air like a scorpion sting. It strikes the woman on the forehead, yanking a cry from her.

She collapses backward, her hands shooting out to break her fall.

"No," she wails as the pod falls into the puddles forming on the ground, blood already streaming down her face.

Kian rushes forward as she scrabbles on all fours. "Get away!" he shouts desperately.

The pod flaps helplessly in the shallow water, flipping itself closer to the pool as if it's seeking refuge. The woman dives after it, clapping both hands around it.

The net snaps in the wind, arcing down once more.

Kian dives, grabbing the woman around the middle as he uses his momentum to yank her away from the pool's edge. The heavy metal clip strikes the water a second later.

The woman clambers away from Kian. "You idiot! I almost lost it!" She looks down at her left hand tightly clasped to her chest. She carefully opens it to inspect the pod, only to have it slip through the gap created by her missing finger.

She gasps but Kian quickly catches it before it hits the ground again. He wraps his hand around it in the way his mother taught him—gently but completely.

The woman's face caves beneath the rivulets of blood and water. "No..." she rasps.

"You're hurt," Kian shouts above the storm. "You need to get help."

The woman looks at him incredulously but then her expression changes. She touches her forehead, pulling her hand back to gaze at the blood on her fingertips. Her shoulders slump. "It doesn't matter. I didn't get the pod."

Kian stands up. "We have to get you to the infirmary."

The woman glares at him. "You listen as well as you lead!" she shouts. "Didn't you hear me? It doesn't matter!"

The pod thrashes against Kian's palm, desperately seeking water so it can live. *Surely one pod can't matter...*

He shoves his hand out. "Here. If I give this to you, will you go to the infirmary?"

The woman stares at him suspiciously through the blood running like two rivers down either side of her nose. "That thing must've hit me harder than I thought. Aren't you the son of Magnus?"

Kian jerks his arm, ignoring her question. "Just take it."

Not needing to be offered twice, the woman extends her hand and Kian drops the pod. It's gelatinous body flaps for a split second before the woman clamps her hands around it.

Wiping the water from his face, Kian takes a step closer. "Now let's get you to the infirmary."

"Fat lot of good that will do," the woman mutters, but she tries to push herself up nevertheless.

Kian reaches down, supporting her as she struggles to get up with her hands clamped around the pod. The moment she's upright she begins to sway.

Her gaze flies to his. Her lips form the word "no" as her eyes roll back in her head.

Kian catches her before her body has a chance to crumple, quickly lifting her into his arms. The pod lands in her lap, her arm flopping down to rest over it.

Even unconscious she's making sure she doesn't lose it.

Striding for the door, Kian awkwardly scans the sensor. The woman's head lolls against his shoulder, her blood smearing across his shirt. She moans quietly, muttering one word. "Sam."

Kian makes his way to the infirmary, forced to walk at an angle carrying the woman through the narrow hallways, when he sees Tory coming toward him.

His eyes widen when he sees Kian carrying a limp woman. He rushes forward. "A Bound?"

Kian shakes his head, not because the woman is Unbound, but because he hates that it matters. "She's hurt herself. We're just on the way to the infirmary."

Tory reaches out. "Let me take her. You have things you need to do."

Kian holds the woman tighter against him. "I've got it. But the net on the pod pool isn't secure."

Tory hesitates but then nods. "I'll make sure it gets done."

With a quick thanks, Kian continues down the hall. He's not sure why he insisted he take her to the infirmary personally. Maybe it's because of the pod she has tucked in her lap...

"Quite the leader, huh?"

Kian looks down in surprise to find the woman looking up at him, eyes bright and shrewd. He focuses his gaze back down the hall. "The pod's in your lap."

He hears her gasp as she picks it up. "We're going to the infirmary?"

Kian nods. "We'll get that cut on your forehead looked at."

The woman is gazing at the pteropod sitting on her palm. It lies still, slowly dying in the dry air. "Are you going to take it away?" she whispers.

His father would. His father would've had Tory carry this woman to the infirmary. His father probably would've been at the gardens by now, caring for Askala rather than one woman, and an Unbound at that.

His father knows that if he lets this woman steal a pod, then others will come. Just like the Remnants, a message has to be sent.

A strong stance must be taken.

Kian's arms tighten. "That pod will be long dead by the time you get it to whoever Sam is. They decompose fast in this heat. It wouldn't be safe to eat."

To his surprise, the woman chuckles. "You guys underestimate us, you know that? You'll never see the league coming."

Kian frowns. That's the second time she's mentioned the league. "What are you talking about?"

"The name's Beatrice by the way. The pod is for my brother."

221

Kian suspected it wasn't for her. He was surprised she didn't stuff it in her mouth the moment she pulled it out of the pool.

"You're changing the subject." Kian's conscious they're almost at the infirmary. "Who, or what, is this league?"

Beatrice angles her chin. "You'll soon find out, son of Magnus. It's much closer that you realize..." She looks away as if she's said too much.

Kian waits but Beatrice doesn't continue. Alarm is worming its way through his muscles. What is Beatrice alluding to? He thought the Unbound understood that they all must make sacrifices.

The door of the infirmary appears and Kian pauses. "You need to tell me what you mean, Beatrice."

But Beatrice allows her head to fall against his shoulder. "This cut is really hurting. I hope it doesn't need stitches"—she slides a bitter glance at him— "considering I'm not allowed them."

Gritting his teeth, Kian enters the infirmary. He'll make sure he gets some answers, but not now.

"Are you okay to stand?" he asks.

His question is followed by a gasp and his gaze flies across the room. That voice is one he could recognize in his sleep.

Nova has shot to her feet, her blue eyes wide and luminous. They widen some more when she registers Kian standing there frozen, but she quickly looks away. She centers her gaze on Beatrice like Kian isn't even in the room.

She rushes over, her limp unmistakable. "Beatrice, what happened?"

Beatrice wriggles so Kian releases her, placing her on her feet. She steps away, adjusting her shoulders. "I'm fine. I could've walked the whole way here, but why do that when you can hitch a ride?"

Nova's eyes are so sad his heart aches. "It's Sam, he's..."

Beatrice extends her arms and opens her hands. "I got him a pod," she whispers reverently.

Nova's eyes well up. "Oh Bea. I'm so sorry." She turns toward the cot she was standing beside. "He's unconscious. It's too late."

"No!" Beatrice rushes to the frail man lying there. She buckles beside him. "Sam, please. Not now."

The man doesn't move, his breath barely visible. Nova walks over to join them, her movements slow and measured. She's trembling, waves of sadness pouring from her.

Kian stands helplessly by the door. Nova's hurting and there's nothing he can do about it.

It's then that he notices Thea sitting in the corner. Her arms are wrapped tightly around her as she almost looks...lost.

Why isn't she helping?

Kian blinks in surprise when Shiloh appears by his side. He hadn't realized she was in the room.

She places a hand on his arm. "Nova knows Sam," she says quietly. "She wants to care for him in his final..."

Her words trail away when Nova's head snaps up as if Shiloh had shouted. Nova's mouth opens but then her gaze flickers to where Shiloh's hand has wrapped around Kian's forearm. Her face tightens as she looks away.

Kian steps to the side and Shiloh's hand falls to her side, leaving behind an icy burn on his skin. He sees Shiloh wince from the corner of his eye as she curls her hand into a fist and tucks it into her apron.

Jamming the heels of his hands into his eyes, Kian welcomes the blackness. What is he supposed to do?

Nova has his heart.

Yet Shiloh is his duty. Just as Askala is.

Everything about this moment feels wrong. Shouldn't the two things be one and the same?

There's a gurgling gasp from the cot and Kian's eyes fly

open. The man, Sam, starts to convulse, red bubbles frothing up from his mouth.

Beatrice watches in horror. "Nova, help him!"

Nova leans over, suddenly calm. She wipes away the bloody foam with a cloth. "We're both going to help him, Bea."

A cough wracks Sam's body and crimson fluid trickles from the corner of his mouth. Nova mops that up, too, her strokes achingly gentle. "It's okay, Sam," she murmurs. "It's almost over."

Sam's body jerks. A gush of blood fountains out of his mouth, soaking his chest, running down past his ears. He collapses again and sounds of suffocation fill the room.

"Sweet, holy hell. He's drowning," moans Bea.

"Hold him, Bea." Nova takes Sam's hand. "He'll know he's not alone."

Heedless of the blood, Bea wraps her arms around Sam. "It's okay, Sam. We'll finish what you started," she chokes past her tears.

Sam's body arches, his face carved with pain. He holds there, curved and choking, before collapsing. With a final gurgle, he goes still.

Silence fills the room, heavy and laden as it blends with the metallic scent of blood.

Bea pushes up, scanning Sam's face. She lifts a hand and goes to stroke his face only to notice it's covered in thick red. Her wail fractures the silence, so full of grief that Shiloh covers her ears.

Bea lifts her other hand, desperate to touch her brother, only to find it's clasping the pod. With tears tumbling down her face, she lays it on Sam's bloody chest. "We'll finish what you started," she whispers fiercely.

Nova's shoulders tremble, then shudder. Within seconds, sobs wrack her body with such force Kian doesn't know how she hasn't collapsed.

He steps forward, aching to comfort her. "Nova..."

Nova shoots up and spins around. "Don't touch me," she shouts. She glances at her mother then Shiloh. "None of you come anywhere near me."

Kian stops where he is, still holding his hand out. "You're hurting, I just want to help."

Nova sucks in a breath, her shoulders yanking back. "Help? Did you just say *help*?"

"You obviously cared for Sam," Kian tries to explain. "I know you, Nova. This would be killing you inside."

Nova takes a step forward, her face suddenly blazing. She's no longer trembling. She's vibrating with fury. "How can you comfort me when your father is the one who killed him, Kian?"

Kian reels back. "What? Just because he's Unbound—"

"Means he doesn't get medical treatment. That pod"—Nova points to the fragile, opaque body soaking in Sam's blood—"could've saved him."

That pod. A single, delicate being he thought couldn't make that much difference. Just like the one his mother brought to his sister…

He shakes his head. "I thought you understood. This is the way it has to be. For Askala."

"Look, Kian."

Nova jabs her finger at Sam again. Beatrice is making a soft noise, part keening, part crooning, as she rests her head beside Sam, heedless of the blood.

"That is the foundation Askala is built on."

Nova's last words explode through Kian.

The words he'd said to her so many times before.

Askala was built on love.

We were forged from love.

Our future will be filled with love.

But Nova isn't finished. She takes another step forward, the motion stilted and uneven. "Askala is built on pain. Its foundations are the suffering and death of those not deemed worthy."

She presses her hand to her belly, opening her mouth as if to speak only to slam it shut again.

She steps past him and Kian has to clench his hands not to reach out to her. It's obvious Nova is injured.

Hurting.

And that he's no longer a person who can comfort her.

She stops at the door, her hand still wrapped around her abdomen. "No one is unworthy, Kian."

Nova limps away, leaving Kian in the infirmary. He feels like his chest has been excavated. He looks down, wondering how he's not covered in blood just like Sam is.

His mind rebels against what Nova just said, but the sound of Bea's grief is as inescapable as the smell of death hanging in the air.

Shiloh steps forward but has the sense not to touch him. "She doesn't understand, Kian. She's forgotten we're doing this for something"—she glances at Bea and lowers her voice to a whisper— "far more important than just a single life."

Kian inhales, but he feels like he's choking on Shiloh's words. They sting his throat, doubling and growing when realizes he's said the exact same thing so many times before.

He's always believed that Askala was built on love.

That it meant he and Nova were forged in love.

That their future would be filled with love.

But the last part never came true.

And now the first part feels more like an assumption than the truth.

Kian jerks away even though Shiloh isn't holding him. He stumbles back toward the door, not sure where he's going, but knowing he needs to get away.

He's lost Nova.

And now it feels like he's losing the very foundations his world was built on.

DEX

*D*ex hadn't needed his father to visit earlier in the day to tell him that a new moon is upon them. He's been staring at the night sky all week, watching the moon grow smaller, until all that remained was a crescent-shaped slither of light hovering above their troubled land.

Tonight, the league of rebels that his father claims he's assembled will meet on the upper deck. It's his chance to find out for himself exactly what his father's been up to.

And how many people stand behind him.

Dex makes as much noise as he can as he lifts the hatch to the secret room and swings himself onto the ladder. The last thing he wants to do is catch Wren and Phoenix by surprise. It's been hard enough observing the obvious bond between them.

Strangely, this has been another thing that's brought him closer to his father. He understands a little better now how he must have felt watching his brother win the affections of the girl they both loved. It would have hurt like hell. It's no wonder his father was never able to fully commit his heart to his mother when it already belonged to someone else. It makes sense now in a way it never has before.

Wren is pacing at the bottom of the ladder. She stops when he sets foot on the ground and rakes her hands through her tangled hair.

"I can't stand it another moment," she says. "You have to get us out of here."

"The little bird needs to fly," Phoenix says from the mattress. The way he's been lounging there all week, he doesn't seem all that bothered by his confinement.

"It's too dangerous," says Dex. "You know that."

"I don't care." Her eyes are wild, her body like a coiled spring ready to release. "I need to get out of here. I'll take the risk."

"There's a meeting tonight." Dex puts his hand on her arm, feeling the tightness in her muscles. She really is stressed. "It's a chance for me to find out more about my father's league. He wants to ask them when they think it's a good time to send another message to your father."

"Now's good. Don't worry about the meeting. Just send it." She picks up her pacing again, breaking contact between them. "Please, Dex."

"You were the one saying we have to wait for the right time," Phoenix reminds her, folding his hands behind his head, making his chest expand. Gees, would it kill him to wear a shirt down here?

"We can wait in the forest," Wren says to him. "You can build us a shelter. Nobody will see if it's far enough away from here."

Dex takes a step toward her, fear for her safety bubbling within. "Wren—"

"Phee's good at building," she says, as if that was his concern. "He's the best at it. He practically built our entire village back home."

Phoenix removes a hand from his head to flex a bicep. "True story. But I'm enjoying my holiday down here, little bird. We'll be okay for a bit longer."

"Then you stay down here." Her voice is harsh. Cold. More

like the tone she'd use with Felicia, not Phoenix. "I'm leaving. Take me to the meeting with you, Dex."

Phoenix leaps to his feet at these words. "No, Wren. That's not a great idea."

"He's right," says Dex, wishing he hadn't stopped in before he left. She's putting him in an impossible position. It's obvious she needs to get out of here. But the meeting is far too risky. They don't know who might be there. "You must be patient."

"I'm done with patience!"

Dex recoils, not having expected her harsh tone to turn on him. He far preferred it when she'd snapped at Phoenix. "You either take me or I'll go by myself."

"Wren!" Phoenix grabs her by the arm. "It's too dangerous. You could be seen."

"There'll be no brig this time," Dex points out, not liking how rough Phoenix is being with her. "Kian will send you straight back out to sea."

"This is worse than the brig." Wren snatches her arm away from Phoenix, proving yet again that she's quite capable of taking care of herself. "When Callix brought me down here, all he did was take me from one prison to another. I may as well be sent back out on a raft. It's gotta be better than this hell."

"Don't say that!" Dex shakes his head. He's fought too hard and risked too much to listen to such words.

"Then help me." Wren's eyes fill with tears, something he's never seen before. "Please, Dex."

"Oh no," groans Phoenix. "She means it."

Dex sighs. It's obvious that if he doesn't let Wren come with him, she'll find her own way, even if she needs to dig out a tunnel using nothing but her fingernails.

"We need to disguise you." Dex turns to the ladder, not at all sure about the decision he just made. "Wait here."

Wren hops up and down on the spot and claps her hands, looking very much like the little bird she's named after. It's no wonder Phoenix uses that as her pet name. He could think of a few pet names for Phoenix, but now probably isn't the right time...

"Get something for me, too," says Phoenix. "So I can watch out for Wren."

"I managed perfectly fine before you got here," she huffs.

"She did, too," says Dex as he climbs the ladder.

He returns to the lab and heads straight for the bunkroom, looking for a fresh set of hemp clothes for Phoenix. Those leather pants are a dead giveaway. Dead being the appropriate word.

He takes a shirt and pants from the shelf Kian had used during the Proving, figuring they're about the same size. It's also sort of amusing to imagine Phoenix wearing Kian's clothing.

Next, he takes a set of his own clothes. They're going to be miles too big for Wren, but that's the idea. The clothes she's been wearing hug the curves of her body just a little too well. It's best if her gender is a little less conspicuous.

Looking under his bunk for his knife, he finds it tucked down the side of his mattress. That will be handy, too. But not for the reason Wren might think when she first sees it. He has a few surprises of his own for that little bird.

He heads back to the hatch, tucking the knife into the back of his pants and throwing the clothes down to Wren below. It's hard enough to go up and down that ladder with one hand, let alone no hands.

"Great disguise," says Wren, frowning as she picks up the clothes and tossing the larger set to Phoenix. "It's exactly what I'm wearing now."

Dex rolls his eyes. "The idea is to blend in. Phoenix needs to look like one of us. You need to look...like a guy. These clothes are larger than the ones you've been wearing."

"A guy?" She unfolds the clothes and holds them out. "Glad to hear you think I can pull that off."

Dex suppresses a smile, not wanting her to know what he really thinks about the way she looks when the hemp clings to her skin.

"Baggy clothes and a new haircut should do the trick given how dark it is out there tonight." He draws out the knife and raises his eyebrows while he waits for her to complain.

"Go for it," she says, turning her back to him and trying to straighten out her mop of dark hair. "It's been driving me crazy anyway."

"Are you serious?" He wonders why he still gets surprised when she does something unexpected. That's one of the reasons he's so drawn to her.

"Wren!" Phoenix darts off the mattress and snatches the knife from Dex's hand.

"What?" Wren spins around and glares at him.

"Turning your back on a dude with a weapon like that isn't exactly the smartest idea." Phoenix studies the knife, turning it over and raising his eyebrows, clearly impressed.

"But…it's Dex." Wren looks genuinely perplexed. "He's even less likely to hurt me than you are."

"Gee, thanks." Phoenix scowls. "I'll cut your hair, though."

"I'd prefer Dex." Wren folds her arms and pouts.

There's a tension between these two that Dex hasn't seen before. Perhaps being in a confined space for so long is starting to get to them. Hating that this thought pleases him, Dex focuses back on Wren.

"It's all good," he says, waving his stump at her. "I'm not all that handy when it comes to cutting hair."

"Oh." Wren sighs. "I forgot."

Dex's eyebrows shoot up. "You forgot I'm missing a hand?"

She shrugs. "It's no biggie."

"Am I doing this or not?" asks Phoenix. "Turn around, little bird."

Wren turns her back to Phoenix and locks eyes with Dex.

Something passes between them in the dim light of this underground room that he can't explain.

No biggie. His hand really isn't a big deal, she's proven that time and time again. So often that he's even started to think of it that way. No matter what transpires between them in the future, she's given him that gift. And it's one of the most precious gifts he can think of.

As Phoenix takes hold of the first tangle of dark hair and slices it from her head, Dex thinks about all the things he wishes he could tell her. There are the big things, like showing her the video his mother left him, but there's the small things, too. He wants her to know everything about him. Every time anything has happened to him after she left his side at the end of the Proving, he's wanted to tell her about it. It's like she's infected his brain with some kind of virus and the only way he can get relief from it, is to share his every moment with her.

More hair falls to the ground. Phoenix is working quickly, his knife skills frighteningly good. In a matter of minutes, he's taken off most of the longer lengths of hair and is working on neatening up what remains.

"How do I look?" Wren asks.

Still beautiful. Even more beautiful. Far too beautiful for someone who just wants to be friends.

"You look fine," he says. "You have a nice head."

"A nice head?" She laughs and it lights something inside him, giving him hope that maybe this night is going to work out okay. "Do I look like a guy though?"

"Yep. We might have to change your name to Rex." He winks at her, trying to make an effort to be more like his old lighthearted self.

"Oh, isn't that cute?" says Phoenix, tilting the knife to use it more like a razor. "Rex and Dex. Adorable."

"I'm going to wait upstairs," says Dex, not trusting himself with a reply. Phoenix has an unusual talent for ruining any moment. "You two get changed and come up when you're ready."

"Sure you don't want to help Wren with that?" Phoenix asks, a coldness creeping into his tone.

"What's your problem with me?" Dex folds his arms and steps around Wren so he's in Phoenix's face. "I've done nothing but help you since you arrived and all you do is make smart comments about me."

"Is it true that Ronan's your true father?" asks Phoenix, letting the knife drop to his side.

"*That's* your problem with me?" Dex takes a step back. "You think we might be brothers and you're not happy about it?"

"Well, is he your dad?" Phoenix bites down on his bottom lip, his resemblance to Dean almost uncanny.

"I don't know." Dex throws out his arms. "Maybe. Maybe not. I have no idea! I don't think so. My dad—Callix—has risked too much for me, which makes me think not. And we don't exactly look like brothers, do we?"

Phoenix shrugs. "Siblings often look nothing alike."

"It's my friendship with Wren that bugs you, isn't it?" Dex sneers. They may as well get this conversation over with properly. "You're worried she might like me more than you."

He watches as Phoenix tips back his head and laughs. "Wren would *never* choose you over me."

"I wouldn't be so sure about that." Dex pokes his finger in Phoenix's chest, only for Phoenix to grip his wrist so hard, he has to fight not to yelp.

"Enough!" Wren steps between them and Phoenix loosens his grip. "You're both being ridiculous."

Dex draws in a breath and steps back, shaking his wrist free and checking it's not broken.

"Is your hand all right?" asks Wren.

"It's okay, I have a spare." He nods. "Oh, that's right…"

"You always have to be the funny bastard, don't you?" says Phoenix.

"Better than always being the asshole," he retorts.

"Dex!" Wren's eyes are wide, but he can see the hint of amusement she's trying to disguise. Without her hair, it's like every one of her features is now highlighted. No more hiding behind that tangled mane. "This isn't like you."

Without another word, Dex climbs the ladder and hauls himself up to his computer lab. The place that used to be so peaceful.

Unable to sit still, he paces, realizing why Wren does this so much. It's like he has energy trying to explode out of every one of his cells.

Wren's right. He's not behaving like himself. He knows why.

And so does she.

She's just so hard to be near. Especially with that oaf of a boyfriend hanging around.

Several minutes later, Wren appears at the top of the ladder, closely followed by Phoenix. He's cut his own hair. So short that it's practically shaved. At least now he looks a little less like Dean, even if he does look tougher. Although, his new outfit isn't helping so much in that department. It's hard to look all that tough while wearing hemp.

"You sure about this?" Dex asks. "It's not too late to back out."

Wren nods solemnly. "Honestly, Dex, I can't stay down there another moment. I'm feeling better already just to be up here. Besides, it's important we're at this meeting if we're going to form an alliance. The Unbound need to see we're on board."

"And we need to see what we're dealing with," says Phoenix, rubbing the stubble on his head.

"Right. We're going to exit via the courtyard and head through the forest." Dex presses his chip to the sensor at the door. "We'll head to the beach and climb up the ladder to the top deck of the Oasis from there. It's best if we walk quickly and remain silent. No torches, no talking. Got it?"

Phoenix salutes him. "Aye, aye, Captain."

"I said *no talking*," Dex reminds him. Phoenix falling silent can't come fast enough.

They head out into the courtyard, two lamps at the exit pooling dim light into the small space.

Wren walks up beside him. It's hard to get used to her new look. He's not sure he'd recognize her at first glance. Especially out here in the night. She could easily pass as a young boy at a distance.

"Fresh air!" she cries in a failed attempt at a whisper, sucking in deep breaths. "This is the happiest day of my life."

She squeezes his arm, then lets her hand fall. It's a gesture that almost breaks his heart. A small sign that everything that's passed between them is still there.

Resisting the urge to pull her into his arms, he goes to the gate and opens it.

"We need to be quiet now," he reminds them.

Stepping out into the forest, he checks to see they're alone, then motions for Wren to follow. Phoenix is close behind her.

As always.

Walking with fast and certain steps, they make their way through the forest. Dex is conscious he's the one making the most noise, no matter how quiet he's trying to be. It seems Wren and Phoenix have had more need to move through the night with stealth.

Without the moon to light their path, or a solar torch clutched in their hands, it's difficult not to trip, and a few stumbles are made. Thankfully, Dex has walked the paths of Askala so many times that he and Kian often joked they could find their way around blindfolded. That's exactly what it feels like he's doing now.

There's a noise as they get closer to the small beach. The three of them stop and listen.

"It's people," says Wren.

Dex listens harder and realizes she's right.

"Who would be on the beach at this hour?" Dex whispers, even though out of the three of them he's the one most likely to be able to answer that. And he has no idea.

They creep closer to the noise, stopping behind a bush, peering out to see what's going on.

There's a group of maybe two dozen people gathered on the small beach. Some have torches and in the soft light he can see a man lying on the ground. No, not a man. A former man. Is that a body?

"You go ahead and look," says Wren, keeping her voice low.

"I'll let you know if it's safe." Dex steps out from behind the bush, making his way across the soft sand toward the group.

Spotting his father's familiar shape, Dex approaches with more confidence.

"What's going on?" he asks.

"Dex!" His father smiles at him. "You're early."

"It doesn't seem like it?" Dex looks down at the body on the sand. It's an old man. An extremely frail looking one. His hands are folded on his chest, his missing finger visible. Several large, flat stones have been strapped to his middle.

"We're just putting one of our fallen out to sea," says his father. "I didn't think you'd be interested in coming to this. You didn't know Sam, did you?"

Dex shakes his head. "Was he part of your league?"

"One of the founding members," his father says. "He recruited many of the people here."

Dex looks across at the faces in the crowd. Not one of them looks familiar. They must all be Unbound. How strange that his father seems to know so many of them.

"When did he die?" Dex asks.

"A few days ago, but his sister hasn't wanted to let him go." His father gestures to a woman kneeling beside the body. "Nova was close to him, too. She was with him when he died, apparently."

"Nova's here?" Dex looks around but Callix shakes his head.

"She's resting. Her leg isn't doing too well."

Dex must look shocked as his father immediately puts a hand on his arm.

"She'll be fine. Thea's taking good care of her."

A woman approaches, the torch in her hand wavering. "Sorry to interrupt, Callix. But we're ready to start."

Dex motions as subtly as he can to the bushes for Wren and Phoenix to stay where they are for now. It's not that it's unsafe. More that their arrival will cause too much of a distraction. From what he's witnessing here, this old man deserves more respect than that. Let his family send him out in peace.

Two of the stronger looking men pick up the man, gently scooping up his rigid body by his ankles and armpits. They carry him to the water's edge and place him on the wet sand, turning their eyes toward Dex's father.

"Thank you for gathering here this evening," his father says as the group of people fall silent. "It seems fitting to be farewelling our friend here on the night of a new moon. We all know how much Sam looked forward to our meetings. Watching our numbers grow in strength, along with our hope for the future."

There's a sob from the woman Dex's father had said was Sam's sister. Dex can see she's not the only one crying. This man was clearly loved.

"It's with sadness that we let Old Sam go tonight," his father continues. "Sam was brave, compassionate and strong. He was our elder. Our founding member. Our brother. Our friend."

There's a rocky beach where the Bound are sent out after they die. Normally Magnus conducts the proceedings and there's much talk about Askala and the sacrifices the deceased made for the greater good. Dex has never really thought too much about how the Unbound are sent out, but he hasn't heard his father mention Askala once so far. It's been all about Sam. He wonders what words were said for his mother when she was sent out.

"Goodbye, Sam," his father says. "Thank you for all you did."

"Goodbye, Sam," the crowd murmurs in response.

The two men pick up Sam once more and carry his frail body out into the shallows. The stones strapped to his middle must weigh more than him. It's hard not to wonder if a few pods might have helped strengthen this man before he died. The men move quickly, knowing they must minimize any time spent in the water.

The beach the Bound use for this purpose has rocks that the men stand on. The body is thrown into the water with little risk to the living, although it can sometimes seem like a brutal final journey for the dead.

This is far gentler. The sacrifice the men are making to send Sam off respectfully is so moving that Dex finds his eyes prickling with tears.

He watches as the men wade further out until the acidic water is almost at their waists. They nod at each other before lowering Sam into the water, the heavy stones ensuring that he's pulled under.

As quickly as they can, the men make their way back to shore.

Turning his gaze to the people on the beach, Dex sees them turn and wrap their arms around each other. His father is included in this. To an observer it would seem they're all one and the same, no matter how many fingers they might have. Is this how the future will look if his father gets his way? Dex has to admit that it isn't all that unpleasant.

One by one, the people break apart and go to the ladder,

beginning their climb to the upper deck. It seems the meeting will go ahead no matter how bereaved they are. From what Dex has just heard, that would be what Sam would have wanted.

Turning to the tree line, Dex motions for Wren and Phoenix to come out.

Only his father is left on the beach now and he walks over to Dex, clutching his torch.

"Who's there?" he asks, seeing two figures emerge from the trees and shining his beam of light on them. "Are these men Unbound?"

Wren and Phoenix shield their eyes and Dex grins at his father, pleased the disguises have worked.

"Oh!" His father gasps as he recognizes who's approaching. "Are you sure this is wise?"

"Not even a bit," says Dex. "But Wren insisted. She was going mad locked up like that."

His father drops his light and nods. "It might be good for the league to meet them."

"That's what Wren seems to think." Dex rubs at his chin. "Will she be safe?"

"Never safer," his father says.

"Surprised to see us, Callix?" Wren asks as they get close enough.

"Nothing surprises me anymore," he replies.

"Not even her hair?" asks Dex, grinning.

"Hurry now. I have some people for you to meet." Callix ignores his question and turns, taking the only light source with him.

Phoenix puts a hand on Wren's back and steers her ahead of him. Dex knows he's held onto his knife. As annoying as Phoenix is, it's nice to know that Wren has someone watching her back. Quite literally. He won't ask for the knife to be returned for now.

Before they're plunged into darkness, they follow Dex's father to the ladder, watching as he climbs up.

Dex goes next, wanting to make sure it's safe at the top before Wren gets up there. He hauls himself up, gripping a rung with his right hand, then looping his stump behind the next. Just another task that would be so much easier with two hands. But after witnessing a body being sent out to sea, it's hard to feel sorry for himself. Each and every one of them is lucky to be alive.

When he gets to the top of the ladder he wonders where everyone is. It's so dark up here without the light of the moon. With only the stars to light the way, he blinks, making out some shadows on the other side of the deck. It seems everyone has turned off their torches. His father wasn't kidding when he said this meeting is top secret.

He turns back and holds out a hand for Wren, half expecting her to ignore his gesture. But she doesn't, slipping her palm into his and allowing him to haul her up. Her hand is warm and soft and he likes the way it fits into his.

Phoenix climbs up behind her and as they walk across to the group of people, Dex decides to wait and see how long it takes for Wren to break away. To his surprise, she doesn't. In the darkness, nobody except the two of them are aware of the contact being made.

Deciding this isn't right, he's the one to let go. Wren knows how he feels. If she decides she feels the same, she needs to step away from Phoenix first. Then she can hold his hand for as long as she likes.

"We need a little light," says Dex's father. "I have two people who want to meet you."

Several torches light up and Dex sees a surprising number of people have gathered for this meeting. Far more than were on the beach. There has to be at least fifty here, all standing before his father like he's some kind of messiah. Magnus would have a fit if he could see this.

Dex leads Wren and Phoenix to the front of the group and they face the expectant crowd. Most are strangers, which isn't surprising, but there are a couple who seem familiar. There's Dean, for one. And Aarov. Which makes Dex wonder if there might be other Bounds here, too. Nova isn't here, but that's expected. As rebellious as she's been lately, getting involved with a league who plan to try to overthrow the guy she loves would be asking just a little too much.

"I'd like you to meet Wren and Phoenix," Dex's father says. "Two people born in the Outlands who've come here to help liberate our people."

Liberate? Wow. Dex hasn't heard his father speak in such strong terms before. Is this how he speaks to his league?

There's a whisper through the crowd and Dex thinks he can make out the words *freedom* and *time*. It's clear these people are just as passionate about the cause as his father.

"There's a reward out for these two," says Dean, standing forward and pointing. "And I sure am hungry for some of those pods. What are you offering us to keep quiet?"

Wren looks aghast. Did she really think that just because Dean is Phoenix's uncle that he would think of anyone but himself?

But it's Phoenix who steps up. "What we can give you is worth more than any number of pods. We can help release you from the tyranny you're currently being ruled under."

"Tyranny?" Dex asks, speaking louder than he intended. This is taking things even further than the liberation his father spoke of.

"Yes, tyranny," says Phoenix. "And yes, I know what it means. It's when people are being governed by cruelty. And what I've seen so far exceeds cruel. Taking fingers and sterilizing people goes far beyond what's necessary. It's a violation of human rights."

A murmur of agreement rushes over the crowd.

Wren pulls back her shoulders and Dex waits, knowing this means she's about to say her piece.

"I've been living amongst you for a while now," she says. "And I've learned that although Askala's laws are brutal, it's a place filled with people who have kind hearts. Bound and Unbound alike. It's not fair and it's not possible to judge a human based on how they perform in one week of their life. I watched as the kindest person I've ever met was deemed not to be worthy enough to be allowed to breed. A person who would've brought nothing but strength to this place. It has to stop and we'd like to work with you to make that happen."

Dex realizes he's nodding along with the crowd and stops himself. He'd come here to learn, not to join their ranks. Although, perhaps it's too late for that.

"It's time to overthrow the Bound," says Phoenix. "To give every person equal rights to food, to pteropods, to decide for themselves what they want to happen to their bodies. You can rat us out for some pods now, if you like"—he fixes his gaze on Dean—"but if you work with us, there will be far more pods for you in the future than the few you might be given as a reward now."

Dean nods from the crowd as he puffs out his chest. "That's my nephew up there."

"How can we trust the son of someone who betrayed us?" asks a woman near the front.

"My father didn't betray anyone," says Phoenix. "He was trying to help you. And for that he was banished. Further proof of the heartlessness of this place. Ronan is no enemy to you. He's your friend. He always has been. Maybe now you'll be able to open your eyes and see that."

The whispering in the crowd grows louder as people try to

decide what they think about this, so Callix steps forward and clears his throat.

"I thank you for coming here tonight. This is the biggest turnout we've had. Which is great but it puts us at risk of discovery. I'd like a show of hands for those who support a message being sent to the Outlands to ask for assistance. Are we ready for a revolution?"

Dex blinks at the sea of hands being raised in the air. Many of the hands are mutilated, just as the voices behind them have been silenced. Until now.

He imagines his own mother in the crowd, a woman who was deemed to be Unbound but fought against the system. He imagines Nova there and thinks of all the injustices she's suffered. Then he imagines the old man they just sent out to the ocean who'd surely still be alive if he'd been offered better care.

He understands the anger that's fueling this meeting. The rules in Askala *aren't* fair. And with these thoughts he finds his own hand in the air, voting in favor of change.

He's ready.

Let the revolution begin.

WREN

*C*limbing down the ladder from the Oasis, Wren knows
she's not ready to go back to that underground hell.
Which means that as much as she hates the idea of it, she needs
to shake Dex. It was a miracle enough that he agreed to her
coming to the meeting. He's never going to let her go for a walk
through the forest before she returns. Not now that she's been
seen by multiple people and she's at even more risk. He'll want
her hidden as soon as possible. And that's not an option.
Breathing this fresh air is just far too sweet.

She pauses on the ladder, waiting for Phoenix to get a little
closer. Guilt surges through the pit of her stomach for what
she's about to do. This isn't the first time she's run off on Dex.
Hopefully, he has it in him to forgive her one more time.

"When we get to the bottom, we run," she hisses, hoping Dex
is high enough above that he can't hear. "If you don't follow, I'm
going on my own."

Phoenix huffs, the only sign he heard what she said. If it
were up to him, he'd be sprawled out on that moldy mattress as
soon as he possibly can. Since when has he gotten so lazy?

She continues to climb down, wondering why she just

invited him to join her. Habit? Safety? Or was it an olive branch? They haven't been getting along lately. Too much time in too little space. His every move has been irritating her.

His snoring. His burping. His farting. The way he picks at his fingernails. The way he chews. The way he breathes.

She's been lying awake fantasizing about putting a pillow over his face.

Which is ridiculous as she'd never hurt him. She loves him too much for that. It seems she really was going crazy down there in Callix's secret room. He's far less annoying out here in the fresh air.

Her feet hit the ground and she darts for the trees, confident Phoenix will be able to follow despite the darkness. It was obvious when they'd walked here how much more experienced he is at moving through the forest than Dex, who'd sounded like a polar grizzly crashing through the trees.

As expected, Phoenix is right behind her.

It will take Dex a few minutes to realize what's happening. They need to use that advantage as best they can.

Her bare feet push across the beach, propelling her forward until sand becomes dirt. With her hands in front of her in case she hits an unexpected obstacle, she continues.

"Wren!" she hears Dex cry from the other side of the beach. "Wren!"

The familiar sound of his voice tugs at her heart and she slows her steps, considering for one crazy moment letting him catch up. But then she remembers the tension between Dex and Phoenix and she knows she has to make a choice. Three's most definitely a crowd when those two are involved.

And Phoenix would be far harder to shake than Dex.

Picking up her pace, she runs faster. She has to get away. She's spent her whole life outdoors. It's not possible to breathe the stale air of that cave. Not yet. Out here, she's free, using all her senses to find her way between the trees.

"I'm sorry," she shouts, not knowing if he can hear her. And she really is. But she doesn't feel like she has another option right now.

Her heart is thumping from the exertion, but she moves forward, deciding to head to the one place she's been thinking of since the day she left there. The place she yearns to show Phoenix.

The cliffs.

When the sun rises in a few hours, Phoenix will see just how special it is. He hadn't understood when she'd tried to explain it to him. He still believes the planet's too far gone to be saved.

But it's not too late. She learned that on the cliffs when she saw that green canopy covering the Earth like a blanket, and it's time for Phoenix to discover it, too. There's far more at stake here than the people who live on this planet. The whole planet itself is depending on them.

Pushing down the thought that maybe Earth would be better off if humans were the next species to become extinct, Wren's feet connect with a path that's unmistakably heading upward. It's hard to tell if it's the right way, but it feels right and that's going to have to be enough for now.

"We've lost him," says Phoenix, jogging up beside her.

"Poor guy never had a hope." Wren drops her pace to a brisk walk, her lungs thanking her for the chance to catch her breath.

"You like him, don't you?" Phoenix asks, his breathlessness covering the animosity she knows is there.

"He's a good guy," she says. "A great guy, in fact. He could be your friend, too, if you were actually nice to him."

"He's the one who has a problem with me!"

"Yes, Mr. Innocent. Dex is the only one with a problem." She stumbles on something and Phoenix catches her by the arm and steadies her. "Admit it. You're jealous of him."

"Me, jealous of a one-armed guy?" Phoenix laughs and Wren shakes herself free of his grasp.

"He has two arms, actually," she says. "One hand. Two arms."

"And one giant crush on you."

There's a pause. She's not going to comment on that. How can she when she knows it's true? It's no wonder Phoenix keeps mentioning it.

"Who do you think his father really is?" she asks, wishing there was some way they could find out for sure.

"Seems there's only one person who knows the answer to that mystery," says Phoenix. "Bit hard for him to answer given he's over the other side of that ocean."

"We need to send that raven." A wave of anxiety sweeps through her. "It could take days for Cy to get everyone organized. Weeks maybe depending on how many people he decides to bring."

"Dean's going to flip out when he sees his long-lost brother," says Phoenix, his breath more even now. "Did you hear the way he was bragging about being my uncle at the meeting?"

"Right after he was talking about dobbing you in for a few pods." Wren huffs.

Phoenix stumbles this time and Wren slips her hand into his and steadies him.

"Thought you hated me." Phoenix squeezes her hand.

"Only a little bit," she says, laughing. "The little bit that's annoying. The rest of you is okay."

"If only I could be more like you." He holds her hand tightly. "You're not annoying at all."

"Good to hear," she chuckles.

"Ready to turn around yet?" he asks. "Surely your legs have had enough? I keep thinking we're going to run into a grizzly."

"Lucky you kept the knife." She lets go of his hand to tap his lower back.

"Your stupid boyfriend didn't even ask for it back."

"He knew you had it," she says, having seen the way Dex's

eyes had been drawn to the bulge of the knife underneath Phoenix's hemp shirt.

"If he knew then why didn't he take it back?" It seems Phoenix really does have it in for Dex.

"Because he thought you might need it." She draws to a halt and throws her hands out. "Honestly, Phee, why can't you see that he's a good guy?"

"I can see it." Phoenix stops beside her, his voice turning serious. "Of course, I can see it. And that scares me even more than if you hated the guy. Does that make sense?"

Wren nods even though she knows she's a mere shadow standing in front of him.

"Back off a little, okay?" he asks. "It's not easy for me seeing that guy drooling all over you."

"Okay." She nods again, knowing there's no way she can ever keep that promise.

"Now can we go back?"

"I'm taking you to the cliffs I told you about. I want you to see what I saw up there. We don't know what's going to happen in the future. This is something you need to see now."

"Thanks for the vote of confidence for my mortality," he laughs.

"We both knew the risks when we climbed onto those rafts. The danger didn't end when we washed up on shore. In many ways, it only just began. It's risky for us out here."

"Fine," he huffs. "Show me the cliffs, then. Before I die."

"It'll be worth it." She tugs on his hand and they break through some trees to a more open part of the path. The sky is starting to lighten. If they hurry, they might make it to the top before sunrise, which has got to make the view even more spectacular than when she saw it last time.

"Got your note for the raven?" he asks.

She pats her pocket. "Yep."

"Always the organized one." He shakes his head.

She's had this note with her all week, ready for the moment she was given the word she could send it. She didn't want to be caught unprepared.

They release hands so they can pick up their pace to a jog. As the sky turns from black to a lighter shade of blue, the climb becomes easier. Although, now that she can see, Wren can't stop her eyes from darting around looking for a polar grizzly in the mood for some breakfast. Thank goodness Phoenix has that knife. Dex is protecting her even when he's not here by allowing him to keep it.

She really hopes Dex forgives her for ditching him like that. Thinking about it now, he's been a whole lot nicer to her than she's been to him since she met him. She's going to need to make that up to him one day, should they both live to co-exist in more peaceful times. A revolution isn't exactly the time to be repaying favors.

It's a time to survive.

There's no doubt it's been harder and harder to fight the feelings she has for Dex. But she has to. Life's already complicated enough. There are questions she needs answered first. And relationships to figure out. It's just not possible to give him what he wants right now. Maybe not ever.

Glancing over her shoulder, she sees Phoenix close behind. They're moving faster than the first time she climbed up to these cliffs during her Proving. Despite his new appreciation for lounging on a mattress, he doesn't seem to have lost any of his fitness.

Enjoying the way her body is responding to the familiarity of being exerted like this, Wren presses on. They've long ago passed the place where Nova was cornered by the polar grizzly and even though that makes them no safer, somehow Wren feels more relaxed.

It isn't long before the path widens out and the vegetation thins, and she knows they're not far.

"It's just up there," she calls to Phoenix.

"About time," he complains, even though he's hardly broken out in a sweat.

Wren bursts through the last of the trees and stops well clear of the cliff, watching as Phoenix jogs right up to the edge.

"Careful!" she calls, having flashbacks of Fern's last moments.

But Phoenix doesn't joke and tease her like Fern did. He has far too much respect for the dangers of their environment for that. Instead, he takes a step back.

"It's okay, little bird." He goes to her and wraps an arm around her. "I can see just fine from here."

This is the Phoenix not many people get to see. The one who cares. The one who'd never want her to feel scared. She wishes he'd let more people see this side of him.

"It's beautiful, isn't it?" she asks, gazing out across the thick, green canopy. It looks so different from up here, like the forest is one large being, rather than something made up of billions of leaves and twigs and branches, all woven together to form these giant lungs of the Earth.

The birds are already up and out of their nests, flitting about, ready to start a new day, Beneath the canopy, Wren knows there are animals, both large and small. Insects and mammals and tiny arachnids, all living their lives, completely unaware of the trouble their planet is in. How delicate their future really is.

Phoenix nods as he stares out across the trees, his eyes widening as the sun peeks up over the horizon, sending spears of golden light toward the heavens.

"Wow," he breathes. "So many trees. And the birds. I never knew so many of them existed."

"The forest is full of life," she says. "When the land's treated with respect, it regenerates."

"Think it's the same for people?" he asks.

Wren tilts her head, turning from the sunrise to look at Phoenix. "What do you mean?"

"People," he says. "The Unbound. They seem so desperate. Do you think if they were given the chance that they'd regenerate, too?"

"That's really deep for you, Phee." Wren punches him in the ribs and giggles.

Phoenix doubles over and lets out a howl. "Careful! I might pick you up and carry you over to the edge."

Wren takes a step back, even though she knows he'd never dare.

"So, do you?" he asks.

"Do I what?" She tilts her head. "Oh. Do I think the Unbound could regenerate, just like these trees?"

Phoenix rolls his eyes. "Yes."

"I do. Anyone has the capacity to heal. Just like this land. All it takes is respect."

Phoenix nods. "That's why we have to help them. It felt good at that meeting, offering them hope like that."

The more the sun rises and lights up the world below them, the more spectacular it looks. There are clouds gathered in the sky and they light up in tones of amber and citrus as they reflect on the tops of the trees.

Phoenix peels off his shirt and ties it around his waist. Wren sees a hint of leather sticking out from the waist of his pants. He may have agreed to wear these hemp clothes as a disguise but he was never going to relinquish his beloved leather pants.

"Feeling hot, are you?" she asks, knowing full well that he's practically allergic to wearing a shirt.

He taps the pendant dangling from his neck. "We might see a raven."

"They do nest up here," she says with thoughts of the final test of the Proving plaguing her. "You never know, we might get lucky."

With no sign of a raven for now, they focus back on the treetops.

"It's hard to believe that this has been here our whole lives," says Wren. "While we've been chopping down trees and burning them for fuel, this forest has been multiplying. Just look at that birdlife."

"Look closer," says Phoenix, edging closer to the ledge and peering down.

"I'm good here, thanks." What is everyone's obsession with getting her to stand closer to the edge?

"Trust me," he says. "You gotta see this. I'll keep you safe."

Wren shuffles closer to Phoenix who puts his arm around her again and leads her up to the ledge. He points down to a clearing below and her stomach lurches to see the drop.

"Check it out," he says.

Wren leans forward just a little and looks down, doing a double take to be sure of what she's seeing.

"What is that?" she asks. "I've never seen anything like it."

There's a small hoofed mammal with slender legs, a short tail and a long body coated in a fine layer of light brown fur. Its large ears are standing upright as it sniffs at the grass.

"I think it's a deer." Phoenix tightens his grip on her. "A baby deer. And look! There's its mother."

"A deer?" Wren leans out a little more. "But they're extinct. It can't be."

They watch in silence as the mother deer goes to her baby and drops her face so their noses touch. Such strange creatures! So unlike the bears that roam the Outlands.

"They're gorgeous," says Wren, unable to tear her eyes away. Never before has she met an animal that not only didn't want to eat her but she didn't want to eat it. There's no way she could hunt these precious animals for food like her ancestors had. To think that one—make that two—of them had survived and managed to breed.

252

"I've got to hand it to Askala," says Phoenix, guiding Wren back from the edge. "They might have issues with how they treat their people, but they sure know what they're doing with the land."

Wren nods, her question of earlier coming back to her. Would this planet be better off without humans to destroy it? Is it even possible to find a way to live in harmony? There has to be some sort of compromise they can arrive at where both are possible.

"I'm glad I brought you up here," she says. "I knew you needed to see it for yourself."

"A raven!" Phoenix gasps, reaching for his pendant and holding it so it reflects the light. "Over here!"

It's already seen them, Wren is sure of that. But is it one of Cy's raven's or the sort who live here and like to protect their nests at any cost?

"Careful," she says. "They like to swoop."

"I think it's one of ours," he says. "It won't swoop."

All she can do is hope he's right, but she pulls back from the edge a little more, not wanting to take any chances.

The raven circles them, getting closer with each loop until it changes course and dives for them.

"Look out!" cries Wren, covering her face with her hands, then remembering how badly battered Shiloh's hands were after her encounter with the raven, she crouches down and buries her face in her knees.

But nothing happens.

"Wren!" Phoenix shouts. "What's got into you?"

She lifts her face from her knees and sees Phoenix a few paces away, a raven on the ground in front of him with a note tied to its leg.

Staying where she is in case she scares the bird away, she waits as Phoenix crouches down and puts out his hand.

"Hello, little guy," he says, using a singsong voice as the raven steps closer. "There's another little bird over there, you know. But she's a scared little bird. I'm not sure what's happened to her. She used to be the bravest little bird I knew."

Wren sighs. "If you want to call me a coward, you're welcome to do that to my face," she mutters.

Phoenix leans forward and unties the note from the raven's leg. "I don't have any food for you today, I'm sorry, but there's plenty out there. All those birds have to be eating something. You should go take a look."

"It's delivering you a note," she says. "It doesn't want to be your best friend."

"Don't listen to her," says Phoenix, still focused on the raven. "She calls me jealous, but really, she's the jealous one. Listen to her, would you?"

With the note safely in Phoenix's hand, Wren approaches him.

"Still want to send your note?" he asks, looking up at her.

"Depends what this one says." She puts out her hand and he passes it to her.

She opens it and deciphers the first line, reading it aloud. "*Got your message.*"

"So, Dex did send it," says Phoenix.

Wren glares at him. "Of course, he did."

"Keep reading," he says. "You know I'm hopeless with that code."

"*Not going to wait.*" Her eyes widen as she reads. "*Must act now. Will arrive on the next storm. Watch the sky. Cy.*"

Phoenix stands up and waves his hands at the raven. They both know there will be no need to send any kind of reply now.

The bird takes to the sky and Wren watches it, trying to still the swirling of her mind.

"He never listens," she says. "He's so stubborn."

"Runs in the family, hey?" Phoenix nudges her.

"We told him to wait and he just goes ahead and comes anyway." She crosses her arms, aware she's pouting.

"But that's what we want, isn't it?" Phoenix shakes his head. "The sooner he arrives, the better. You said as much yourself earlier."

"You know what it means if he said to wait for the storm, don't you?" she asks.

Phoenix nods. "No rafts this time."

A sick feeling builds in Wren's gut. It's happening. It's really happening.

Cy is on his way.

NOVA

"Good morning, Nova."

Nova struggles to throw off the hold of sleep as someone says her name again. Despite the sunlight trying to penetrate her eyelids, it feels like she only just climbed into bed. She doesn't remember ever feeling this tired.

"I've brought you something." Nova opens her eyes to her mother smiling at her, the tilt of her lips slight and uncertain. "Well, two things actually."

Pushing herself up in bed, Nova wishes her stomach would stop moving as if the Oasis was still out at sea. Her mother has a small hemp bag slung over her shoulder and Nova suspects she knows one of the things in there. "I wish you hadn't," she mutters, all traces of sleep now gone.

"I don't remember you being this...tenacious," her mother jokes.

This is what her mother has done since she stitched up Nova's leg and she returned to her cabin. Visits three times a day, although this has been the earliest so far. Kept things light. Pretending as if it's the days they shared a living space—uncomplicated.

Nova moves to sit up a little straighter, her body wishing she could just climb back under the covers. Being tired seems to be her new baseline. "I didn't have anything to fight for back then."

She stops herself from placing her hand on her abdomen. That's a movement she only allows herself when she's alone. Is the impossible true?

Does she have a baby that she's going to have to fight for?

Her mother sighs as she slips into the seat at the desk. "You don't have to do this alone, Nova."

Nova looks at her but doesn't answer. She's right, but so wrong. Nova isn't alone, but not because her mother is here. She's never felt so distanced from her, and not just because her mother's Bound. High Bound, no less.

It's because her mother believes in a system that let Sam die.

Nova rubs her temples, then promptly stops. Any circular motion isn't a good idea right now. "The cut has healed well," she tells her mother, hoping that's all she wants. "It barely hurts anymore."

"I'm glad. I checked it last night while you were asleep. You're right, the sap combined with the stitches has worked quickly."

"You were in here last night?"

Nova doesn't mean for the question to sound so accusing, but her mother doesn't appreciate what an invasion that is. Just like her appearance right now. Her mother's chip allows her to go wherever she wants. Nova doesn't have the same privilege— her chip wouldn't open the door to her mother's cabin.

Her old cabin.

"You were asleep very deeply. I didn't want to disturb you." Her gaze flickers to Nova's belly and Nova has to stop herself from covering it protectively. "You need your rest."

Nova works to keep her tone soft. "Like I said, I'm feeling better."

"Good, because I want you to have this."

257

Her mother's hand slips into the bag and there's a clink of jars telling Nova there's at least two in there. Her stomach clenches.

Her mother pulls out the first. It's a small jar, one Nova's seen before. One used for carrying pods.

Nova pushes herself back on the bed. "I don't want it."

Her mother is already pushing it toward her. "It was a large cut, Nova, and you lost a lot of blood when it reopened. Your body needs this." She holds out the jar, the gelatinous pod flapping against the clear sides.

Nova shakes her head as vehemently as she can considering her constant nausea. "No."

"Please," her mother pleads, keeping the jar dangling between them.

Nova looks at her mother, at her desperate desire to help her, and she wonders if she can make her understand. "You're treating me like a Bound."

"I'm treating you like my daughter."

"I'm Unbound first." She clenches her hands. "Just like Sam was."

Her mother's shoulders sag. "You were always stronger than me."

Nova looks away. It's not about strength. It's about heart.

With a sigh, her mother retracts the jar and Nova hopes she's given up. If her mother were to freely give that pod to any Unbound, irrespective of whether she knows them, then she would've considered it. But not when it's special treatment.

Just like no one is less, no one is more.

"Maybe this will help you decide," her mother says as she pulls out the second jar.

Nova braces herself as if her mother is about to withdraw an explosive. She frowns when she sees it's another, smaller jar, this one half-full of fine white granules.

"You brought sugar? Because you knew I wouldn't eat the

"You did it for my grandchild, Nova. A child we'll need to keep safe."

She's talking about planning how they'll hide this pregnancy. How they'll raise the child of an Unbound in a society that predicts that child will be...less.

Nova shakes her head. "I don't want to talk about it now. I need time to process this." To spend time with the precious life growing inside of her.

Warmth unfurls deep within Nova, blossoming in what others decided should be a wasteland. It grows, fierce and bright, blazing with the knowledge that despite the chasm that exists between her and Kian, their love forged something.

A child.

Her mother's about to object when there's a knock at the door. She looks at Nova who shrugs. Many of the Unbound come to check on her at all times of the day, it could be any of them.

"Come in," Nova calls out, glad for the reprieve.

The door slides open and Nova stands in surprise. "Flick."

Felicia rushes in, curls bouncing with excitement "I have big news to share, Nova." She freezes when she sees Nova's mother standing by the desk. "Oh, you have company. Hi, Thea."

"How lovely to see you, Felicia. Why, you're practically glowing."

Felicia's gaze slides away. "Thanks, Thea," she responds, taking on the subdued appearance many of the Unbounds have around the Bound. "I was...ah...I was hoping I could talk to Nova." Felicia looks at Nova meaningfully. "Alone."

Nova's mother smiles graciously. "Luckily, I was just leaving." She walks to Nova, pressing a kiss to her head. "No one can know," she whispers against her forehead.

Felicia watches Nova's mother leave, sagging as the door slides closed. "She really loves you, Nova. You're lucky. My mother hasn't visited me once."

Nova grits her teeth at the contradictions that comment holds. Her mother barely visited her before that day Nova brought Sam to the infirmary. Unquestioningly, she accepted that Nova was Unbound. Unquestioningly, she refused to treat Sam with more than basic healthcare.

And yet, the moment Nova was injured, her mother ignored the rules she's spent her life living by. She stitched her up. She brought her a pod.

She's willing to protect her child.

What does that even mean?

Nova sighs as she sits back down on the bed. "It's complicated." She rubs her forehead as if that can wipe away all the unanswered questions. "You wanted to tell me something?"

"I'm going to get straight to the point." Felicia straightens her shoulders and looks Nova in the eye. "Do you think it's impossible for an Unbound to fall pregnant?"

The words slam through Nova. Alarm shoots hot and fast down her spine—Felicia looked so surprised to see her mother there, but she must've heard them through the walls. "I'm not pregnant!"

"Not you, silly," Felicia flaps her hand. "Me. I'm pregnant."

"You're pregnant? But…how?"

Felicia flushes. "I doubt you need the details. It's more the who that you're going to be blown away by."

Nova tries to remember the males she'd seen around their halls. Felicia has barely been out of her cabin since the Proving. But no one's face stands out as a regular visitor. "Who?"

"Let me show you."

Felicia gets up and walks to the wall, rapping on it three times in quick succession. Confused, Nova watches, glad it gives her time to process this.

Felicia's also pregnant. What are the chances that *both* their chips were faulty?

Nova startles when her door slides open and a body rushes

through, quickly plastering themselves against the wall of her cabin. She pushes to her feet, gasping in shock as she recognizes who it is.

"Thom!" His name is part exclamation, part question. "We thought you were dead!"

Thom grins as he straightens. "It's not that easy to get rid of me."

Felicia rushes to his side, wrapping herself around his arm. "He survived in the woods for two days," she states proudly. "Then he snuck onto the upper decks looking for food. I found him, hid him"—she caresses her stomach gently—"and the rest is history."

The last time Nova saw Thom was when he was running away as she was cornered by the polar grizzly. Not only has he survived, but he also missed the final day of the Proving. He's neither Bound nor Unbound.

Nova drops back onto the bed, her knees suddenly weak. "But you're Unbound..."

The glow Nova's mother commented on returns to Felicia's face. "Isn't it amazing? My chip must've failed or something." She looks at Nova earnestly. "I know I'm right. I was due two weeks ago and I've always been regular. You've got to believe me."

Of all the people Flick chose to tell. Of all the days. "I believe you, Flick. I know it shouldn't be possible, but I believe you."

Felicia relaxes. "I knew you would." She releases Thom so she can come to sit by Nova. "I wanted to tell you before... before we say goodbye."

Nova turns to her in surprise. "You're leaving?"

Surely they can't think they'll survive in the forest.

"Each night we've been working, back down by the beach." Felicia pulls in a breath. "We've built a raft. We're going to the Outlands."

Thom nods. "The last storm has cleared, so we'll be leaving tonight or tomorrow night."

Nova recoils in shock. "You can't! It's too dangerous!"

Thom strides over to stand beside Felicia. "The moment I'm found, I'll be banished." He laces a protective arm around her shoulder. "And what's stopping them from banishing Felicia, and our child?"

Nova's body clenches, as if it's wrapping itself around her own baby. *Banished?*

"The forest is too dangerous to live in on our own." Felicia takes Nova's hand in hers. "We can't stay, Nova."

Nova glances at Thom. His square body is certainly leaner, but that would make sense if he and Felicia have been sharing her food. Each Unbound's rations are barely enough for one person. And with so many storms lately she wouldn't be surprised if those rations become even more meager...

And Flick's right. They'd never survive in the forest. If a grizzly didn't kill them, they'd die of starvation.

But the Outlands?

"We can't keep living like this. Like we're...wrong." Felicia grasps her stomach. "Like our child is wrong."

Nova shakes her head, desperately trying to think of another solution. "You don't know what's over there. What you're getting yourself into."

Thom squares his shoulders. "It's a risk we have no choice but to take."

Nova stands, needing to move. Felicia and Thom stay close together as they watch her mull this over. They don't realize this isn't the first revelation Nova's been dealt today.

Going to the Outlands is a desperate move. A risky move. And Felicia is pregnant.

Just like Nova.

Nova straightens as an idea strikes her. "Wait here. I'm going to find out exactly what you're going to get yourself into. You need to make an informed decision."

Felicia pushes upright. "But how?"

Nova is already out the door as Felicia realizes what she's talking about. Who she's talking about.

As Nova heads for the stairs, she acknowledges she hasn't seen Wren since she helped her escape the brig. For all Nova knows, she might not even be in Askala anymore. As she exits the upper decks, though, she knows there's one person who would know exactly where Wren is.

Dex.

The walk to the lab isn't as strenuous as Nova expected. The cut on her leg aches but her mother was right, it's healing well. Her stomach continues to twist around itself, but now it's a reminder of the special gift she's carrying. Her lips turn up. As unpleasant as it is, she wouldn't choose to lose the nausea.

Nova keeps her face deep in her shawl as she follows the track, not wanting to have to stop and talk. Keeping her head down, she focuses on getting to the lab, not wanting to think of where she'll have to go next if Dex isn't there.

The lower decks would have to be her next stop. A place Nova can't access on her own. A place where Kian might be.

Kian. The father of her child. How ironically poignant. It's as if their love has transcended the laws of Askala so their child could be conceived.

Nova knocks on the door to the lab, counting out the *rap, rap, raps* so she doesn't sound impatient. She waits for long seconds, breath held, but the door remains closed. She's just lifted her hand to knock again, determined to get a response, when it slides open.

Dex's face fills with surprise. "Nova!" He engulfs her in a warm hug. "You're up and about! I'm so glad."

Nova hugs him back, loving the sense of familiarity with her old friend. "Thanks, it's good to be out of the cabin for a change."

Dex pulls back, studying her at arm's length. "How are you?"

Nauseous thanks to morning sickness...because I'm carrying Kian's child. "My leg has almost healed," she says with a smile.

"That's great news." Dex grins wryly. "Foot-long gashes don't seem to agree with you. And considering it was Phoenix you were saving, I'm not sure it's going to be worth the scar."

Nova relaxes, enjoying Dex's banter. She holds up her left hand, wriggling her four fingers. "Seems I'm collecting scars."

Dex lifts his stump. "I win," he states, grinning at his victory.

Nova shakes her head with a soft giggle. "I've missed you, Dex."

He slips an arm around her shoulder, leading her into the labs as if they're nothing but old friends catching up. As if they're equals. "I can't blame you. I'm one of the few people in this colony who has fewer fingers than you!"

Nova shoves him with her shoulder. "Actually, I've discovered that the number of fingers you have doesn't define you."

Dex glances down at her as they enter the computer room. "Haven't we all." He sobers as he steps back. "What brings you here, Nova?"

She sighs. The joking was a nice reprieve, but they both know that light-hearted world is short-lived. Too much has happened. "I need to talk to Wren."

Dex stills. "Wren isn't exactly taking visitors right now."

Which means she's still in Askala. "I know. But this is important."

"I can't take the risk, Nova. Magnus is tearing Askala apart looking for her."

Nova doesn't take Dex's refusal personally. He's protecting Wren. In the same way she's protecting her child by keeping it a secret.

She takes a seat, sending a sign she's not planning on leaving. "Flick came and saw me today."

"She's come out of hibernation, huh?"

"Yeah, well, I found out why she's been MIA." Nova looks Dex in the eye, trepidation tight in her chest. "She came to tell me she's pregnant."

The color rushes from Dex's face and he flops into the seat behind him. "Pregnant?" he whispers hoarsely.

"I know it's a shock but hear me out," Nova rushes to explain. "She's sure. She thinks her chip must've been faulty."

Dex is rubbing his stump although Nova doubts he's aware of it. "I suppose it's possible."

Relieved that Dex believes her, Nova continues. "She's scared about what could happen to her baby because she's Unbound. She's planning on going to the Outlands."

"That's crazy!" Dex exclaims. He shakes his head. "Felicia was always a bit flaky, but never crazy."

Nova's lips tip up in a half-smile. "See why I need to talk to Wren?"

Still looking stunned and pale, Dex nods. He wheels his chair back, and Nova watches in amazement as Dex opens a trap door in the section of floor he was sitting on. He leans over the black hole he just exposed. "Phoenix, get your shirt on, you've got company!"

Dex clambers down the ladder and Nova follows him. Inside, she finds herself in a small room, a single bulb hanging from the center of the roof—which is also the floor they were just standing on.

Looking around, she spots Phoenix lounging on a mattress in the corner of the room, his arms behind his head. He grins at her, looking like the lord of his domain, having clearly ignored Dex's instruction to put on a shirt.

"Hey, Blondie. Looks like my healing hands worked their magic—you're looking good!"

Nova smiles, ignoring the cockiness. It was a gentle, caring Phoenix who tended her for two days while she burned up with fever. "Hey Phoenix. Nice place."

"The east wing is my favorite. You could explore it for days," he quips.

"Ah, Phoenix..." Dex is scanning the tiny quarters. "Where's Wren?"

Dex is right. Wren isn't here, and there's not enough space for someone even as small as her to hide in. Apprehension twists along Nova's nerves. She really needs to talk to her.

"You mean she's not with you?" Phoenix's grin fades.

Dex shakes his head. "Last time I saw her, she was down here with you."

"I knew I should have gone with her!" Phoenix punches the air.

"Where the hell is she then?" asks Dex.

"Now isn't that the million-pod question." Phoenix pushes up from the mattress and paces. "She left sometime during the night, saying she needed to get out before she killed me."

Dex's hand clenches by his side. "I'm pretty sure she's going to be the death of me first," he mutters under his breath.

Phoenix frowns. "She promised she wouldn't go far. She said she'd be with you."

Nova twists the hem of her shirt. "We need to find her, Dex."

Dex pauses, his face suddenly transforming. His eyes widen as his features light up. "I know exactly where she is." He turns toward the ladder, already heading back out.

"I'm coming with you." Phoenix says, right behind him.

Dex shakes his head. "She told the truth. She hasn't gone far. She's safe. If I'm not back in an hour, you can come looking."

Phoenix hesitates but then must realize it's safer for both him and Wren if he stays put. "I'll give you forty-five minutes."

Dex is already climbing the ladder. "And when I come back, I'll bring dinner," he calls down to him.

"Go easy on the green stuff," Phoenix shoots back.

Nova follows, throwing Phoenix a smile as she's about to climb up after Dex. "Look after yourself, Phoenix."

"Will do, Blondie." He winks at her. "It's the first rule of the Outlands."

Once they're back up at ground level Dex closes the trap door and wheels his chair back over it. "Of all the impulsive, stupid, careless, frustratingly understandable, foolish—"

"We don't have much time, Dex. Felicia was talking about leaving tonight."

He's out the door without an explanation so Nova follows, hoping they're not going hiking through the forest. Wren's always been drawn to the outdoors, but Nova isn't sure her leg is ready for that sort of exertion.

Except Dex stops at the door to their old bunkroom during the Proving. He scans the sensor and they step through, standing in the empty room as the door slides shut. Nova's about to ask him if he's here to get anything when Dex speaks.

"I know you're in here, Wren. Get out from under there."

Amazed for the second time in such a short period, Nova watches as Wren frowns from under Dex's old bunk. "A girl needs to get some sleep, you know." A smile breaks out as she sees Dex has company. "Oh, hey Nova."

Nova's brows shoot up at Wren's shortened hair. "You've had a haircut. I like it."

"Thanks, so much more practical." Wren shuffles her way from under the bed, dusting herself off once she's standing before them. She glances at Dex. "Good guess, finding me here."

He arches a brow at her. "I slept in here last night."

"Just like old times." Wren wrinkles her nose at him, her eyes twinkling. "I promised Phoenix I'd be with you. I never promised that you'd know about it."

Dex angles his head as he scratches his chin, a gesture Nova knows means he's about to deal Wren a dose of truth. "It seems that you chose to spend the night with me instead of Phoenix."

Wren's mouth pop's open but Nova jumps in before she can speak. They don't have time for her token objections. Eventually Wren has got to realize that her feelings are far more than friendship, but now isn't the time.

Nova steps forward. "Felicia came to see me."

Wren frowns. "What's got that girl's curls in a twist?"

"She's pregnant."

Wren's eyes widen. "She's what?"

Nova glances at Dex, conscious she hasn't shared this part with him yet. "And Thom is the father. He's been hiding out in her cabin this whole time."

It's Dex's turn to go all wide-eyed. Nova almost smiles at their identical expressions, but then she remembers that there's still one more thing Wren needs to know. "And they're thinking of running away to the Outlands."

Except Wren doesn't seem to balk at the idea like Dex and Nova did. She shrugs as she takes a seat in the chair nearby. "I can see why they'd consider it. Many of us live in villages. There are families." She glances pointedly at Nova's left hand. "Freedom."

Except Dex is already shaking his head. He sits on the bunk, but then leans forward, pinning Wren with his gaze. "What about food? Fresh water?"

Wren narrows her eyes at Dex. "They don't come to you from neat little rows of tomatoes or pretty lakes. You have to work for them."

"Or fight for them?" he counters.

Nova sits on the bunk beside Dex, realizing she already has to fight for those.

"And the forests?" Dex asks.

Wren looks away. "Much of it is burned or cleared—"

"To build your villages."

"Look, I'm not saying it's all gardens and pods. Survival isn't a game out there, it's a daily battle. But we're not savages. We're not the dregs of humanity you've painted us to be."

Dex falls silent and Nova wonders if he's mulling over the fact he's fallen for a girl who they once called a Remnant.

"Babies and children," Nova asks quietly. "How do they survive?"

"They're cared for by parents who love them. Who would do anything to make sure they thrive."

"And these villages? What are they like?"

"I wouldn't recommend a girl wander around on her own, but they provide shelter and protection in the form of numbers. If a polar grizzly is killed, then the meat is shared."

"Because they haven't figured out how to preserve it," mutters Dex.

Nova places her hand over his. "We need to know as much as we can so Felicia and Thom can make the right decision."

A muscle twitches in Dex's jaw. "She'll be safe to stay here. I know she would be."

Wren shoves forward. "How do you know that, Dex? She's Unbound. There's no way she'd be allowed to keep that child."

Dex shoots up. "Just because she's Unbound doesn't mean her child will be!" Looking startled at the strength those words flung out, Dex sits again, modulating his voice. "Change is coming, they'll see that."

Nova frowns. Sam spoke the same words, talking of change. Surely that can't be a coincidence.

"Can you guarantee that child's safety, Dex?" Wren asks. "That it won't be collateral damage in this rebellion? What do you think Magnus will do when he learns an Unbound is pregnant?"

Collateral damage? Rebellion? Sweet Terra. What would Magnus do when he learned that she's carrying his son's child?

Nova hasn't realized she's gasped until Dex and Wren both look at her.

Dex's gaze is full of concern as he peers at her. "Are you okay? Is it your leg?"

Nova smiles weakly. "Just a twinge." She turns back to Wren. "Maybe a few more questions—so Flick and Thom know what they're getting into. If something is coming, they'll need to make the best decision for their child."

Wren's back curves into the seat as she relaxes. "The Outlands isn't an easy place to raise a child, but at least everyone's equal in their fight to survive."

No one is less...

Nova grips her hands around each other. "What do you eat out there? Grizzlies wouldn't be regular fare."

"We forage what we can," Wren shrugs. "It's all very hunter and gatherer."

Even that has Dex's interest piqued. "Please don't tell me you make soup from mangrove pinecones. Kian and Nova tried that once and I'd prefer to eat my only hand rather than try that stuff again."

Wren rolls her eyes. "The cones are poisonous, but there are other plants to eat."

Nova leans forward, ready to absorb this information. As she asks more and more questions, she realizes she's not just asking for Felicia and Thom.

That it's not their baby she's planning for.

She's asking for herself.

KIAN

*K*ian wipes the humidity away from his face as he makes his way down the gangplank, the morning sun already heating his skin. He smiles politely at the people he passes as they nod respectfully, but he doesn't slow, hoping he'll be left alone to fulfill his task.

He's on his way to the lab. To talk to Dex.

A couple of people try to make eye contact but Kian keeps moving. Gone are the days he could walk around the Oasis or its surrounds without being interrupted. Now people stop him to ask how the pods are going as they hold their stomachs, to tell him their child will take part in the Proving next year with wringing hands, to excitedly share that they're off to the infirmary to confirm whether they're pregnant.

Unlike the Unbound.

Kian's rounds have extended beyond a cursory sweep of the upper decks. Ever since Sam died.

Ever since Nova threw those words at him and walked away.

The Unbound don't come to him with their worries or good news. Some smile politely. Many avoid his gaze. A couple turned around and walked the other way when they saw him approaching.

It hasn't stopped him from trying to make conversation. From visiting Beatrice as she mourns the loss of her brother. She hasn't welcomed him, but she hasn't shunned him either. He's sat in her cabin, crammed with others as he's surrounded by the undeniable sense of community as they share stories of Sam. It seems he was a generous heart who intuitively cared for others.

Just like Nova.

Which is why Kian needs to talk to Dex.

Nova's words haven't left him since the moment she walked out on him. *No one is unworthy*. Like roots of the mangrove pine, they've twisted and penetrated his mind. Insidious and troubling, they've continued to erode his foundations.

Kian hasn't spoken to his father about it, and he's not sure why. Just like he's not sure what he'll say to Dex. All he has is an unsettled, burning feeling worming through him.

And an aching heart.

Dex is his cousin and best friend. He understands what Askala asks of them. How hard this is.

Kian's just stepped onto the path when the inevitable happens.

"Kian!"

His steps falter for the briefest of seconds as he considers pretending he didn't hear.

Not only does he not want to talk, but he's been avoiding the owner of that voice.

He turns, his duty constraining him like it has from the moment his father appointed him his successor.

Shiloh is rushing up to him, happiness keeping her footsteps light. She stops before him, her cheeks flushed, rosy lips tipped up in a smile. "I'm glad I ran into you. Have you changed the times of your rounds?"

Guilt pierces Kian. Why is it so hard to let Nova go? Why can't he do the one last thing Askala is asking of him? "The storm has kept me busy in the gardens."

Luckily, the rains and winds didn't wreak much damage. The plants look weary and battered, but they've survived.

Shiloh nods, her eyes glowing as she takes him in. "You work so hard, Kian." She places a hand on his arm, the sensation feeling cold and heavy. "Is there anything I can do to help?"

Kian's about to shake his head but he stops himself. If he's going to consider making this final choice, there's something he needs to know.

"Tell me, Shiloh, how do you *not* treat the Unbound?"

Her hand flutters to her throat. "I'm sorry?"

Kian can see he's unsettled her, but he doesn't back down. He needs to know. "If an Unbound comes in and they have a deep cut. Or if the broth you gave them hasn't made their cough go away. What do you do?"

"I do what I know I have to." She clenches her jaw. "For the planet we're working to save."

Except it's not that simple. "So we just ignore their humanity? Their rights?"

We decide they're unworthy?

Shiloh's blue eyes flash. "What's the alternative? Do what Nova did for Sam? Stitching him up?"

Kian draws back in shock. "She wouldn't do that."

Shiloh shakes her head. "She thought no one saw. But Sam was the only one there that afternoon, and I was doing stocktake. We had less thread than we should've, a needle that needed sterilizing." Shiloh huffs. "I didn't think she'd tell you. She wasted precious supplies. She knew it was wrong."

Kian knows he shouldn't ask the next question, but it's out before he can stop it. "Helping someone is wrong?"

Shiloh's hand fists as she twists the material at her throat. "Helping the right people is what's right."

"You didn't answer the question."

"At that second test of our Proving, Kian, when the Bound and the Unbound were both cut and bleeding, who would you have chosen if Nova didn't speak first?"

Kian's nostrils flare as he draws in a sharp breath. Shiloh knows exactly who he would've chosen.

He would've chosen the Bound.

Shiloh moves closer, her hand stroking down his bicep. "Don't let one loss"—her eyes flicker—"the loss of Nova, undermine what you know is right."

Kian steps back, still uncomfortable with Shiloh's touch. That feels like a long time ago.

And like he's lost more than just Nova.

"I have to keep going. I was on my way to talk to Dex."

"Of course." Shiloh bites her lip as if she's considering saying more.

Kian takes a few more steps away, knowing he doesn't want to hear whatever she's contemplating. He spins on his heel, realizing talking to Shiloh is like talking to his father.

And yet it's Dex he wants to see.

One of the two people who *didn't* agree with Kian's decision to send the Remnants back.

"Kian?"

He turns at the hitch in Shiloh's voice, bracing himself.

Shiloh clasps her hands in front of her, smiling with self-assurance. "You'll never lose me."

He nods, respecting the strength and commitment in her words. "Thanks, Shiloh," he responds, knowing gratitude isn't what she's looking for. "Your support is…impressive."

Shiloh's smile grows, blazing like the sun. Kian disappears around a bend in the path before it can burn him.

He hopes the painful clenching in his chest goes away before he gets to Dex. It's making it hard to breathe.

He's only made it a few yards when his name is called again.

"Kian!"

Stopping his shoulders from drooping takes a Herculean effort as Kian turns around to see who's calling him. Zali is waving, trying to get his attention as she runs up the path.

"Kian, I've been searching everywhere for you. Your father says you need to see this."

"Is something wrong?" he asks with a frown.

Panting, Zali doubles over before him. "It's…the…gardens," she huffs between breaths.

Kian grasps her arm, steadying her. "Just give yourself a second."

Zali shakes her head. "There's no time." She straightens, looking Kian in the eye. "Locusts went through last night."

"Locusts? But there hasn't been more than the usual number. We've been managing them."

"I'll show you."

Zali's eyes are grave as she heads back the way she came. Kian follows her, a sick feeling lodged in the back of his throat. The gardens aren't far, meaning it's not long before Zali shows him exactly what she's talking about.

She pushes open the gate and steps back. Kian's eyes widen at the devastation.

Entire sections of the gardens have been stripped, nothing but a handful of stalks left standing like scrawny spines.

This is what it would've looked like when humans cleared entire tracts of forest. Naked. Barren. Emaciated.

Kian walks to the worst affected section, brushing his hands over the single, shredded stem left standing. "The sweetcorn?"

Zali nods. "Then the amaranth."

Kian works not to frown. The corn provides their flour as well as a proportion of their protein. The amaranth provides both green leaves and grain. They were both key foods in their diets. And their reserves.

"We cleared them before they could do any more damage,

277

thank Terra." Kian can hear the strain in Zali's voice. "And we'll put netting in place in case they return."

He stops himself from snapping the last stalk as frustration tightens his muscles. "If we plant straight away, how long before we'll have another harvest?"

"Weeks." Zali crosses her arms. "Assuming nothing else goes wrong."

Like another insect swarm. Or a storm.

Although, surely with the two storms in quick succession they're due for a break on that front. Even for this broken planet that's unusual.

She sags a little. "We're going to have to use some of the corn kernels we have to seed another crop."

Mentally, Kian crosses a large part of their corn reserves off the ledgers. Corn flour won't be on the menu anytime soon.

"Of course. Do what needs to be done."

Zali nods. "I'll get started right away." She turns to walk away then stops. "Your father said he wanted to talk to you after you'd seen this."

Kian pauses. He'd almost forgotten she'd mentioned his father when she approached him. "Dad's been here already?"

"Yes, he comes by most mornings, usually quite early. He said he'd be in the boardroom."

Kian smiles, although his jaw feels like it's been wired with steel. "Thanks."

As he heads back to the Oasis, Kian reflects on what Zali just told him. It seems his father has been doing rounds this whole time. Early in the morning. Ahead of Kian.

And he's not sure what that means, but it leaves an uneasy feeling in Kian's gut. Is that because his father doesn't trust him? Or was appointing his son as Askala's leader just an illusion?

As he reaches the boardroom, Kian pulls in a calming breath. This probably isn't the time to ask those questions. Their food

278

reserves have never been this low. The survival of their colony takes precedence.

And Kian can already guess what his father is going to suggest as a solution.

The door's open, as he expected it would be. Inside, his father is sitting at the table, the open ledgers laying in front of him. He looks up. "Ah, Kian. I'm glad you're here. You've seen the gardens?"

Kian pulls up a chair across from him as he nods. "Locusts."

"Yes, Zali said it can happen if there's been more rain than usual. Must be all these storms we keep getting. Causes a population boom. Although it's not something we saw in all the time I was leader."

Kian glances at the ledgers, wondering if his father still is the leader. "The sweet corn and amaranth are gone."

His father pushes the ledgers toward Kian. "Yes, you'll have some decisions to make."

Glancing down, Kian sees the numbers have already been altered. Amaranth zero. What's left of the sweet corn to be used as seed. He swallows the words that would've pointed out it's his role to adjust the numbers. He doesn't want to look petty.

Instead, he states the inevitable. "We're going to have to ration food."

"For everyone?"

"Yes. Everyone."

His father's brows contract, the motion darkening his eyes. "I thought you realized how dire this is."

"Of course I do." Kian points to the dangerously low tallies in the columns before him. "We're going to have quite serious restrictions until we can harvest more crops."

"And if there's another storm? More locusts? A polar grizzly gets through the fences and destroys it all?"

Kian doesn't like the feeling of defensiveness that has his

spine straightening as each question is thrown at him. "We do what we can. At least we have the pods."

"I spoke to your mother about that—"

"You spoke to Mom? Why didn't you speak to me?"

His father blinks. "Because I thought her perspective would be valuable. She said we have a healthy pod population but we need to be careful."

"Which is what I would've told you. Their numbers are strong. We can keep the colony going until the crops grow again."

"As long as nothing happens to the pods like it did with Ronan," his father counters darkly.

"You dealt with Ronan. You banished him. I won't limit our pods on a *what if*, Dad."

His father pushes up from his seat. "You're risking too much."

Kian remains in his chair, telling himself his father has always been passionate about this. It's what he's always respected about him. "What are you suggesting, Dad?"

"What needs to be done, Kian. The Unbound will receive basic rations. No ability to earn pods. We need to ensure Bound survival. That has always been what Askala was about."

"The Unbound are barely surviving as it is. Who knows how many will die if you do that."

His father slams his fist on the table. "Sacrifices are inevitable. Askala needs a strong leader who is willing to make them."

Just like his father was.

Still is in many ways.

As he sits there, his father standing over him, Kian realizes he needs to make a decision. That the direction of Askala teeters on the edge of this moment.

Does he continue what he's done since the moment his father chose him to lead Askala? Does he follow in the path that's been carved for him? The one he believed was true and necessary?

The one that no longer feels right…

Kian shakes his head, a little disbelieving that he's taking a cautious step away from that route. "You aren't making the sacrifices, Dad. The Unbound are."

Nova is. Sam did. Bea is mourning what she had to lose in the name of Askala.

"You haven't had to lose anything for Askala. You have Mom. You have"—Kian spreads out his hands—"children to love and hold. Food on your plate." His hands clench as he stares at his father, wondering if he really understands. "You have the promise of a future."

"None of the decisions I've had to make were easy, son." His father pushes further forward. "You're talking like this because you're grieving for Nova. Don't let your love for one person dictate the fate of many."

Kian pauses. Shiloh said the same thing. Is that what he's doing? Letting what he feels for Nova—that broken, aching part of him—decide what's best for Askala?

His father must sense something, because he leans forward even more, his face tight with intensity. "Askala proves humans can heal rather than destroy. Everything we've created is evidence we can give rather than take. There's nothing more important than that."

Slowly, Kian rises to meet his father's gaze, eye to eye. He splays his fingers on the table, knowing he's going to need a firm foundation to say what he has to say.

"Except who gives and who takes, Dad?" Kian presses his face forward, seeing a kaleidoscope of emotions fragment through his father's dark eyes. Shock. Anger. Disappointment.

But it doesn't stop him. Nothing has ever felt more right in his life.

Just like he never doubted what he felt for Nova was right.

"What if there's something even bigger than Askala? Something you've taken for granted as you led us."

His father narrows his eyes, confused, but unwilling to admit it. "You need to consider what you're saying, Kian. What you're talking about—"

"I'm talking about something that transcends the laws that have been laid in Askala. Something that is the very core of humanity." Kian narrows his eyes, too, lasering his father with his gaze. "Love."

Kian steps back before his father can respond. He walks to the door, only stopping after he's scanned the sensor and it's slid open.

He turns back to his father. "The food will be rationed equally, amongst Bound and Unbound." He straightens as he says the words Nova threw at him, liking the feeling as they flow past his lips. "No one is unworthy."

Kian strides away, not wanting an answer or a debate or an argument. He won't be changing his mind.

Everything about this moment tells him this is right.

The words that seem to want to be shouted from the top of the cliffs for all to hear.

The blazing light that's exploded in his chest.

The smile that graces his face, after feeling like it was never going to gain life again.

As he heads for the exit, Kian realizes he needs to talk to Dex more than ever. They need to call a High Bound meeting. The rations will be discussed and voted on. Dex will help him make sure the Unbound are treated as equals.

Kian realized that's why he wanted to see Dex all along. He wanted to talk to someone who hasn't blindly followed the edicts of Askala. He wanted to be questioned.

The sweet, relieved feeling grows again as Kian realizes he'll make a second suggestion for them to vote on. If more Remnants arrive in peace, they will welcome them. They will act in line with the values they defend so righteously. They'll be kind and generous and smart.

Together, they'll work toward healing Earth.

But before he finds Dex, he has to find Nova.

He's going to tell her he was wrong.

Askala wasn't built on love. Their love was never forged by Askala.

The truth is, their love has forged Askala.

Kian takes a sharp right as he heads for the upper decks.

He can't wait to tell her.

Maybe, just maybe, it's not too late.

DEX

*A*voiding Kian in Askala is like trying to avoid the sun. Dex has been hiding in dark corners as his cousin moves from one side of the Oasis to the other, his leadership like a beacon to the Bound who follow him, if not with their feet then their eyes.

They're waiting to see what kind of leader he's going to be.

The Unbound aren't waiting for Kian, though. Instead, they're waiting for a sign of the liberation they've been promised. Word of a revolution is quickly spreading throughout the upper corridors of the old ship. If the league were to meet again, Dex is certain they'd have more than double the attendees.

Hunger is what eventually drives Dex from the shadows and has him walking to the dining hall, despite the certainty that Kian will likely find him there. He can't hide from him forever. Eventually, he's going to need to look him in the eye and betray him to his face. Pretend that he stands beside him when in reality he'd stood on the upper deck and stabbed him in the back.

Walking into the dining hall, Dex nods at Milli, who's already seated at one of the tables.

Letting a carrot fall from her lips, Milli's brows dart up. "Kian's looking for you."

"Thanks," he says, not pausing his steps.

"He says it's urgent!" Milli calls after him.

Waving over his shoulder, Dex makes his way to the food counter. Milli isn't the first one to tell him of Kian's desperation to see him. And he's sure she won't be the last.

Zali is behind the counter that connects to her kitchen. She gives him a sad smile when she sees him and passes him a plate containing one scrawny carrot sitting on an aibika leaf.

"Are you trying to tell me something?" Dex pats his belly. Meals in Askala aren't ever of feast-like proportions, but he's never seen anything this stingy. "I know I don't quite have Kian's six-pack, but I didn't think I'd let myself go that much."

His joke falls flat, along with Zali's pretense at a smile.

"It was locusts," she says. "They wiped out the corn and amaranth. I'm afraid it's desperate. Especially with the new storm that's just getting started out there."

"New storm?" There'd been some rain outside earlier, but he'd been too tired to pay much attention to it. "But surely there can't be another so soon?"

"I'm afraid so," says Zali. "This one looks even worse than the last. Kian's put us on rations. He wants to call a High Bound meeting to discuss it."

Realizing this is more serious than he'd thought, Dex looks around at the other tables to see what the Unbound are eating.

"We all get the same," Zali says. "No matter how many fingers we have."

Dex nods, slowly. If things are that desperate, he would've expected Kian to ration the Unbound first. This seems like an awfully *fair* decision for the leader of Askala.

"He's looking for you," says Zali.

"Well, he'd better hurry up." Dex grins at her. "If this is all I'm eating I'll be a lot harder to find soon."

"You know I'd give you extra if I could." Zali's eyes fill with tears. "But it wouldn't be right."

"No, Zali." Dex sets down his plate to reach out and touch her on the arm. "I wasn't suggesting that. I'm sure we'll figure something out."

She nods. "I hope so."

"If you don't mind, I think I'll get this to go." Dex wraps the carrot in the leaf and scoops it up, taking a bite and wincing at the bitterness.

"Find Kian," she says, wiping her tears to smile at the next person to approach the counter. "He needs you."

"I'll keep an eye out for him," Dex says as honestly as he can. He's been keeping an eye out for Kian for days now already. It's hard to avoid someone if you don't know where they are.

Putting what remains of the carrot in his mouth, he takes one of the rear exits and heads for his father's cabin, hoping to find him alone. There's always someone hanging off him lately. And what he has to talk to him about isn't something for anyone else to hear.

A wave of fatigue washes over him as he takes to the dimly lit corridor and he yawns, certain if he were to sleep for the next forty-eight hours, he'd still wake up tired.

It's been hard to drift off ever since Wren disappeared with Phoenix after the meeting of the league. Even her coming back the next day hadn't taken the sting out of it.

He feels just like Felicia must have when Wren grabbed her by the throat in the Proving.

Betrayed. Worried. And more than a little pissed off.

Just when he'd thought they were finally on the same side, she'd proven otherwise by running off.

With *him*. That red-headed wall of muscle he couldn't win a fight against if Phoenix had both hands tied behind his back.

Turning the corner, he sighs. It's not Phoenix's fault, he supposes. Although, if Dex can't be with Wren, Phoenix isn't exactly the kind of guy he'd choose for her.

Who's he kidding? He wouldn't choose any guy for her, unless it's him.

He approaches his father's cabin to find a group of people outside the door.

Unbounds. No doubt, all lining up to speak to their illustrious leader.

"He's with someone," says a woman when he goes to press his stump to the sensor. "And we were here first."

"He's Callix's son," hisses a man Dex has never seen before.

"Oh." The woman flushes and looks at Dex's infamously missing hand as if needing proof. "Sorry. It was dark the other night. I didn't recognize you."

"That's fair enough." Dex scans his chip and waits for the door to open. "I'm far more handsome in the daylight."

The open door reveals his father sitting on the edge of the bed with two Unbound standing in front of him.

"Dex!" his father says, looking across at him. "I've been looking for you."

"Here I am." Dex steps into the room and shoots his father's visitors a smile.

"You remember Bea and Vern from the meeting?" His father waves a hand toward them.

Dex nods as the memory of Bea crouched over her brother's body comes back to him. She has a large scab on the top of her head that he hadn't noticed in the darkness of the beach but now's not the time to ask her what happened.

"I'm sorry for your loss," he says.

"Thank you. I'm sorry for your loss, too." She looks down at his missing hand.

"It's okay. I have another one." He waves his right hand at her.

"I meant your mother," she says flatly.

"Oh." Dex looks down at his feet, ashamed. Of course, that's what she meant. Wren's right. It really is time he stopped making jokes about his missing hand.

"Could you give us a moment please?" Dex's father asks.

Dex glances up at him. "Sure." He'd hoped that after everything that'd happened lately that his father wouldn't keep him waiting. It seems it was too much to wish for that he'd be his priority for once.

"Not you," his father says. "I meant Bea and Vern."

Dex pulls his shoulders back as the feeling of pleasant surprise washes over him.

"Would you two mind waiting outside?" his father asks his guests. "Keep a watch on the door so that nobody disturbs us."

"Of course, Callix," says Bea, taking Vern by the hand and stepping outside.

"Since when have you needed guards outside your room?" Dex flops down on the bed and props himself up with his elbows.

"Since the last meeting." His father turns, locking his blue eyes on him. "They're anxious. And somehow they see me as their leader."

"Somehow?" Dex shakes his head. "I dunno, but maybe promising to lead them to freedom had something to do with that."

"It's no different than if my father had appointed me as leader in the first place." There's ice in his voice and it has Dex pulling himself up into a seated position on the bed.

"Why did you want to see me?" Dex asks.

"There's something you need to know." His father stands and paces the small space at the end of the bed. "It's about the chips used in your Proving."

"I already know." Dex shakes his head. "That's what I came here to talk to you about. I figured it out."

"What?" His father draws to a halt and stares at him. "What did you figure out?"

"You messed with the sterilizing agent," says Dex. "It's the only way to explain the pregnancy."

"Nova's pregnant?" His father's hands fly to his chest as a light behind his eyes seems to switch on. "That was what I wanted to ask you about."

"What?" Now it's Dex's turn to stand. "No, not Nova. Felicia."

His father nods, not seeming as surprised as he should be.

"She's pregnant to Thom of all people," Dex adds.

"Thom's alive?" Now the surprise kicks in and it has his father's brows shooting for the ceiling. "But I looked everywhere for him!"

"Everywhere?" Dex huffs. "Next time try looking in Felicia's bed."

"That's wonderful news." His father is smiling broadly, the weight of one less death on his shoulders visibly lifting. "And how is Felicia? Is it a strong pregnancy? I wasn't sure if I did it right, but if she's pregnant then it must have worked."

"Dad?" A thought crosses Dex's mind and he sits on the edge of the bed as if the pieces of a puzzle are trying to fit together inside his sleep-deprived brain. "You thought I was talking about Nova just now. How many chips did you mess with?"

"Just the Unbound," his father says. "Felicia and Nova. Admittedly, it was Nova I was thinking of, but it just didn't seem right to spare her fertility without sparing Felicia's."

Dex is barely listening now, his father's voice becoming a background buzzing as he remembers the night he came upon Nova and Kian on the beach.

He'd seen a whole lot more than he'd let Kian know. He'd turned away as soon as he'd realized, of course, and run right back to Magnus to steer him in the opposite direction. Then he'd returned to warn them, not for a moment thinking they'd be foolish enough to still be lying on the sand exposed like that. The rush of hormones had clearly inhibited their ability to think.

But had that rush of hormones also resulted in something else? Could there have been more behind Nova questioning Wren about the Outlands? Because if those puzzle pieces fit together in the way he fears they do, it's very possible Felicia isn't the only one looking for a way to escape.

"Dex!" His father is shaking him by the shoulders now. "What's wrong with you?"

Dex looks up, bringing his eyes into focus.

"Why?" Dex asks. "Why Nova? Why would you do that to her? You've put her in danger. If Magnus finds out..."

His father steps back. "Is she pregnant?"

"I don't know." Dex shrugs. "Maybe? She hasn't been well lately. I thought it was her leg, but I guess she could be."

He watches his father rub his hands together.

"Why?" Dex shakes his head as he asks again. "Answer my question! Why would you do that to Nova?"

"Lots of reasons. I wanted Magnus to see that an Unbound can give birth to a Bound. You're proof of that. We know it's possible, but Magnus won't believe it. Besides, I could never reveal your mother's secret." His father lets his hands fall as he sits beside Dex on the bed. "But if it were Magnus's own grandchild, he might look at things through a different lens. He wouldn't banish his grandchild."

"You reckon?" Dex shuffles over, needing his space while he thinks this through. "Because I don't know, Dad. I think he might."

"Well, he can't banish Nova if he's not the leader, can he?" his father says. "Kian would never let her go. Besides, none of this really matters anymore. Not now that the revolution's coming. Nobody will get banished once Askala is overthrown."

Dex draws in a deep breath as he stands. His father means

well. He knows that. But he sure has a special talent for going about things the wrong way.

"Was Nova really Unbound?" he asks, remembering the way her Proving scores had never really sat right. "Or was this your plan all along? To make her Unbound, then have her fall pregnant? You knew she and Kian wouldn't be able to keep away from each other."

His father throws his hands up in the air. "Dex, you've been raised to value the greater good. But did you ever really stop to think about what that is? Sometimes sacrifices have to be made, but they aren't the ones you might think of first."

Now it's Dex's turn to hold up his hand. "I've had enough of this."

He goes to the door and pauses at the sensor.

"Where are you going?" His father follows and grabs him gently on the arm.

"I need to find Kian." Dex pulls his arm free.

"Kian? Are you mad?" His father takes hold of him a little more forcefully this time. "You can't talk to Kian about this!"

"Did you go to breakfast this morning?" Dex asks.

His father nods, his brows furrowed. "Yes, and so?"

"Did you notice anything odd, other than the rations?"

"Not especially." His father shrugs.

"The Bound and Unbound were being rationed in the same way," says Dex. "Which tells me one thing."

"What?" His father releases his grip on him.

"That Kian is *not* his father."

Dex presses his chip to the sensor and marches out of the room.

"He's all yours," he says to Bea and Vern as he passes them and heads down the corridor, aware that his father is trying to follow but being accosted by the swarm of Unbounds wanting their turn.

Dex takes the opportunity to break into a run, swerving

around the labyrinth of corners until he's certain he's lost him. He doesn't need his father's input into this conversation. He's done quite enough already.

Pressing himself against a wall while he catches his breath, he decides to check the most obvious place first. The boardroom. But when he gets there, he finds it empty apart from Kian's ledgers lying open on the table.

He heads back out to the ballroom, deciding if he's going to find Kian, then he needs to think like him. Which means he'll be in one of two places. Either on the upper decks looking for Nova. Or in the lab waiting for him.

"Dex!"

He spins around to find Thea running into the ballroom.

"Have you seen Nova?" she asks, coming to a breathless stop and clutching her chest. "I can't find her anywhere."

Dex takes a step back, feeling like he's been punched in the gut. Surely, Nova hasn't left already? He'd thought he had more time to talk her out of whatever crazy idea she'd come up with. This could be a disaster if the storm Zali was predicting is true.

"What about Felicia?" he asks. "Have you found her?"

Thea shakes her head. "Her cabin was empty, too. Do you think they're together?"

"This is going to sound strange." Dex lowers his voice and leans down to Thea's short frame. "But is Nova pregnant?"

Thea's eyes fly open and she shakes her head. "Nova is Unbound. It's impossible."

"You need to trust me," he says, looking her directly in the eye. "Felicia's pregnant. I think they might have escaped to the Outlands together to protect their babies. You have to tell me the truth if I'm going to be able to help. Is Nova pregnant? I'm on her side, Thea."

Thea nods, her eyes filling with tears. "She is. But please, you have to find her."

"Does Kian know?" he asks.

"No." Her voice is a whisper. "But he's looking for her. He's looking for you, too."

"Wait in the infirmary so we can find you," he says, taking a step back. "If there's a way to fix this, I will. I promise."

Thea nods through her tears as he runs toward the door on the stage used in their Announcement. That has to be the fastest way to the lab. But he quickly realizes there's no sensor on the interior of this door. It's for one-way traffic only, a symbol of the new life the participants of the Proving are stepping into.

This leaves only two possible exits. The ladder on the upper deck, or the gangplank. Sweet Terra will need to help them if there's ever an evacuation needed on this rotting hulk of metal.

He dashes down the stairs and heads for the gangplank, desperately hoping his father isn't waiting for him there.

The rain outside is heavy now and a clap of thunder pierces the air, sending him scurrying down the gangplank with speed. It would be just his luck to be struck by lightning. Zali was right. This storm is coming in fast. Soon walking around out here will be too dangerous. Let alone paddling on a raft.

If in fact that's what Nova is doing.

Desperately hoping he's wrong, he reaches the path to the lab, wiping the rain out of his eyes as he runs. His feet pound the dirt like he's greeting an old friend. This is a path he's taken so many times before, but never in such a hurry.

Pressing his chip to the sensor at the lab he wills the door to slide open faster, slipping through when the gap is only a couple of feet wide.

"Kian!" he calls. "It's me! Are you in here?"

There's a noise, followed by the most disheveled version of Kian that Dex has ever seen. His hair is mussed and his eyes are bloodshot, his normally well-kept shirt is skewed across his chest like he's just wrestled a leatherskin.

"Dex, where have you been?" Kian goes to him and Dex feels his heart break right down the middle.

This is his cousin. His best friend. The one who's stood beside him his whole life as they learned about the world. And he's let him down in the worst kind of way, right when he needed him most.

"I'm sorry." Dex holds out his arms, half expecting Kian to give him a playful punch in the ribs. But instead, Kian wraps his arms around him, drawing comfort from him in a way he's only needed to once before. And that time was about Nova, too.

Dex pats him on the back. "Okay, mate. I know I give the best brugs in Askala, but we need to talk."

"Actually, you smell like a wet bear," says Kian as he lets go of him.

"I do the jokes around here," says Dex, pleased to see this familiar glimpse of the Kian he knows.

"I can't find Nova." Kian gets straight to the point. "She's vanished."

"I know. I just ran into Thea." Dex leads him to the bunkroom, bending to look under his mattress out of habit. It seems Wren's stayed with Phoenix in the secret room for once.

Kian sits on his old bunk while Dex changes into a dry set of clothes, trying to come up with the right words to let Kian know that the situation is even more serious than he might think.

"Kian, she's pregnant," he says, deciding just to spit it out.

"Wren?" Kian asks, his face lighting up. "I knew you had her hidden somewhere! Good for you."

"No!" Dex shakes his head, amazed that Kian would think he'd gotten that far with Wren. She hasn't even let him kiss her, let alone...

"Then who?" asks Kian, his brow furrowed.

"Nova."

"But..." Kian's face washes over with the pale complexion of a man in shock.

"Felicia's pregnant, too. They're not sterile. Their chips

malfunctioned." Dex decides not to bring his father into this mess just now. There's already enough for Kian to take in.

Kian leaps to his feet. "Are you certain?"

"Thea told me," he says. "I'm certain."

"We have to find her." Kian wrings his hands and paces the room. "Now more than ever."

"I think it might be too late for that. You see—"

"What? Tell me?" Kian grinds to a stop. "Do you know where she is? Is she with Wren?"

"Hold up!" Dex raises his palm. "Too many questions. Let me explain."

Kian nods, standing still, waiting for him to speak.

"She's not with Wren." Dex draws in a breath, deciding it's time to let Kian in on a few facts. "Wren's with Phoenix."

"Phoenix? But he's dead!" Kian throws his hands in the air.

"Yeah, about that." Dex winces. "He's sort of not dead."

"But Nova told me he was." Kian shakes his head. "Does she know he's alive?"

Dex bites down on his lip. Telling Kian that Nova lied to him is even harder than it was to tell him she's pregnant.

"Yes." It's one simple word, but it feels like he just slapped Kian. "She had no choice. Listen, there's a lot we need to talk about, but let's just focus on finding Nova for now."

Kian exhales, taking this news so much better than Dex had expected. "Do you know where she is?"

"I haven't seen her since yesterday. She came here looking for Wren."

"But you just said Wren's with Phoenix?" Kian shakes his head, doing his best to keep up. "Are they here?"

Dex hesitates, not wanting to reveal to Kian just how close he is to Wren and Phoenix right now.

"They were here when they spoke to Nova," he says, using Wren's technique of lying by omission, then moving on quickly before the other person has a chance to give it much thought.

"Nova told Wren that Felicia was thinking of escaping to the Outlands with Thom. He's the father of Felicia's baby, by the way."

"But, Thom…"

"Yeah, also not dead," Dex adds, ignoring the baffled look on Kian's face. "The point is that Nova asked Wren a lot of questions. Too many. When I think about it now, it was obvious she was asking them for herself. I just couldn't see it at the time. I never thought…"

"Why didn't you tell me?" Kian looks at him with nothing but the utter betrayal he must be feeling. "I thought I could trust you."

"I only just found out about Nova's baby now." He knows it sounds pathetic, but he has to try. "I've just put it all together. I swear it. I'd never keep something like that from you."

"Are you certain about that?" Kian pulls his hands into fists by his side. "Because it sure feels like you've been keeping plenty of other things from me. I'm supposed to be the leader of Askala, Dex. So, why does it feel like I have no clue about anything that's happening here right now?"

"It's complicated." Dex swallows down his guilt. It's a fair accusation.

"Do you think it's possible they've already gone?"

Dex nods. "We can't find her anywhere in Askala. I can't imagine where else she might be. The weather was clear last night. She must have left then."

"But the Remnants are the ones desperate to come here for refuge!" Kian shakes his head, the angst that's building up within him seeping from his pores. "We don't go *there*."

"We do if we're desperate," says Dex. "Being an Unbound isn't—"

"I know what it isn't!" Kian's shock has turned to anger now. "I know exactly what it isn't. Nobody is unworthy. I get that now. I just got it too late."

"It's not too late." Dex isn't sure what he means by this, but he's certain it's the truth. It can't be too late. Nova means too much to Kian—to all of them—to just let her go.

"What if she's hurt?" Kian's eyes spill over with tears. "What if our baby…"

"Nova's strong. Don't underestimate her." Dex hates that this is the best he can say to reassure him.

"I'm not underestimating her. But I'm also not going to just sit here and do nothing." Kian takes a step toward the door. "I'm going after her."

"Have you seen the weather out there?" Dex points to his damp clothes in a pile on the floor. "It's suicide! If you're serious about that, you're going to have to wait for this new storm to blow over."

"Nova is out there! In that very same storm." Kian points in the direction of the Outlands. "Do you not understand that?"

"You can't help her if you're dead, that's all I'm saying."

There's a crash in the hallway and Dex turns from Kian to run out to the entryway.

"Dex!" It's his father, hair wet and plastered to his head, clothes dripping in a puddle at his feet. "The storm's coming in fast now. I'm glad I found you. Listen, I don't think it's a good idea to talk to…"

Dex looks over his shoulder to see what has his father's words pausing.

Kian is behind him, staring at his uncle. "You don't think it's a good idea to talk to who, Callix?"

"Nobody. Nothing." Dex's father rakes a hand through his hair, sending water droplets flying. "It doesn't matter."

Kian sighs loudly, then marches toward the exit. Dex is close behind him, almost crashing into his back when he turns.

"No, Dex." The distraught look on Kian's face would have been enough without the words. "Don't follow me.

"It's too dangerous out there." He's practically pleading now, but he doesn't care.

"But *she's* out there."

"Don't do it, Kian." Dex puts a tentative hand on his arm. "She needs you too much for you to do anything stupid."

Kian lets out a long sigh. "Then I'll wait for the storm to blow over. But, then I go."

"Don't stop him, Dex." Dex's father steps forward. "Let him go after her."

"You know what, Callix," says Kian, as he presses his hand to the sensor at the door. "There's only one job you were worse at than being a father. And that's being an uncle."

Kian steps through the door, the storm seeming to gather him in its arms and sweeping him along the path back to the Oasis.

Dex stands in shock as the door slides closed.

"He's right, you know," he says to his father. "You really are—"

"Enough, Dex!" His father turns toward the computer lab but stops to have his final say. "I wanted you to let Kian go for his own safety. What do you think the Remnants are going to do to him when they arrive here? Bake him a cake? Shake his hand?"

"I...I...I don't know." Dex never thought about this.

"They'll kill him," his father says, plainly. "It's better that he gets out of here while he still can."

His father leaves Dex standing at the door, his legs shaking with such force he leans against the wall and slides down until he's seated on the cold floor.

When he'd raised his hand to vote with the league to allow Wren's people to come here, never once did he think about the impact that would have on Kian. He'd been too wrapped up thinking about the liberation of the Unbound.

It seems that there's no right answer with how to move

298

forward. No answer that's right for all the people, Bound, Unbound and Remnants alike.

His mom had told him to trust his father, but that doesn't seem to be getting him anywhere.

With Nova in the Outlands, Kian certain to soon be on his way after her, and Wren in the muscled arms of another man, he doesn't know which way to turn or where his loyalties lie.

All he ever wanted was to do the right thing.

So, why does it feel like he's done everything wrong?

WREN

*W*ren hates that she's done it again.

That's three times she's run away from Dex, even if for now he's probably oblivious to the third. Maybe she can get back to him before he finds her missing?

No, that's a stupid idea. Because this time when she returns she'll have Cy with her. He's going to notice that.

Cy had said he'd be arriving on the next storm and given the fierce howling at her eardrums, it's a good bet that this is the one he meant. The last couple of storms weren't big enough. If there's one thing Cy likes, it's a grand entrance. *This* is the kind of storm he's been dreaming of.

Wren had been in the bunkroom taking a break from Phoenix by having a nap underneath Dex's bed when she'd heard the wind outside. It's just as well, really. She'd never have heard it from down in Callix's claustrophobic pit of hell.

Thankfully, Dex had been over in the Oasis and she'd been able to get Phoenix and leave without being seen. They'd headed straight for the lake where Phoenix had constructed a shelter to keep the worst of the rain off them.

"It can't be long now, little bird." Phoenix wraps his arm around her and she sighs.

"What if something went wrong?" She shivers as the temperature seems to plummet a few more degrees.

"Nothing will have gone wrong," Phoenix reassures her. "Cy's been planning this for years. He knows what he's doing."

They sit in silence, eyes glued to the stretch of sky above the lake. Rain splashes at their faces, but at least their backs are keeping dry.

A flash of lightning breaks through the clouds, just as a massive gust of wind collects the roof of their shelter and sends it skittering across the lake. Not even one of Phoenix's constructions can compete with Mother Nature in a bad mood.

The boom of thunder that follows is so loud Wren's hands fly to her ears. Phoenix leaps to his feet, tugging at her arm as he pulls her upward.

"This is crazy!" she screams as the rain pelts at her.

But Phoenix isn't listening. He's pointing at the sky with one hand and pumping his fist with the other.

Wren's eyes lift and she sees what he's pointing at. A plane is approaching from behind the cliffs.

After all this time waiting, it's finally happening.

She shakes her head, amazed that Cy has actually managed to get that rust bucket into the air. But she should know better than to have doubted him. He'd said that plane would fly again, and there it is like an eagle soaring beneath the clouds.

"He did it!" Phoenix is jumping up and down now, waving his arms like he actually thinks anyone up there could possibly see him.

Wren lets out a whoop, trying to show the excitement she knows she's meant to be feeling. Maybe she's just too cold, or too nervous, or too tired to be excited? Because she can't help but recognize that her dominant feeling right now is one made up of nerves.

It's because of Wren that this moment is happening. When she'd agreed to go on ahead of Cy and find out what they were up against in Askala, she'd helped set this plan in motion. The plane wasn't ready back then, nor did they have quite enough fuel. Not that she'd have agreed to hover that far above the Earth in that thing. Even the thought of it makes her feel ill. A raft had been more her style. It still is. Should she ever return to the Outlands, it will be in exactly the same way she arrived.

"How cool is that!" Phoenix is shouting over the noise of the storm, seeming oblivious to the way the wind is tearing at his hair and clothes.

"Maybe you should have waited," she calls back.

He doesn't hear, but it doesn't matter. She knows he'd have far preferred to arrive by plane, but his need to know she was okay had been more important.

Slipping her hand into his, she squeezes it, comforted by the knowledge that he loves her. There's a safety in their relationship that she's never had with anyone else.

The plane angles closer, turbulence sending its wings rising and dipping as the pilot struggles to keep control. The sound of the engine is muffled by the storm, just as Cy had intended. He didn't care what risk that put everyone at. For him, the element of surprise was always more important. In his mind, it was either a bumpy ride and arriving undetected, or a smoother journey with an audience awaiting him on the shore.

Wren squints through the rain, no longer trying to shelter any part of her sodden body. It feels like even her insides are wet through.

"Here they come!" shouts Phoenix as a door on the plane opens and someone leaps from the aircraft, a parachute opening behind them as they begin their descent. More follow in quick succession.

"How many has he brought with him?" Wren's jaw falls open. She'd expected maybe six people in total, but this is insane.

There are perhaps two dozen parachutes opening underneath the plane as her father's soldiers float toward the lake. If the sight weren't so ominous, it would be beautiful. The white billowing fabric makes the soldiers look more like falling angels than a group of people intent on turning the world on its head.

Phoenix pulls on her hand and they run around the lake, trying to get closer to the landing site.

With their cargo unloaded, the plane flies away, the weather too dangerous for it to stay a moment longer than necessary. Wren pushes away the thought of how fair it was for Cy to ask that pilot to fly in this storm. Before she left the Outlands she never really thought too much about what was fair. But everything's different now. She just has to hope that she can convince Cy to see things in the same way. Surely, he'll listen to her? Why else would he have sent her ahead?

The first of the parachutes hits the water, quickly followed by the others and now the lake looks like it's covered in giant white lily pads. Releasing themselves from the weight of the parachutes, the soldiers swim for the shore.

Phoenix is already wading out to them and Wren follows close behind. It's not like she could possibly get any wetter. If anyone's hurt, they're going to need to be dragged to shore.

The warmth of the water is a blessing on her cold skin and she curses herself for not thinking of this earlier. Of course it would be warmer in here with Askala's normally humid temperatures.

She spots Cy swimming ahead of his men and her stomach clenches at the sight of him. He powers through the water toward her, his brute strength propelling him at an impressive speed. He may have put her through an intense training regime, but it was never any less than what he put himself through. She's never seen anyone else like him, not even Phoenix.

Running through the water, she hates how desperate she is to see him. Despite all his flaws and the harsh way he raised her, he's the only parent she has. He'd do anything for her. Protect her at any cost. And for that alone, she loves him.

The water's up to her waist now and she stops, waiting for Cy to close the gap between them.

Tears run down her face, the salt mingling with the acid of the rain and she holds out her arms as her father emerges from the water. After so long apart, it's hard to believe he's standing right before her.

Cy.

The man who had to fight for every privilege he ever had in his life.

The man who's the Commander of the Outlands, despite the fact he wasn't born there.

The man who changed his name to honor the only woman he ever loved by taking the last two letters of her name and making them his own.

The man once known as Ronan.

Father to Wren and father to her twin brother, Phoenix, this man should never have been so underestimated. The time has come for him to show Askala exactly what they banished.

Taking her in his arms, Cy pulls her to his chest and holds her close, water cascading from the mop of red hair plastered to the sides of his face.

"Hey, little bird," he says, releasing her so he can cup her face in his calloused hands. "Terrible haircut."

"Dad!" Phoenix is beside them now and Cy releases her to give his son a far less gentle hug. They slap each other on the back with loud thumps, audible even over the noise of the storm.

Seeing the two of them embrace like this has Wren aching all over. Before she came here, these two men were her whole world. The only people she'd ever loved.

But her world has expanded now in the same way her heart has had to. For she's had to make room for both Dex and Nova.

She even loves Kian in his golden-boy Askala-loving kind of way.

And this is why she's crying. Because these people offered her love and she gave them nothing but half-truths in return.

She allowed them to believe Phoenix was her boyfriend, taking advantage of the fact they've never looked alike. She let them think that Cy and Ronan were different people, when they're one and the same. And she convinced Dex that she doesn't care for him in the same way he cares for her, knowing that first she has to find out if the son of Mercy is also the son of Ronan.

Because as much as she'd like to have a brother like Dex, that's the last thing she wants him to be. Her feelings run far too deep for that.

Cy and Phoenix let go of each other and turn to her, raindrops dripping from their brows. They grin at her and before she knows what she's doing, she's smiling in return.

There are more questions to answer, but for now, she needs to just be happy with what she has.

"Home, sweet home," says Cy, looping an arm around each of his children and scanning the line of trees on the shore. "Let the fun and games begin."

THE END
Ready for the next installment?
Check out Book 3, FALLING, now!
http://mybook.to/FallingThaw

BOOK THREE - FALLING

Only the chosen shall breed.

Nova. Kian. Dex. Wren.

Four divided hearts. Four teens no longer sure what they're fighting for.

Their society was meant to mold human evolution. Their future, and that of Earth, was to be decided by the kindest and smartest. Askala was supposed to be a beacon of hope in a flooded, desecrated world.

Except the line between the Bound and Unbound is blurring. The Outlands is no longer some distant, faceless world. And the Remnants have a leader who knows more about them than any Remnant before.

In a world devastated by global warming, the fight for survival has always been deadly. Now, the battle for Askala is about to define the very future of humanity.

But...does the greatest threat lie within?

Lovers of Divergent, The Hunger Games, and The Maze Runner will be blown away by the breathtaking new series from USA Today best-selling author Tamar Sloan and award-winning author Heidi Catherine.

Grab your copy now!
http://mybook.to/FallingThaw

WANT TO STAY IN TOUCH?

If you'd like to be the first for to hear all the news from Tamar and Heidi, be sure to sign up to our newsletter. Subscribers receive bonus content, early cover reveals and sneaky snippets of upcoming books. We'd love you to join us!

SIGN UP HERE:

https://sendfox.com/tamarandheidi

ABOUT THE AUTHORS

Tamar Sloan hasn't decided whether she's a psychologist who loves writing, or a writer with a lifelong fascination with psychology. She must have been someone pretty awesome in a previous life (past life regression indicated a Care Bear), because she gets to do both. When not reading, writing or working with teens, Tamar can be found with her husband and two children enjoying country life in their small slice of the Australian bush.

Heidi Catherine loves the way her books give her the opportunity to escape into worlds vastly different to her own life in the burbs. While she quite enjoys killing her characters (especially the awful ones), she promises she's far better behaved in real life. Other than writing and reading, Heidi's current obsessions include watching far too much reality TV with the excuse that it's research for her books.

MORE SERIES TO FALL IN LOVE WITH...

ALSO BY TAMAR SLOAN

Keepers of the Grail

Keepers of the Light

Keepers of the Chalice

Keepers of the Excalibur

Zodiac Guardians

Descendants of the Gods

Prime Prophecy

ALSO BY HEIDI CATHERINE

The Kingdoms of Evernow

The Soulweaver

The Woman Who Didn't (written as HC Michaels)

The Girl Who Never (written as HC Michaels)